Taking the Oath

※

Quickly, before she could start to feel silly, she read it out loud.

"'In Life's name, and for Life's sake,'" she read, "'I say that I will use the Art for nothing but the service of that Life...'" The words seemed to echo slightly, as if the room were larger than it really was....

The next morning, the sun on her face woke Nita up as usual. She sat up and pulled the book out, felt around for her glasses. The book fell open in her hand at the listing for the wizards in the New York metropolitan area, which Nita had glanced at the afternoon before. Now she looked down the first column of names, and her breath caught.

CALLAHAN, Juanita L.
(novice, pre-rating)

Her mouth fell open. She shut it.
I'm going to be a wizard! she thought.

Diane Duane's
Young Wizards Series

DIANE DUANE

So You Want to Be a Wizard

Magic Carpet Books
Harcourt, Inc.
*Orlando Austin New York San Diego
Toronto London*

www.HarcourtBooks.com

First Magic Carpet Books edition 1996
First published by Delacorte Press in 1983

Magic Carpet Books is a trademark of Harcourt, Inc., registered in the
United States of America and/or other jurisdictions.

Library of Congress Cataloging-in-Publication Data
Duane, Diane.
So you want to be a wizard/Diane Duane.
p. cm.—(The young wizards series; 1)
"Magic Carpet Books."
Sequel: Deep wizardry.
Summary: Thirteen-year-old Nita, tormented by a gang of bullies
because she won't fight back, finds the help she needs in a library book
on wizardry which guides her into another dimension.
[1. Wizards—Fiction. 2. Bullies—Fiction. 3. Fantasy.] I. Title.
PZ7.D84915So 2001
[Fic]—dc21   2001016696
ISBN 0-15-216250-X pb   ISBN 0-15-204940-1 digest pb

Text set in Stempel Garamond
Designed by Trina Stahl

A C E G H F D B

Printed in the United States of America

For Sam's friend

Contents

ACKNOWLEDGMENT

David Gerrold is responsible for the creation of several images found in this book, upon which the writer has elaborated slightly. He's also responsible for beating the writer with a club until the words came out right—a matter of several years' nonstop exertion. It would take several more years to fully acknowledge his contributions to both the writer and the written; but brevity is probably best. Old friend, big brother, thanks and love, again and always.

By necessity every book must have at least one flaw; a misprint, a missing page, one imperfection. ... the Rabbis ... point out that even in the holiest of books, the scroll resting inside the Ark, the Name of Names is inscribed in code so that no one might say it out loud, and chance to pronounce properly the Word that once divided the waters from the waters and the day from the night. ... As it is, some books, nearly perfect, are known to become transparent when opened under the influence of the proper constellation, when the full Moon rests in place. Then it is not uncommon for a man to become lost in a single letter, or to hear a voice rise up from the silent page; and then only one imperfect letter, one missing page, can bring him back to the land where a book, once opened, may still be closed, can permit him to pull up the covers around his head and smile once before he falls asleep.

—*Midrashim*, by Howard Schwartz

I have been a word in a book.
—"The Song of Taliesin"
in *The Black Book of Caermarthen*

So You
Want to Be
a Wizard

Prologue

PART OF THE PROBLEM, Nita thought as she tore desperately down Rose Avenue, *is that I can't keep my mouth shut.*

She had been running for five minutes now, hopping fences, sliding sideways through hedges, but she was losing her wind. Some ways behind her she could hear Joanne and Glenda and the rest of them pounding along in pursuit, threatening to replace her latest, now-fading black eye. Well, Joanne *would* come up to her with that new bike, all chrome and silver and gearshift levers and speedometer/odometer and toe clips and water bottle, and ask what she thought of it. So Nita had *told*

1

her. Actually, she had told Joanne what she thought of *her*. The bike was all right. In fact, it had been almost exactly the one that Nita had wanted so much for her last birthday—the birthday when she got nothing but clothes.

Life can be really rotten sometimes, Nita thought. She wasn't really so irritated about that at the moment, however. Running away from a beating was taking up most of her attention.

"Callahan," came a yell from behind her, "I'm gonna pound you up and mail you home in bottles!"

I wonder how many bottles it'll take, Nita thought, without much humor. She couldn't afford to laugh. With their bikes, they'd catch up to her pretty quickly. And then . . .

She tried not to think of the scene there would be later at home—her father raising hands and eyes to the ceiling, wondering loudly enough for the whole house to hear, "Why didn't you hit them *back*?"; her sister making belligerent noises over her new battle scars; her mother shaking her head, looking away silently, because she understood. It was her sad look that would hurt Nita more than the bruises and scrapes and swollen face would. Her mom would shake her head, and clean the hurts up, and sigh. ...

Crud! Nita thought. The breath was coming hard to her now. She was going to have to try to hide, to wait them out. But where? Most of the people around here didn't want kids running through their yards. There was Old Crazy Swale's house with its big landscaped yard, but the rumors among the neighborhood kids said that weird things happened in there. Nita herself had noticed that the guy didn't go to work like normal people. *Better to get beat up again than go in* there. *But where can I hide?*

She kept on running down Rose Avenue, and the answer presented itself to her: a little brown-brick building with windows warmly alight—refuge, safety, sanctuary. The library. *It's open, it's open. I forgot it was open late on Saturday! Oh, thank Heaven!* The sight of it gave Nita a new burst of energy. She cut across its tidy lawn, loped up the walk, took the five stairs to the porch in two jumps, bumped open the front door, and closed it behind her, a little too loudly.

The library had been a private home once, and it hadn't lost the look of one despite the crowding of all its rooms with bookshelves. The walls were paneled in mahogany and oak, and the place smelled warm and brown and booky. At the thump of the door Mrs. Lesser, the weekend librarian, glanced up from her desk, about to say something sharp. Then she saw who was standing there and how hard she was breathing. Mrs. Lesser frowned at Nita and then grinned. She didn't miss much.

"There's no one downstairs," she said, nodding at the door that led to the children's library in the single big basement room. "Keep quiet and I'll get rid of them."

"Thanks," Nita said, and went thumping down the cement stairs. As she reached the bottom, she heard the bump and squeak of the front door opening again.

Nita paused to try to hear voices and found that she couldn't. Doubting that her pursuers could hear her either, she walked on into the children's library, smiling slightly at the books and the bright posters.

She still loved the place. She loved any library, big or little; there was something about all that knowledge, all those facts waiting patiently to be found that never failed to give her a shiver. When friends couldn't be found, the books were always waiting with something new to tell. Life that was getting too much the same could be shaken up in a few minutes by the picture in a book of some ancient temple newly discovered deep in a rain forest, a fuzzy photo of Uranus with its up-and-down rings, or a prismed picture taken through the faceted eye of a bee.

And though she would rather have died than admit it—no respectable thirteen-year-old *ever* set foot down there—she still loved the children's library too. Nita had gone through every book in the place when she was younger, reading everything in sight—fiction and nonfiction alike, fairy tales, science books, horse stories, dog stories, music books, art books, even the encyclopedias.

Bookworm, she heard the old jeering

voices go in her head, *four eyes, smart-ass, hide-in-the-house-and-read. Walking encyclopedia. Think you're so hot.* "No," she remembered herself answering once, "I just like to find things out!" And she sighed, feeling rueful. *That* time she had found out about being punched in the stomach.

She strolled between shelves, looking at titles, smiling as she met old friends—books she had read three times or five times or a dozen. Just a title, or an author's name, would be enough to summon up happy images. Strange creatures like phoenixes and psammeads, moving under smoky London daylight of a hundred years before, in company with groups of bemused children; starships and new worlds and the limitless vistas of interstellar night, outer space challenged but never conquered; princesses in silver and golden dresses, princes and heroes carrying swords like sharpened lines of light, monsters rising out of weedy tarns, wild creatures that talked and tricked one another. . . .

I used to think the world would be like that when I got older. Wonderful all the

*time, exciting, happy. Instead of the way
it is....*

Something stopped Nita's hand as it ran
along the bookshelf. She looked and found
that one of the books, a little library-bound
volume in shiny red buckram, had a loose
thread at the top of its spine, on which her
finger had caught. She pulled the finger
free, glanced at the title. It was one of those
So You Want to Be a...books, a series
on careers. *So You Want to Be a Pilot* there
had been, and *So You Want to Be a Scien-
tist...a Nurse...a Writer...*

But this one said, *So You Want to Be a
Wizard.*

A what?

Nita pulled the book off the shelf, surprised not so much by the title as by the
fact that she'd never seen it before. She
thought she knew the whole stock of the
children's library. Yet this wasn't a new
book. It had plainly been there for some
time—the pages had that yellow look
about their edges, the color of aging, and
the top of the book was dusty. SO YOU
WANT TO BE A WIZARD. HEARNSSEN, the

spine said: that was the author's name. Phoenix Press, the publisher. And then in white ink in Mrs. Lesser's tidy handwriting, 793.4: the Dewey decimal number.

This has to be a joke, Nita said to herself. But the book looked exactly like all the others in the series. She opened it carefully, so as not to crack the binding, and turned the first few pages to the table of contents. Normally Nita was a fast reader and would quickly have finished a page with only a few lines on it; but what she found on that contents page slowed her down a great deal. "Preliminary Determinations: A Question of Aptitude." "Wizardly Preoccupations and Predilections." "Basic Equipment and Milieus." "Introduction to Spells, Bindings, and *Geasa.*" "Familiars and Helpmeets: Advice to the Initiate." "Psychotropic Spelling."

Psychowhat? Nita turned to the page on which that chapter began, looking at the boldface paragraph beneath its title.

WARNING

Spells of power sufficient to make temporary changes in the human mind are always subject to sudden and unpredictable back-lash on the user. The practitioner is cau-tioned to make sure that his/her motives are benevolent before attempting spelling aimed at . . .

I don't believe this, Nita thought. She shut the book and stood there holding it in her hand, confused, amazed, suspicious—and delighted. If it was a joke, it was a great one. If it wasn't . . .

No, don't be silly.

But if it isn't . . .

People were clumping around upstairs, but Nita hardly heard them. She sat down at one of the low tables and started reading the book in earnest.

The first couple of pages were a fore-word.

Wizardry is one of the most ancient and misunderstood of arts. Its public image for centuries has been one of a mysterious pur-suit, practiced in occult surroundings, and usually used at the peril of one's soul. The modern wizard, who works with tools more advanced than bat's blood and beings more complex than medieval demons, knows how far from the truth that image is. Wizardry, though exciting and interesting, is not a glamorous business, especially these days, when a wizard must work quietly so as not to attract undue attention.

For those willing to assume the Art's responsibilities and do the work, though, wizardry has many rewards. The sight of a formerly twisted growing thing now growing straight, of a snarled motivation untangled, the satisfaction of hearing what a plant is thinking or a dog is saying, of talking to a stone or a star, is thought by most to be well worth the labor.

Not everyone is suited to be a wizard. Those without enough of the necessary personality traits will never see this manual for what it is. That you have found it at all says a great deal for your potential.

The reader is invited to examine the next few chapters and determine his/her wizardly potential in detail—to become familiar with the scope of the Art—and finally to decide whether to become a wizard.

Good luck!

It's a joke, Nita thought. *Really.* And to her own amazement, she wouldn't believe herself—she was too fascinated. She turned to the next chapter.

PRELIMINARY DETERMINATIONS

An aptitude for wizardry requires more than just the desire to practice the art. There are certain inborn tendencies, and some acquired ones, that enable a person to become a wizard. This chapter will list some of the better documented of wizardly characteristics. Please bear in mind that it isn't necessary to possess all the qualities listed, or even most of them. Some of the greatest wizards have been lacking in the qualities possessed by almost all others and have still achieved startling competence levels....

Slowly at first, then more eagerly, Nita began working her way through the assessment chapter, pausing only to get a pencil and scrap paper from the checkout desk, so that she could make notes on her aptitude. She was brought up short by the footnote to one page:

*Where ratings are not assigned, as in rural areas, the area of greatest population density will usually produce the most wizards, due to the thinning of worldwalls with increased population concentration. . . .

Nita stopped reading, amazed. "Thinning of worldwalls"—were they saying that there are other worlds, other dimensions, and that things could get through? Things, or people?

She sat there and wondered. All the old fairy tales about people falling down wells into magical countries, or slipping backward in time, or forward into it—did this mean that such things could actually happen? If you could actually go into other worlds, other places, and come back again. . . .

Aww—who would believe anybody who came back and told a story like that? Even if they took pictures?

But who cares! she answered herself fiercely. *If only it could be true. . . .*

She turned her attention back to the book and went on reading, though skeptically—the whole thing still felt like a game, but abruptly it stopped being a game, with one paragraph:

Wizards love words. Most of them read a great deal, and indeed one strong sign of a potential wizard is the inability to get to sleep without reading something first. But their love for and fluency with words is what makes wizards a force to be reckoned with. Their ability to convince a piece of the world—a tree, say, or a stone—that it's not what it thinks it is, that it's something else, is the very heart of wizardry. Words skillfully used, the persuasive voice, the persuading mind, are the wizard's most basic tools. With them a wizard can stop a tidal wave, talk a tree out of growing, or into it—freeze fire, burn rain—even slow down the death of the Universe.

That last, of course, is the reason there are wizards. See the next chapter.

Nita stopped short. The universe was running down; all the energy in it was slowly being used up. She knew that from studying astronomy. The process was called *entropy*. But she'd never heard anyone talk about slowing it down before.

She shook her head in amazement and went on to the "correlation" section at the end of that chapter, where all the factors involved in the makeup of a potential wizard were listed. Nita found that she had a lot of them—enough to be a wizard, if she wanted to.

With rising excitement she turned to the next chapter. "Theory and Implications of Wizardry," the heading said. *"History, Philosophy, and the Wizards' Oath."*

Fifty or sixty eons ago, when life brought itself about, it also brought about to accompany it many Powers and Potentialities to manage the business of creation. One of the greatest of these Powers held aloof for a long time, watching its companions work, not wishing to enter into Creation until it could contribute something unlike anything the other Powers had made, something completely new and original. Finally the Lone Power found what it was looking for. Others had invented planets, light, gravity, space. The Lone Power invented death, and bound it irrevocably into the worlds. Shortly thereafter the other Powers joined forces and cast the Lone One out.

Many versions of this story are related among the many worlds, assigning blame or praise to one party or another. However, none of the stories change the fact that entropy and its symptom, death, are here now. To attempt to halt or remove them is as futile as attempting to ignore them.

Therefore there are wizards—to handle them.

A wizard's business is to conserve energy—to keep it from being wasted. On the simplest level this includes such unmagical-looking actions as paying one's bills on time, turning off the lights when you go out, and supporting the people around you in getting their lives to work. It also includes a great deal more.

Because wizardly people tend to be good with language, they can also become skillful with the Speech, the magical tongue in which objects and living creatures can be described with more accuracy than in any human language. And what can be so accurately described can also be preserved—

or freed to become yet greater. A wizard can cause an inanimate object or animate creature to grow, or stop growing—to be what it is, or something else. A wizard, using the Speech, can cause death to slow down, or go somewhere else and come back later—just as the Lone Power caused it to come about in the first place. Creation, preservation, destruction, transformation—all are a matter of causing the fabric of being to do what you want it to. And the Speech is the key.

Nita stopped to think this over for a moment. *It sounds like, if you know what something is, truly* know, *you don't have any trouble working with it. Like my telescope—if it acts up, I know every piece of it, and it only takes a second to get it working again. To have that kind of control over—over* everything—*live things, the world, even* . . . She took a deep breath and looked back at the book, beginning to get an idea of what kind of power was implied there.

The power conferred by use of the Speech has, of course, one insurmountable limita-

tion: the existence of death itself. As one renowned Senior Wizard has remarked, "Entropy has us outnumbered." No matter how much preserving we do, the Universe will eventually die. But it will last longer because of our efforts—and since no one knows for sure whether another Universe will be born from the ashes of this one, the effort seems worthwhile.

No one should take the Wizards' Oath who is not committed to making wizardry a lifelong pursuit. The energy invested in a beginning wizard is too precious to be thrown away. Yet there are no penalties for withdrawal from the Art, except the knowledge that the Universe will die a little faster because of energy lost. On the other hand, there are no prizes for the service of Life—except life itself. The wizard gets the delight of working in a specialized area—magic—and gets a good look at the foundations of the Universe, the way things really work. It should be stated here that there are people who consider the latter more of a curse than a blessing. Such wizards usually lose their art. Magic does not live in the unwilling soul.

Should you decide to go ahead and take

the Oath, be warned that an ordeal of sorts will follow, a test of aptitude. If you pass, wizardry will ensue....

Yeah? Nita thought. *And what if you* don't *pass?*

"Nita?" Mrs. Lesser's voice came floating down the stairs, and a moment later she herself appeared, a large brunette lady with kind eyes and a look of eternal concern. "You still alive?"

"I was reading."

"So what else is new? They're gone."

"Thanks, Mrs. L."

"What was all that about, anyway?"

"Oh ... Joanne was looking to pick a fight again."

Mrs. Lesser raised an eyebrow at Nita, and Nita smiled back at her shamefacedly. She *didn't* miss much.

"Well, I might have helped her a little."

"I guess it's hard," Mrs. Lesser said. "I doubt *I* could be nice all the time, myself, if I had that lot on my back. That the only one you want today, or should I just have the nonfiction section boxed and sent over to your house?"

"No, this is enough," Nita said. "If my father sees too many books he'll just make me bring them back."

Mrs. Lesser sighed. "Reading one book is like eating one potato chip," she said. "So you'll be back Monday. There's more where that came from. I'll check it out for you."

Nita felt in her pockets hurriedly. "Oh, crud. Mrs. L., I don't have my card."

"So you'll bring it back Monday," she said, handing her back the book as they reached the landing, "and I'll stamp it then. I trust you."

"Thanks," Nita said.

"Don't mention it. Be careful going home," Mrs. Lesser said, "and have a nice read."

"I will."

Nita went out and stood on the door-step, looking around in the deepening gloom. Dinnertime was getting close, and the wind was getting cold, with a smell of rain to it. The book in her hand seemed to prickle a little, as if it were impatient to be read.

She started jogging toward home,

taking a circuitous route—up Washington from Rose Avenue, then through town along Nassau Road and down East Clinton, a path meant to confound pursuit. She didn't expect that they would be waiting for her only a block away from her house, where there were no alternate routes to take. And when they were through with her, the six of them, one of Nita's eyes was blackened and the knee Joanne had so carefully stomped on felt swollen with liquid fire.

Nita just lay there for a long while, on the spot where they left her, behind the O'Donnells' hedge; the O'Donnells were out of town. There she lay, and cried, as she would not in front of Joanne and the rest, as she would not until she was safely in bed and out of her family's earshot. Whether she provoked these situations or not, they kept happening, and there was nothing she could do about them. Joanne and her hangers-on had found out that Nita didn't like to fight, wouldn't try until her rage broke loose—and then it was too late, she was too hurt to fight well. All her self-defense lessons went out of her head with the pain. And they knew it, and at least once a week found a way to sucker her into a fight—or, if that failed, they would simply ambush her. All right, she had purposely baited Joanne today, but there'd been a fight coming anyway, and *she* had chosen to start it rather than wait, getting angrier and angrier, while they baited *her*. But this would keep happening, again and again, and there was nothing she could do about it. *Oh, I wish we could move. I wish Dad would say something to Joanne's father—no, that would just make it worse. If only something could just happen to make it stop!*

Underneath her, where it had fallen, the book dug into Nita's sore ribs. The memory of what she had been reading flooded back through her pain and was followed by a wash of wild surmise. *If there are spells to keep things from dying, then I bet there are spells to keep people from hurting you. . . .*

Then Nita scowled at herself in contempt for actually believing for a moment what couldn't possibly be more than an elaborate joke. She put aside thoughts of the book and slowly got up, brushing herself off and discovering some new bruises. She also discovered something else. Her favorite pen was gone. Her space pen, a present from her Uncle Joel, the pen that could write on butter or glass or upside down, her pen with which she had never failed a test, even in math. She patted herself all over, checked the ground, searched in pockets where she knew the pen couldn't be. No use; it was gone. Or taken, rather— for it had been securely clipped to her front jacket pocket when Joanne and her group jumped her. It must have fallen out, and one of them picked it up.

"Aaaaaagh!" Nita moaned, feeling bitter enough to start crying again. But she was all cried out, and she ached too much, and it was a waste. She stepped around the hedge and limped the little distance home.

Her house was pretty much like any other on the block, a white frame house with fake shutters; but where other houses had their lawns, Nita's had a beautifully landscaped garden. Ivy carpeted the ground, and the flowerbeds against the house had something blooming in every season except the dead of winter. Nita trudged up the driveway without bothering to smell any of the spring flowers, went up the stairs to the back door, pushed it open, and walked into the kitchen as nonchalantly as she could.

Her mother was elsewhere, but the delicious smells of her cooking filled the place; veal cutlets tonight. Nita peered into the oven, saw potatoes baking, lifted a pot lid and found corn on the cob in the steamer.

Her father looked up from the newspaper he was reading at the dining-room table. He was a big, blunt, good-looking man, with startling silver hair and large capable hands—"an artist's hands!" he would chuckle as he pieced together a flower arrangement. He owned the smaller of the town's two flower shops, and he loved his work dearly. He had done all the landscaping around the house in his spare time, and around several neighbors' houses too, refusing to take anything in return but the satisfaction of being up to his elbows in a flowerbed. Whatever he touched grew. "I have an understanding with the plants," he would say, and it certainly seemed that way. It was people he sometimes had trouble understanding, and particularly his eldest daughter.

"My Lord, Nita!" her father exclaimed, putting the paper down flat on the table. His voice was shocked. "What happened?"

As if you don't know! Nita thought. She could clearly see the expressions going across her father's face. *MiGod*, they said, *she's done it again! Why doesn't she fight back? What's wrong with her?* He would get around to asking that question at one point or another, and Nita would try to explain it again, and as usual her father would try to understand and would fail. Nita turned away and opened the refrigerator door, peering at nothing in particular, so that her father wouldn't see the grimace of impatience and irritation on her face. She was tired of the whole ritual, but she had to put up with it. It was as inevitable as being beaten up.

"I was in a fight," she said, the second verse of the ritual, the second line of the scene. Tiredly she closed the refrigerator door, put the book down on the counter beside the stove, and peeled off her jacket, examining it for rips and ground-in dirt and blood.

"So how many of them did you take out?" her father said, turning his eyes back to the newspaper. His face still showed exasperation and puzzlement, and Nita sighed. *He looks about as tired of this as I am. But really, he* knows *the answers.* "I'm not sure," Nita said. "There were six of them."

"Six!" Nita's mother came around the corner from the living room and into the bright kitchen—danced in, actually. Just watching her made Nita smile sometimes, and it did now, though changing expressions hurt. She had been a dancer before she married Dad, and the grace with which she moved made her every action around the house seem polished, endlessly rehearsed, lovely to look at. She glided with the laundry, floated while she cooked. "Loading the odds a bit, weren't they?"

"Yeah." Nita was hurting almost too much to feel like responding to the gentle humor. Her mother caught the pain in her voice and stopped to touch Nita's face as she passed, assessing the damage and conveying how she felt about it in one brief gesture, without saying anything that anyone else but the two of them might hear.

"No sitting up for you tonight, kidlet," her mother said. "Bed, and ice on that, before you swell up like a balloon."

"What started it?" her dad asked from the dining room.

"Joanne Virella," Nita said. "She has a new bike, and I didn't get as excited about it as she thought I should."

Nita's father looked up from the paper again, and this time there was discomfort in his face, and regret. "Nita," he said, "I couldn't afford it this month, really. I thought I was going to be able to earlier, but I couldn't. I *wish* I could have. Next time for sure."

Nita nodded. "It's okay," she said, even though it wasn't really. She'd *wanted* that bike, wanted it so badly—but Joanne's father owned the big five-and-dime on Nassau Road and *could* afford three-hundred-dollar bikes for his children at the drop of a birthday. Nita's father's business was a lot smaller and was prone to what he called (in front of most people) "cash-flow problems" or (in front of his family) "being broke most of the time."

But what does Joanne care about cash flow, or any of the rest of it? I wanted that bike!

"Here, dreamer," her mother said, tapping her on the shoulder and breaking her thought. She handed Nita an icepack and turned back toward the stove. "Go lie down or you'll swell worse. I'll bring you something in a while."

"Shouldn't she stay sitting up?" Nita's father said. "Seems as if the fluid would drain better or something."

"You didn't get beat up enough when you were younger, Harry," her mother said. "If she doesn't lie down, she'll blow up like a basketball. Scoot, Nita."

She scooted, around the corner into the dining room, around the second corner into the living room, and straight into her little sister, bumping loose one of the textbooks she was carrying and scattering half her armload of pink plastic curlers. Nita bent to help pick things up again. Her sister, bent down beside her, didn't take long to figure out what had happened.

"Virella again, huh?" she asked. Dairine was eleven years old, redheaded like her mother, gray-eyed like Nita, and precocious; she was taking tenth-grade English courses and breezing through them, and Nita was teaching her some algebra on the side. Dairine had her father's square-boned build and her mother's grace, and a perpetual, cocky grin. She was a great sister, as far as Nita was concerned, even if she was a little too smart for her own good.

"Yeah," Nita said. "Look out, kid, I've gotta go lie down."

"Don't call me kid. You want me to beat up Virella for you?"

"Be my guest," Nita said. She went on through the house, back to her room. Bumping the door open, she fumbled for the light switch and flipped it on. The familiar maps and pictures looked down at her—the *National Geographic* map of the Moon and some enlarged *Voyager* photos of Jupiter and Saturn and their moons.

Nita eased herself down onto the bottom bunk bed, groaning softly—the deep bruises were beginning to bother her now. *Lord,* she thought, *what did I say? If Dari does beat Joanne up, I'll never hear the end of it.* Dairine had once been small and fragile and subject to being beaten up—mostly because she had never learned to curb her mouth either—and Nita's parents had sent her to jujitsu lessons at the same time they sent Nita. On Dari, though, the lessons took. One or two overconfident kids had gone after her, about a month and a half into her lessons, and had been thoroughly and painfully surprised. She was protective enough to take Joanne on and, horrors, throw her clear over the horizon. It would be all over school; Nita Callahan's little sister beat up the girl who beat *Nita* up.

Oh no! Nita thought.

Her door opened slightly, and Dari stuck her head in. "Of course," she said, "if you'd rather do it yourself, I'll let her off this time."

"Yeah," Nita said, "thanks."

Dairine made a face. "Here," she said, and pitched Nita's jacket in at her, and then right after it the book. Nita managed to field it while holding the icepack in place with her left hand. "You left it in the kitchen," Dairine said. "Gonna be a magician, huh? Make yourself vanish when they chase you?"

"Sure. Go curl your hair, runt."

Nita sat back against the headboard of the bed, staring at the book. *Why not? Who knows what kinds of spells you could do? Maybe I could turn Joanne into a turkey. As if she isn't one already. Or maybe there's a spell for getting lost pens back.*

Though the book made it sound awfully serious, as if the wizardry were for big things. Maybe it's not right to do spells for little stuff like this—and anyway, you can't do the spells until you've taken the Oath, and once you've taken it, that's supposed to be forever.

Oh, come on, it's a joke! What harm can there be in saying the words if it's a joke? And if it's not, then ...

Then I'll be a wizard.

Her father knocked on her door, then walked in with a plate loaded with dinner and a glass of cola. Nita grinned up at him, not too widely, for it hurt. "Thanks, Dad."

"Here," he said after Nita took the plate and the glass, and handed her a couple of aspirin. "Your mother says to take these."

"Thanks." Nita took them with the Coke, while her father sat down on the edge of the bed.

"Nita," he said, "is there something going on that I should know about?"

"Huh?"

"It's been once a week now, sometimes twice, for quite a while. Do you want me to speak to Joe Virella and ask him to have a word with Joanne?"

"Uh, no, sir."

Nita's father stared at his hands for a moment. "What should we do, then? I really can't afford to start you in karate lessons again—"

"Jujitsu."

"Whatever. Nita, what *is* it? Why does this keep happening? *Why don't you hit them back?*"

"I *used* to! Do you think it made a difference? Joanne would just get more kids to help." Her father stared at her, and Nita flushed hot at the stern look on his face.

"I'm sorry, Daddy, I didn't mean to yell at you. But fighting back just gets them madder, it doesn't help."

"It might help keep you from getting mangled every week, if you'd just keep trying!" her father said angrily. "I hate to admit it, but I'd love to see you wipe the ground up with that loudmouth rich kid."

So would I, Nita thought. *That's the problem.* She swallowed, feeling guilty over how much she wanted to get back at Joanne somehow. "Dad, Joanne and her bunch just don't like me. I don't do the things they do, or play the games they play, or like the things they like—and I don't *want* to. So they don't like me. That's all."

Her father looked at her and shook his head sadly. "I just don't want to see you hurt. Kidling, I don't know...if you could just be a little more like them, if you could try to..." He trailed off, running one hand through his silver hair. "What am I saying?" he muttered. "Look. If there's anything I can do to help, will you tell me?"

"Yessir."

"Okay. If you feel better tomorrow, would you rake up the backyard a little? I want to go over the lawn around the rowan tree with the aerator, maybe put down some seed."

"Sure. I'll be okay, Dad. They didn't break anything."

"My girl." He got up. "Don't read so much it hurts your eyes, now."

"I won't," Nita said. Her father strode out the door, forgetting to close it behind himself as usual.

She ate her supper slowly, for it hurt to chew, and she tried to think about something besides Joanne or that book.

The Moon was at first quarter tonight; it would be a good night to take the telescope out and have a look at the shadows in the craters. Or there was that fuzzy little comet, maybe it had more tail than it did last week.

It was completely useless. The book lay there on her bed and stared at her, daring her to do something childlike, something silly, something absolutely ridiculous.

Nita put aside her empty plate, picked up the book, and stared back at it.

"All right," she said under her breath. "All right."

She opened the book at random. And on the page to which she opened, there was the Oath.

It was not decorated in any way. It stood there, a plain block of type all by itself in the middle of the page, looking serious and important. Nita read the Oath to herself first, to make sure of the words. Then, quickly, before she could start to feel silly, she read it out loud.

" 'In Life's name, and for Life's sake,' " she read, " 'I say that I will use the Art for nothing but the service of that Life. I will guard growth and ease pain. I will fight to preserve what grows and lives well in its own way; and I will change no object or creature unless its growth and life, or that of the system of which it is part, are threatened. To these ends, in the practice of my Art, I will put aside fear for courage, and death for life, when it is right to do so— till Universe's end.' "

The words seemed to echo slightly, as if the room were larger than it really was. Nita sat very still, wondering what the ordeal would be like, wondering what would happen now. Only the wind spoke softly in the leaves of the trees outside the bedroom window; nothing else seemed to stir anywhere. Nita sat there, and slowly the tension began to drain out of her as she realized that she hadn't been hit by lightning, nor had anything strange at all happened to her. *Now* she felt silly—and tired too, she discovered. The effects of her beating were catching up with her. Wearily, Nita shoved the book under her pillow, then lay back against the headboard and closed her hurting eyes. So much for the joke. She would have a nap, and then later she'd get up and take the telescope out back. But right now . . . right now. . . .

After a while, night was not night anymore; that was what brought Nita to the window, much later. She leaned on the sill and gazed out in calm wonder at her backyard, which didn't look quite the same as usual. A blaze of undying morning lay over everything, bushes and trees cast light instead of shadow, and she could see the wind. Standing in the ivy under her window, she turned her eyes up to the silver-glowing sky to get used to the brilliance. *How about that,* she said. *The backyard's here, too.* Next to her, the lesser brilliance that gazed up at that same sky shrugged slightly. *Of course,* it said. *This is Timeheart, after all. Yes,* Nita said anxiously as they passed across the yard and out into the bright shadow of the steel and crystal towers, *but did I do right?* Her companion shrugged again. *Go find out,* it said, and glanced up again. Nita wasn't sure she wanted to follow the glance. Once she had looked up and seen—*I dreamed you were gone,* she said suddenly. *The magic stayed, but you went away.* She hurt inside, enough to cry, but her companion flickered with laughter. *No one ever goes away forever,* it said. *Especially not here.* Nita looked up, then, into the bright morning and the brighter shadows. The day went on and on and would not end, the sky blazed now like molten silver....

The Sun on her face woke Nita up as usual. Someone, her mother probably, had come in late last night to cover her up and

take the dishes away. She turned over slowly, stiff but not in too much pain, and felt the hardness under her pillow. Nita sat up and pulled the book out, felt around for her glasses. The book fell open in her hand at the listing for the wizards in the New York metropolitan area, which Nita had glanced at the afternoon before. Now she looked down the first column of names, and her breath caught.

CALLAHAN, Juanita L.,
243 E. Clinton Ave.,
Hempstead, NY 11575
(516) 555-6786. (novice, pre-rating)

Her mouth fell open. She shut it.
I'm going to be a wizard! she thought.
Nita got up and got dressed in a hurry.

Preliminary
Exercises

SHE DID HER CHORES that morning and got out of the house with the book as fast as she could, heading for one of her secret places in the woods. *If weird things start happening,* she thought, *no one will see them there. Oh, I'm going to get that pen back! And then...*

Behind the high school around the corner from Nita's house was a large tract of undeveloped woodland, the usual Long Island combination of scrub oak, white pine, and sassafras. Nita detoured around the school, pausing to scramble over a couple of chain-link fences. There was a path on the other side; after a few minutes she

38

turned off it to pick her way carefully through low underbrush and among fallen logs and tree stumps. Then there was a solid wall of clumped sassafras and twining wild blackberry bushes. It looked totally impassable, and the blackberries threatened Nita with their thorns, but she turned sideways and pushed through the wall of greenery undaunted.

She emerged into a glade walled all around with blackberry and gooseberry and pine, sheltered by the overhanging branches of several trees. One, a large crab-apple, stood near the edge of the glade, and there was a flattish half-buried boulder at the base of its trunk. Here she could be sure no one was watching.

Nita sat down on the rock with a sigh, put her back up against the tree, and spent a few moments getting comfortable—then opened the book and started to read.

She found herself not just reading, after a while, but studying—cramming the facts into her head with that particular mental *stomp* she used when she knew she was going to have to know something by heart. The things the book was telling her now were not vague and abstract, as the initial discussion of theory had been, but straightforward as the repair manual for a new car, and nearly as complex. There were tables and lists of needed resources for working spells. There were formulas and equations and rules. There was a syllabary and pronunciation guide for the 418 symbols used in the wizardly Speech to describe relationships and effects that other human languages had no specific words for.

The information went on and on—the book was printed small, and there seemed no end to the things Nita was going to have to know about. She read about the hierarchy of practicing wizards—her book listed only those practicing in the U.S. and Canada, though wizards were working everywhere in the world—and she scanned down the listing for the New York area, noticing the presence of Advisory wizards, Area Supervisors, Senior wizards. She read through a list of the "otherworlds" closest to her own, alternate earths where the capital of the United States was named Huictilopochtli or Lafayette City or Hrafnkell or New Washington, and where the people still called themselves Americans, though they didn't match Nita's ideas about the term.

She learned the Horseman's Word, which gets the attention of any member of the genus *Equus*, even the zebras; and the two forms of the Mason's Word, which give stone the appearance of life for short periods. One chapter told her about the magical creatures living in cities, whose presence even the nonwizardly people suspect sometimes—creatures like the steam-breathing fireworms, packratty little lizards that creep through cracks in building walls to steal treasures and trash for their lair-hoards under the streets. Nita thought about all the steam she had seen coming up from manhole covers in Manhattan and smiled, for now she knew what was causing it.

She read on, finding out how to bridle the Nightmare and learning what questions to ask the Transcendent Pig, should she meet him. She read about the Trees' Battle—who fought in it, who won it, and why. She read about the forty basic classes of spells and their subclasses. She read about Timeheart, the unreal and eternal realm where the places and things people remember affectionately are preserved as they remember them, forever.

In the middle of the description of things preserved in their fullest beauty forever, and still growing, Nita found herself feeling a faint tingle of unease. She was also getting tired. She dropped the book in her lap with an annoyed sigh, for there was just too much to absorb at one sitting, and she had no clear idea of where to begin. "Crud," she said under her breath. "I thought I'd be able to make Joanne vanish by tomorrow morning."

Nita picked the manual up again and leafed through it to the section labeled "Preliminary Exercises."

The first one was set in a small block of type in the middle of an otherwise empty page.

To change something, you must first describe it. To describe something, you must first see it. Hold still in one place for as long as it takes to see something.

Nita felt puzzled and slightly annoyed. This didn't sound much like magic. But obediently she put the book down, settled herself more comfortably against the tree, folded her arms, and sighed. *It's almost too warm to think about anything serious.... What should I look at? That rock over there? Naah, it's kind of a dull-looking rock. That weed... look how its leaves go up around the stem in a spiral....* Nita leaned her head back, stared up through the crabtree's branches. *That rotten Joanne. Where would she have hidden that pen? I wonder. Maybe if I could sneak into her house somehow, maybe there's a spell for that.... Have to do it after dark, I guess. Maybe I could do it tonight.... Wish it didn't take so long to get dark this time of year.* Nita looked at the sky where it showed between the leaves, a hot blue mosaic of light with here and there the fire-flicker of sun showing through, shifting with the shift of leaves in the wind. There are kinds of patterns—the wind never goes through the same way twice, and there are patterns in the branches but they're never quite the same either. And look at the changes in the brightness. The sky is the same but the leaves cover sometimes more and sometimes less ... the patterns ... the patterns, they ... they ...

(They won't let you have a moment's rest,) the crabapple tree said irritably. Nita jumped, scraping her back against the trunk as she sat up straight. She had heard the tree quite plainly in some way that had nothing to do with spoken words. It was light patterns she had heard, and wind movements, leafrustle, fireflicker.

(Finally paid attention, did you?) said the tree. (As if one of them isn't enough, messing up someone's fallen-leaf pattern that's been in progress for fifteen years, drawing circles all over the ground and messing up the matrices. Well? What's *your* excuse?)

Nita sat there with her mouth open, looking up at the words the tree was making with cranky light and shadow. *It works. It works!* "Uh," she said, not knowing whether the tree could understand her, "I didn't draw any circles on your leaves—"

(No, but that other one did,) the tree

said. (Made circles and stars and diagrams all over Telerilarch's collage, doing some kind of power spell. You people don't have the proper respect for artwork. Okay, so we're amateurs,) it added, a touch of belligerence creeping into its voice. (So none of us have been here more than thirty years. Well, our work is still valid, and—)

"Uh, listen, do you mean that there's a, uh, a wizard out here somewhere doing magic?"

(What else?) the tree snapped. (And let me tell you, if you people don't—)

"Where? Where is she?"

(He,) the tree said. (In the middle of all those made-stone roads. I remember when those roads went in, and they took a pattern Kimber had been working on for eighty years and scraped it bare and poured that black rock over it. One of the most complex, most—)

He? Nita thought, and her heart sank slightly. She had trouble talking to boys. "You mean across the freeway, in the middle of the interchange? That green place?"

(Didn't you hear me? Are you deaf?

Silly question. That other one *must* be deaf not to have heard Teleri yelling at him. And now I suppose *you'll* start scratching up the ground and invoking powers and ruining *my* collage. Well, let me tell you—)

"I, uh—listen, I'll talk to you later," Nita said hurriedly. She got to her feet, brushed herself off, and started away through the woods at a trot. *Another wizard? And my God, the trees—* Their laughter at her amazement was all around her as she ran, the merriment of everything from foot-high weeds to hundred-foot oaks, rustling in the wind—grave chuckling of maples and alders, titters from groves of sapling sassafras, silly giggling in the raspberry bushes, a huge belly laugh from the oldest hollow ash tree before the freeway interchange. *How could I never have heard them before!*

Nita stopped at the freeway's edge and made sure that there were no cars coming before she tried to cross. The interchange was a cloverleaf, and the circle formed by one of the off-ramps held a stand of the original pre-freeway trees within it, in a kind of sunken bowl. Nita dashed across the concrete and stood a moment, breathless, at the edge of the downslope, before starting down it slantwise.

This was another of her secret places, a spot shaded and peaceful in summer and winter both because of the pine trees that roofed in the hollow. But there was nothing peaceful about it today. Something was in the air, and the trees, irritated, were muttering among themselves. Even on a foot-thick cushion of pine needles, Nita's feet seemed to be making too much noise. She tried to walk softly and wished the trees wouldn't stare at her so.

Where the slope bottomed out she stopped, looking around her nervously, and that was when she saw him. The boy was holding a stick in one hand and staring intently at the ground underneath a huge larch on one side of the grove. He was shorter than she was, and looked younger, and he also looked familiar somehow. *Now who* is *that?* she thought, feeling more nervous still. No one had ever been in one of her secret places when *she* came there.

But the boy just kept frowning at the ground, as if it were a test paper and he was trying to scowl the right answer out of it. A very ordinary-looking kid, with straight black hair and a Hispanic look to his face, wearing a beat-up green windbreaker and jeans and sneakers, holding a willow wand of a type that Nita's book recommended for certain types of spelling.

He let out what looked like a breath of irritation and put his hands on his hips. *"Cojones,"* he muttered, shaking his head—and halfway through the shake, he caught sight of Nita.

He looked surprised and embarrassed for a moment, then his face steadied down to a simple worried look. There he stood regarding Nita, and she realized with a shock that he wasn't going to yell at her, or chase her, or call her names, or run away himself. He was going to let her explain herself. Nita was amazed. It didn't seem quite normal.

"Hi," she said.

The boy looked at her uncertainly, as if trying to place her. "Hi."

Nita wasn't sure quite where to begin. But the marks on the ground, and the willow wand, seemed to confirm that a power spell was in progress. "Uh," she said, "I, uh, I don't see the oak leaves. Or the string."

The boy's dark eyes widened. "So *that's* how you got through!"

"Through what?"

"I put a binding spell around the edges of this place," he said. "I've tried this spell once or twice before, but people kept showing up just as I was getting busy, and I couldn't finish."

Nita suddenly recognized him. "You're the one they were calling crazy last week."

The boy's eyes narrowed again. He looked annoyed. "Uh, yeah. A couple of the eighth graders found me last Monday. They were shooting up the woods with BB guns, and there I was working. And they couldn't figure out what I was doing, so at lunch the next day they said—"

"I know what they said." It had been a badly rhymed song about the kid who played by himself in the woods, because no one else would play with him. She remembered feeling vaguely sorry for the kid, whoever he was; boys could be as bad as girls sometimes.

"I thought I blew the binding, too," he said. "You surprised me."

"Maybe you can't bind another wizard out," Nita said. *That was it,* she thought. *If he's not one—*

"Uhh . . . I guess not." He paused. "I'm Kit," he said then. "Christopher, really, but I hate Christopher."

"Nita," she said. "It's short for Juanita. I hate that, too. Listen—the trees are mad at you."

Kit stared at her. "The *trees?*"

"Uh, mostly this one." She looked up into the branches of the larch, which were trembling with more force than the wind could lend them. "See, the trees do—I don't know, it's artwork, sort of, with their fallen leaves—and you started doing your power schematic all over their work, and, uh—"

"Trees?" Kit said. "Rocks I knew about, I talked to a rock last week—or it talked to me, actually—though it wasn't talking, really . . ." He looked up at the tree. "Well, hey, I'm sorry," he said. "I didn't know. I'll try to put things back the way I found them. But I might as well not have bothered with the spell," he said, looking again at Nita. "It got caught. It's not working. You know anything about this?"

He gestured at the diagram he had drawn on the cleared ground, and Nita went to crouch down by it. The pattern was one she had seen in her book, a basic design of interlocking circles and woven parallelograms. There were symbols drawn inside the angles and outside the curves, some of them letters or words in the Roman alphabet, some of them the graceful characters of the wizardly Speech. "I just got my book yesterday," she said. "I doubt I'll be much help. What were you trying to get? The power part of it I can see."

She glanced up and found Kit looking with somber interest at her black eye. "I'm getting tired of being beat up just because I have a Spanish accent," he said. "I was going to attract enough power to me so that the big kids would just leave me alone and not start anything. An 'aura,' the book called it. But the spell got stuck a couple of steps in, and when I checked the book it said that I was missing an element." He looked questioningly at Nita. "Maybe you're it?"

"Uhh—" She shook her head. "I don't know. I was looking for a spell for something different. Someone beat me up and stole my best pen. It was a space pen, the kind the astronauts have, and it writes on anything, and I always took all my tests with it and I always pass when I use it, and I want it *back*." She stopped, then added, "And I guess I wouldn't mind if they didn't beat me up anymore either."

"We could make a finding spell and tie it into this one," Kit said.

"Yeah? Well, we better put these needles back first."

"Yeah."

Kit stuck the willow wand in his back pocket as he and Nita worked to push the larch's needles back over the cleared ground. "Where'd you get your book?" Nita said.

"In the city, about a month ago. My mother and father went out antique hunting. There's this one part of Second Avenue where all the little shops are—and one place had this box of secondhand books, and I stopped to look at them because I always look at old books—and this one caught my eye. My hand, actually. I was going after a Tom Swift book underneath it and it pinched me...."

Nita chuckled. "Mine snagged me in the library," she said. "I don't know...I didn't want Joanne—she's the one who beat me up—I didn't want her to get my pen, but I'm glad she didn't get *this*." She pulled her copy of the book out of her jacket as Kit straightened up beside her. She looked over at him. "Does it work?" she demanded. "Does it really *work?*"

Kit stood there for a moment, looking at the replaced needles. "I fixed my dog's nose," he said. "A wasp stung him and I made it go down right away. And I talked to the rock." He looked up at Nita again. "C'mon," he said. "There's a place in the middle where the ground is bare. Let's see what happens."

Together they walked to the center of the hollow, where the pine trees made a circle open to the sky and the ground was bare dirt. Kit pulled out his willow wand and began drawing the diagram again.

"This one I know by heart," he said. "I've started it so many times. Well, this time for sure." He got his book out of his back pocket and consulted it, beginning to write symbols into the diagram. "Would you look and see if there's anything else we need for a finding spell?"

"Sure." Nita found the necessary section in the index of her book and checked it. "Just an image of the thing to be found," she said. "I have to make it while you're spelling. Kit, do you know *why* this works? Leaves, pieces of string, designs on the ground. It doesn't make sense."

Kit kept drawing. "There's a chapter on advanced theory in there, but I couldn't get through it all the way. The magic is supposed to have something to do with interrupting space—"

"Huh?"

"Listen, that's all I could get out of it. There was this one phrase that kept turning up, 'temporospatial claudication.' I think that's how you say it. It's something like, space isn't really empty, it folds around objects—or words—and if you put the right things in the right place and do the right things with them, and say the right things in the Speech, magic happens. Where's the string?"

"This one with all the knots in it?" Nita reached down and picked it up.

"Must have fallen out of my pocket. Stand on this end, okay?" He dropped one end of the string into the middle of the diagram, and Nita stepped onto it. Kit walked around her and the diagram with it, using the end of the string to trace a circle. Just before he came to the place where he had started, he used the willow wand to make a sort of figure-eight mark—a "wizards' knot," the book had called it—and closed the circle with it. Kit tugged at the string as he stood up. Nita let it go, and Kit coiled it and put it away.

"You've got to do this part yourself," Kit said. "I can't write your name for you—each person in a spelling does their own. There's a table in there with all the symbols in it."

Nita scuffed some pages aside and found it, a long list of English letters and numbers, and symbols in the Speech. She got down to look at Kit's name, so that she could see how to write hers, and group by group began to puzzle the symbols out. "Your birthday's August twenty-fifth?"

"Uh-huh."

Nita looked at the symbol for the year. "They skipped you a couple grades, huh?"

"Yeah. It's rotten," Kit said, sounding entirely too cheerful as he said it. Nita knew that tone of voice—it was the one in which she usually answered Joanne, while trying to hide her own fear of what was sure to happen next. "It wouldn't be so bad if they were my age," Kit went on, looking over Nita's shoulder and speaking absently. "But they keep saying things like 'If you're so smart, 'ow come you talk so fonny?' " His imitation of their imitation of his accent was precise and bitter. "They make me sick. Trouble is, they outweigh me."

Nita nodded and started to draw her name on the ground, using the substitutions and symbols that appeared in her manual. Some of them were simple and brief; some of them were almost more complex than she believed possible, crazy amalgams of curls and twists and angles like those an insane stenographer might produce. She did her best to reproduce them, and tied all the symbols together, fastening them into a circle with the same wizards' knot that Kit had used on the outer circle and on his own name.

"Done?" Kit asked. He was standing up again, tracing the outer circle around one more time.

"Yup."

"Okay." He finished the tracing with another repetition of the wizards' knot and straightened up; then he put his hand out as if to feel something in the air. "Good," he said. "Here, come check this."

"Check what?" Nita got up and went over to Kit. She put out her hand as he had, and found that something was resisting the movement of her hand through the air—something that gave slightly under increased pressure, like a mattress being pushed down and then springing back again. Nita felt momentarily nervous. "Can air get through this?"

"I think so. I didn't have any trouble the last couple of times I did it. It's only supposed to seal out unfriendly influences."

Nita stood there with her hand resting against nothing, and the nothing supported her weight. The last of her doubts about the existence of magic went away. She might have imagined the contents of the book, or been purposely misreading. She might have dozed off and dreamed the talking tree. But *this* was daylight, the waking world, and she was leaning one-handed on empty air!

"Those guys who came across you when you had this up," she said, "what did they think?"

"Oh, it worked on them, too. They didn't even understand why they couldn't get at me—they thought it was their idea to yell at me from a distance. They thought they were missing me with the BB guns on purpose, too, to scare me. It's true, what the book said. There are people who couldn't see a magic if it bit them." He glanced around the finished circle. "There are other spells like this that don't need drawings after you do them the first time, and when you need them, they're there really fast—like if someone's about to try beating you up. People just kind of skid away from you."

"I bet," Nita said, with relish. Thoughts of what else she might be able to do to Joanne flickered through her head, but she pushed them aside for the moment. "What next?"

"Next," Kit said, going to the middle of the circle and sitting down carefully so as not to smudge any of the marks he'd made, "we read it. Or I read most of it, and you read your name. Though first you have to check my figuring."

"How come?" Nita joined him, avoiding the lines and angles.

"Two-person spell—both people always check each other's work. But your name, you check again after I do."

Kit was already squinting at Nita's squiggles, so she pulled out her book again and began looking at the symbols Kit had drawn in the dirt. There were clearly two sides to the diagram, and the book said they both had to balance like a chemical equation. Most of the symbols had numerical values attached, for ease in balancing, and Nita started doing addition in her head, making sure both sides matched. Eventually she was satisfied. She looked again at her name, seeing nothing wrong. "Is it okay?"

"Yeah." Kit leaned back a little. "You have to be careful with names, it says. They're a way of saying what you *are*— and if you write something in a spell that's *not* what you are, well . . ."

"You mean . . . *you* change . . . because the spell says you're something else than what you are? You *become* that?"

Kit shrugged, but he looked uneasy. "A spell is saying that you want something to happen," he said. "If you say your name wrong—"

Nita shuddered. "And now?"

"Now we start. You do your name when I come to it. Then, the goal part down there—since it's a joint goal, we say it together. Think you can do it okay if I go slow?"

"Yeah."

Kit took a deep breath with his eyes closed, then opened his eyes and began to read.

Nita had never heard a voice speaking a spell aloud before, and the effect was strange. Ever so slightly, ever so slowly, things began to change around her. The tree-sheltered quiet grew quieter. The cool light that filtered through the canopy of branches grew expectant, fringed with secrecy the way things seen through the edge of a lens are fringed with rainbows. Nita began to feel as if she was caught in the moment between a very vivid dream and the awakening from it. There was that feeling of living in a body—of being aware of familiar surroundings and the realities of the daylight world waiting to be resumed—yet at the same time seeing those surroundings differently, colored with another sort of light, another kind of time. On one level Nita heard Kit reciting a string of polysyllables that should have been meaningless to her—words for symbols, pieces of words, babble. Yet she could also hear Kit talking, saying casually, and, it seemed, in English, "We need to know something, and we suggest this particular method of finding the information . . ." And the words didn't break the expectancy, the listening silence. For once, for the first time, the dream was *real* while Nita was awake. Power stirred in the air around her and waited for her to shape it.

Magic.

She sat and listened to Kit. With each passing second she could catch more clearly the clean metallic taste of the equation as it began to form itself, flickering chill and bright in her mind. Kit's speech was giving it life, and with quiet, flowing efficiency it was going about its purpose. It was invoking the attention of what Nita might have called physical laws, except that there was nothing physical about them—they had to do with flows of a kind of power as different from ordinary energy as energy was from matter. The equation stretched and coiled and caught those powers within itself as the words wove it. Nita and Kit were caught in it, too. To Nita it seemed as if, without moving, she held out her hands, and they were taken—by Kit, and by the spell itself, and by the ponderous powers caught across from her in the dance. There was a pause: Kit looked across the diagrams at her.

Nita scowled at the symbols beside her and began to read them, slowly and with some hesitation—naming herself one concept or one symbol at a time, binding herself into the spell. At first she was scared, for she could feel the strangeness folding in close around her. But then she realized that nothing awful was happening, and as her name became part of the spell, *that* was what was sliding down around her, protecting her. She finished, and she was out of breath, and excited, and she had never been happier in her life.

Kit's voice came in again then, picking up the weave, rejoining the dance. So it went for a while, the strange words and the half-seen, half-felt movements and images falling into a rhythm of light and sound and texture, a song, a poem, a spell. It began to come whole all around them, and all around the tingling air stayed still to better hold the words, and the trees bent close to listen.

Kit came to the set of symbols that stood for his name and who he was, and read them slowly and carefully. Nita felt the spell settle down around him, too. He

finished it and glanced up at Nita, and together they began the goal section of the
spell. Nita did her best to make a clear image of the pen as she spoke—the silver case,
gone a little scratched and grubby now, her
initials incised up on the top. She hardly
had time to wonder at the harmony their
paired voices made before things began to
change again. The shadows of the trees
around them seemed to grow darker; the
aura of expectancy grew sharp enough to
taste. The silence became total, and their
voices fell into it as into a great depth.

The formula for their goal, though
longer than either of their names had been,
seemed to take less time to say—and even
stranger, it began to sound like much more
than just finding a pen and being left alone.
It began to taste of starfire and night
and motion, huge and controlled, utterly
strange. Saying the formula left Kit and
Nita breathless and drained, as if something
powerful had briefly been living and speaking through them and had worn them
down. They finished the formula together,
and gulped for air, and looked at each other

in half-frightened expectation, wondering what would happen next.

The completed spell took effect. Nita had thought that she would gradually begin to see something, the way things had changed gradually in the grove. The spell, though, had its own ideas. Quick as a gasp it slammed them both out of one moment and into another, a shocking, wrenching transition like dreaming that you've fallen out of bed, *wham!* Instinctively they both hung on to the spell as if onto a railing, clutching it until their surroundings steadied down. The darkness had been replaced by a lowering, sullen-feeling gloom. They looked down as if from a high balcony onto a shadowed island prisoned between chill rivers and studded with sharp spikes of iron and cold stone.

(Manhattan?) Kit asked anxiously, without words. Nita felt frozen in place like a statue and couldn't turn to answer him—the spell was holding her immobile.

(It looks like Manhattan,) she said, feeling just as uneasy. (But what's my pen doing *there*?)

Kit would have shaken his head if he could have. (I don't get it. What's wrong here? This *is* New York City—but it never looked this awful, this dirty and nasty and...) He trailed off in confusion and dismay.

Nita looked around her. It was hard to make out anything on the island—there was a murky pall over the city that seemed more than just fog. There was hardly any traffic that she could see, and almost no light—in fact, in all of Manhattan there were only two light sources. In one place on the island—the east Fifties, it looked like—a small point of brittle light seemed to pulse right through steel and stone, throbbing dully like a sown seed of wildfire waiting to explode. The pulses were irregular and distressing, and the light was painful to look at. Some blocks to the south, well into the financial district near the south end of the island, another fire burned, a clear white spark like a sun seed, beating regularly as a heart. It was consoling, but it was very small.

(Now what?) Nita said. (Why would my pen be in this place?) She looked down

67

at the dark grainy air below them, listened to the brooding silence like that of a beast of prey ready to spring, felt the sullen buildings hunching themselves against the oppressive sky—and then felt the *something* malevolent and alive that lay in wait below—a something that *saw* them, was conscious of them, and was darkly pleased.

(Kit, what's *that?*)

(It *knows!*) Kit's thought sang with alarm like a plucked string. (It knows we're here! It shouldn't be able to, but—Nita, the spell's not balanced for this. If that thing grabs us or holds us somehow, we won't be able to get back!)

Nita felt Kit's mind start to flick frantically through the memories of what he had read in his wizards' manual, looking for an idea, for something they could do to protect themselves.

She held very still and looked over his shoulder at his thoughts, even though part of her trembled at the thought of that dark presence that was even now reaching out toward them, lazy, curious, deadly. Abruptly she saw something that looked useful.

(Kit, stop! No, go back one. That's it. Look, it says if you've got an imbalance, you can open out your side of the spell to attract some more power.)

(Yeah, but if the wrong kind of power answers, we're in for it!)

(We're in for it for *sure* if that gets us,) Nita said, indicating the huge, hungry darkness billowing upward toward them like a cloud. (Look, we'll make a hole through the spell big enough for something friendly to fall into, and we'll take potluck.)

Nita could feel Kit's uncertainty as he started choosing from memory the words and symbols he would need. (All right, but I dunno. If something worse happens . . .)

(*What could be worse?*) Nita hollered at Kit, half in amusement, half in fear. The hungry something drew closer.

Kit started to answer, then forgot about it. (There,) he said, laying the equation out in his mind, (I think that's all we need.)

(Go ahead,) Nita said, watching anxiously as their pursuer got closer and the air around them seemed to grow thicker and darker yet. (You say it. Just tell me what to do and when.)

(Right,) Kit said, and began speaking in his mind, much faster than he had during the initial spelling. If that first magic had felt like the weaving of a whole, this one felt like ripping something apart. Their surroundings seemed to shimmer uncertainly, the dark skyline and lead gray sky rippled like a wind-stirred curtain; even that stalking presence seemed to hesitate in momentary confusion. (Push,) Kit said suddenly, (push right there.) Nita felt the torn place that Kit had made in the spell, and she shoved clumsily at it with her mind, trying to make the hole larger.

(It's . . . giving . . .)

(Now, *hard!*) Kit said, and Nita pushed until pain stabbed and stabbed again behind where her eyes should have been, and at the moment she thought she couldn't possibly push anymore, Kit said one short sharp syllable and threw the spell wide open like a door.

It was like standing at the core of a tornado which, rather than spinning you away to Oz, strips the roof off your home, opens the house walls out flat as the petals of a plaster flower, and leaves you standing confused and disbelieving in the heart of a howling of smoke and damned voices; or like moving through a roomful of people, every one of whom tries to catch your eye and tell you the most important thing that ever happened to him. Nita found herself deluged in fragments of sights and sounds and tastes and feelings and thoughts not her own, a madly coexisting maelstrom of imageries from other universes, other earths, other times. Most of them she managed to shut out by squeezing her mind shut like eyes and hanging on to the spell. She sensed that Kit was doing the same and that their stalker was momentarily as bewildered as they were by what was happening. The whirling confusion seemed to be funneling through the hole in the spell like water going down a drain—things, concepts, creatures too large or too small for the hole fell through it, or past it, or around it. But sooner or later something just the right size would catch. (Hope we get something useful,) Nita thought desperately. (Something bigger than that *thing*, anyway.)

And *thump*, something fitted into the

hole with snug precision, and the crazy whirling died away, and the two of them had company in the spellweb. Something small, Nita felt; very small, *too* small— but no, it was big, too . . . Confused, she reached out to Kit.

(Is that it? Can we get out now? Before that what's-its-name—)

The what's-its-name shook itself with a ripple of rage and hunger that Kit and Nita could feel even at a distance. It headed toward them again, quickly, done with playing with them.

(Uh-oh!) Kit said. (Let's get outta here!)

(What do we—)

(What in the—) said a voice that neither of them recognized.

(Out!) Kit said, and hooked the spell into the added power that the newcomer provided, and *pulled*. . . .

. . . Plain pale daylight came down around them, heavy as a collapsed tent. Gravity yanked at them. Kit fell over sideways and lay there panting on the ground like someone who's run a race. Nita sagged, covered her face, bent over double right down to the ground, struggling for breath.

Eventually she began to recover, but she put off moving or opening her eyes. The book had warned that spelling had its prices, and one of them was the physical exhaustion that goes along with any large, mostly mental work of creation. Nita felt as if she had just been through about a hundred English tests with essay questions, one after another. "Kit?" she said, worried by his silence.

"Nnngggg," Kit said, and rolled over into a sort of crouch, holding his head in his hands. "Ooooh. Turn off the *Sun*."

"It's not that bad," Nita said, opening her eyes. Then she winced and shut them in a hurry. It was.

"How long've we been here?" Kit muttered. "The Sun shouldn't be showing here yet."

"It's—" Nita said. She opened her eyes again to check her watch and was distracted by a bright light to her right that was entirely too low to be the Sun. She squinted at it and then forgot what she had started to say.

Hanging in midair about three feet away from her, inside the circle, was a spark of eye-searing white fire. It looked no bigger than a pinhead, but it was brilliant all out of proportion to its size, and was giving off light about as bright as that of a two-hundred-watt bulb without a shade. The light bobbed gently in midair, up and down, looking like a will-o'-the-wisp plugged into too powerful a current and about to blow out. Nita sat there with her mouth open and *stared.*

The bright point dimmed slightly, appeared to describe a small tight circle so that it could take in Kit, the drawn circle, trees and leaves and sky; then it came to rest again, staring back at Nita. Though she couldn't catch what Kit was feeling, now that the spell was over, she could feel the light's emotions quite clearly—amazement, growing swiftly into unbelieving pleasure. Suddenly it blazed up white-hot again.

(Dear Artificer,) it said in bemused delight, (I've blown my quanta and gone to the Good Place!)

Nita sat there in silence for a moment, thinking a great many things at once.

Uhh, . . . she thought. And, *So I wanted to be a wizard, huh? Serves me right. Something falls into my world and thinks it's gone to Heaven. Boy, is it gonna get a shock.* And, *What in the world is it, anyway?*

"Kit," Nita said. "Excuse me a moment," she added, nodding with abrupt courtesy at the light source. "Kit." She turned slightly and reached down to shake him by the shoulder. "Kit. C'mon, get up. We have company."

"Mmmp?" Kit said, scrubbing at his eyes and starting to straighten up. "Oh no, the binding didn't blow, did it?"

"Nope. It's the extra power you called in. I think it came back with us."

"Well, it—oh," Kit said, as he finally managed to focus on the sedately hovering brightness. "*Oh.* It's—uh . . ."

"Right," Nita said. "It says," she added, "that it's blown its quanta. Is that dangerous?" she asked the light.

(Dangerous?) It laughed inside, a crackling sound like an overstimulated Geiger counter. (Artificer, child, it means I'm *dead.*) "Child" wasn't precisely the concept it used; Nita got a fleeting impression of a huge volume of dust and gas contracting gradually toward a common center, slow, confused, and nebulous. She wasn't flattered.

"Maybe you won't like hearing this," Nita said, "but I'm not sure this is the Good Place. It doesn't seem that way to *us*, anyhow."

The light drew a figure eight in the air, a shrug. (It looks that way to *me*,) it said. (Look how orderly everything is! And how much life there is in just one place! Where I come from, even a spore's worth of life is scarcer than atoms in a comet's tail.)

"Excuse me," Kit asked, "but what *are* you?"

It said something Nita could make little sense of. The concept she got looked like page after page of mathematical equations. Kit raised his eyebrows. "It uses the Speech, too," he commented as he listened.

"So what is it?"

Kit looked confused. "Its name says that it came from way out in space somewhere, and it has a mass equal to—to five or six blue-white giant stars and a few thousand-odd planets, and it emits all up and down the matter-energy spectrum, all kinds of light and radiation and even some subatomic particles." He shrugged. "You have any idea what that is?"

Nita stared at the light in growing disbelief. "Where's all your mass?" she asked. "If you have that much, the gravity should have crushed us up against you the minute you showed up."

(Elsewhere,) the light said offhandedly. (I have a singularity-class temporospatial claudication.)

"A warp," Nita whispered. "A tunnel through space–time. Are you a white hole?"

It stopped bobbing, stared at her as if she had said something derogatory. (Do I look like a hole?)

"Do I look like a cloud of gas?" Nita snapped back, and then sighed—her mouth was getting the better of her again. "I'm sorry. That's just what we call your kind of—uh—creature. Because you act like a hole in the Universe that light and radiation come through. I know you're not, really. But, Kit," she said, turning, "where's my

pen? And where's the power you were after? Didn't the spell work?"

"Spells always work," Kit said. "That's
what the book says. When you ask for
something, you always get back something
that'll help you solve your problem, or be
the solution itself." He looked entirely
confused. "I asked for that power aura for
me, and your pen for you—that was all. If
we got a white hole, it means he's the
answer—"

"If he's the answer," Nita said, bemused, "I'm not sure I understand the
question."

(This is all fascinating,) the white hole
said, (but I have to find a functional-
Advisory nexus in a hurry. I found out that
the *Naming of Lights* has gone missing, and
I managed to find a paradimensional net
with enough empty loci to get me to an
Advisory in a hurry. But something seems
to have gone wrong. Somehow I don't
think you're Advisories.)

"Uh, no," Kit said. "I think we called
you—"

(*You* called me?) The white hole regarded Kit with mixed reverence and

amazement. (You're one of the Powers born of Life? Oh, I'm sorry I didn't recognize You—I know You can take any shape but somehow I'd always thought of You as being bigger. A quasar, or a meganova.) The white hole made a feeling of rueful amusement. (It's *confusing* being dead!)

"Oh, brother," Kit said. "Look, I'm not—you're not—just *not*. We made a spell and we called you. I don't think you're dead."

(If you say so,) the white hole said, polite but doubtful. (You called *me*, though? Me personally? I don't think we've met before.)

"No, we haven't," Nita said. "But we were doing this spell, and we found something, but something found us, too, and we wouldn't have been able to get back here unless we called in some extra power—so we did, and it was you, I guess. You're not mad, are you?" she asked timidly. The thought of what a live, intelligent white hole might be able to do if it got annoyed scared her badly.

(Mad? No. As I said, I was trying to

get out of my own space to get the news to someone who could use it, and then all of a sudden there was a paranet with enough loci to handle all the dimensions I carry, so I grabbed it.) The white hole made another small circle, looking around him curiously. (Maybe it did work. Are there Advisories in this—on this— What is this, anyway?)

Kit looked at Nita. "Huh?"

(This,) the white hole said, (all of this.) He made another circle.

"Oh! A planet," Nita said. "See, there's our star." She pointed, and the white hole rotated slightly to look.

(Artificer within us,) he said, (maybe I *have* blown my quanta, after all. I always wanted to see a planet, but I never got around to it. Habit, I guess. You get used to sitting around emitting X rays after a while, and you don't think of doing any-thing else. You want to see some?) he asked suddenly. He sounded a little insecure.

"Uh, maybe you'd better not," Nita said.

(How come? They're really pretty.)

"We can't see them—and besides, we're

not built to take hard radiation. Our atmosphere shuts most of it out."

(A real planet,) the white hole said, wondering and delighted, (with a real atmosphere. Well! If this is a planet, there has to be an Advisory around here somewhere. Could you help me find one?)

"Uhh—" Kit looked uncertainly at the white hole. "Sure. But do you think you could help me find some power? And Nita get her pen back?"

The white hole looked Kit up and down. (Some potential, some potential,) he muttered. (I could probably have you emitting light pretty quickly, if we worked together on a regular basis. Maybe even some alpha. We'll see. What's a pen?)

"What's your name?" Kit asked. "I mean, we can't just call you 'hey you' all the time."

(True,) the white hole said. (My name is Khairelikoblepharehglukumeilichephreidosd'enagouni—) and at the same time he went flickering through a pattern of colors that was evidently the visual translation.

"Ky—elik—" Nita began.

"Fred," Kit said quickly. "Well," he

added as they looked at him again, "if we have to yell for help or something, the other way's too long. And that was the only part I got, anyway."

"Is that okay with you?" Nita asked.

The white hole made his figure-eight shrug again. (Better than having my truename mangled, I guess,) he said, and chuckled silently. (Fred, then. And you are?)

"Nita."

"Kit."

(I see why you like them short,) Fred said. (All right. Tell me what a 'pen' is, and I'll try to help you find it. But we really must get to an Advisory as fast as we can.)

"Okay," Kit said. "Let's break the circle and go talk."

"Sounds good," Nita said, and began to erase the diagrams they had drawn. Kit cut the wizards' knot and scuffed the circle open in a few places, while Nita took a moment to wave her hand through the now empty air. "Not bad for a first spell," she said with satisfaction.

(I meant to ask,) Fred said politely, (what's a spell?)

Nita sighed, and smiled, and picked up her book, motioning Fred to follow her over to where Kit sat. It was going to be a long afternoon, but she didn't care. Magic was loose in the world.

Research and
Development

THEY WERE AT THE schoolyard early the
next morning, to be sure they wouldn't
miss Joanne and her crew. Nita and Kit sat
on the curb by the front door to the school,
staring across at the packed dirt and dull
grass of the athletic field next to the building. Kit leafed through his wizards' manual, while Fred hung over his shoulder and
looked around with mild interest at everything. (Will it be long?) he said, his light
flickering slightly.

"No," Nita said. She was shaking. After the other day, she didn't want anything
to do with Joanne at all. But she wanted
that pen back, so . . .

"Look, it'll be all right," Kit said, paging through his manual. "Just do it the way we decided last night. Get close to her, keep her busy for a little while. Fred'll do the rest."

"It's keeping her busy that worries me," Nita muttered. "Her idea of busy usually involves her fists and my face."

(I don't understand,) Fred said, and Nita had to laugh briefly—she and Kit had heard that phrase about a hundred times since Fred arrived. He used it on almost everything. (What are you afraid of?)

"This," Nita said, pointing to her black eye. "And this—" uncovering a bruise. "And this, and this—"

Fred regarded her with a moment's discomfiture. (I thought you came that way. Joanne makes this happen?)

"Uh-huh. And it hurts *getting* this way."

(But she only changes your outsides. Aren't your insides still the same afterward?)

Nita had to stop and think about that one.

"Okay," Kit said suddenly, "here's the

Advisory list for our area." He ran a finger down the page. "And here's the one in town. Twenty-seven Hundred Rose—"

"That's up the hill past the school. What's the name?"

"Lessee. 'Swale, T.B., and Romeo, C.J. Research Advisories, temporospatial adjustments, entastics, nonspecific scry-ings—' "

"Wait a minute," Nita said hurriedly. " 'Swale'? You mean Crazy Swale? We can't go in there, Kit, that place is haunted! Everybody knows that! Weird noises are always coming out of there—"

"If it's haunted," Kit said, "it's haunted by wizards. We might as well go after school, it's only five or six blocks up the road."

They were quiet for a while. It was about twenty minutes before the bell would ring for the doors to open, and a few early kids were gathering around the doors. "Maybe we could rig you a defense against getting hit," Kit said, as he kept looking through his manual. "How about this?" He pointed at one page, and both Nita and Fred looked at the formula he was indicating. All it needed was the right words. It would be something of a strain to carry the shield for long, but Nita wouldn't have to; and any attempt to hit her would just glance off.

(The problem is,) Fred said, (that spell will alter the field slightly around this Joanne person. I'm going to have a hard enough time matching my pattern to that of your pen so that I can get it off her—if indeed she has it. Her own field is going to interfere, and so will yours, Nita. More stress on the space in the area and I might not be able to get your pen back at all.)

Nita shook her head. She could tolerate another black eye if it meant getting that pen back. "Forget it," she said, still shaking, and leaned forward a bit, elbows on knees and face in hands, trying to relax. Above her the old maple trees were muttering morning thoughts in the early sunlight, languid observations on the weather and the decreasing quality of the tenant birds who built nests in their branches. Out in the field the grass was singing a scratchy soprano chorus—(grow-growgrowgrowgrowgrow)—which broke off abruptly and turned into an annoyed mob sound of boos and razzes as one of the groundskeepers, way across the field, started up a lawn mower. *I'm good with plants,* Nita thought. *I guess I take after Dad. I wonder if I'll ever be able to hear people this way*

Kit nudged her. "You're on," he said, and Nita looked up and saw Joanne walking into the schoolyard. Their eyes met. Joanne recognized her handiwork on Nita's face and smiled. *Now or never!* Nita thought, and got right up before she had a chance to chicken out and blow everything. She walked over to Joanne without a pause, fast, to keep the tremor in her knees from showing. *Oh, Fred, please be behind me. And what in the world can I say to her?*

"I want my pen back, Joanne," she said—or rather it fell out of her mouth, and she went hot at her own stupidity. Yet the momentary shocked look on Joanne's face made her think that maybe saying what was on her mind hadn't been so stupid after all. Joanne's shock didn't last; a second later she was smiling again. "Callahan," she said slowly, "are you looking for another black eye to match that one?"

"Lllp. No," Nita said, "just my pen, thanks."

"I don't know what you're talking about," Joanne said, and then grinned. "You always were a little odd. I guess you've finally flipped out."

"I had a space pen on me the other day, and it was gone afterward. One of you took it. I want it back." Nita was shaking worse than ever, but she was also surprised that the fist hadn't hit yet. And there over Joanne's shoulder was a flicker, a pinpoint of light, hardly to be seen, looking at her.

(Don't react. Make me a picture of the thing now.)

"What makes you think I would want anything of *yours?*" Joanne was saying, still with that smile. Nita looked straight at her and thought about the pen. Silver barrel, grooved all around the lower half to keep the user's fingers from slipping. Her initials engraved on it. *Hers,* her pen.

(Enough. Now then—)

"But now that I think of it, I do remember finding a pen on the ground last week. Let's see." Joanne was enjoying this so much that she actually flipped open the top of her backpack and began rummaging around. "Let's see, *here*—" She came up with something. Silver barrel, grooved— and Nita went hot again, not with embarrassment this time.

"It's mine!"

"Come and get it, then," Joanne said, dropping her backpack, keeping her smile, holding the pen back a little.

And a spark of white light seemed to light on the end of the pen as Joanne held it up, and then both were gone with a *pop* and a breath of air. Joanne spun to see who had plucked the pen out of her fingers, then whirled on Nita again. Nita smiled and held out her hands, empty.

Joanne was not amused. She stepped in close, and Nita took a few hurried steps back, unable to stop grinning even though she knew she was going to get hit. Heads were turning all around the schoolyard at the prospect of a fight. "Callahan," Joanne hissed, "you're in for it now!"

The eight-thirty bell went off so suddenly they both jumped. Joanne stared at Nita for a long long moment, then turned and went to pick up her backpack. "Why hurry things?" she said, straightening. "Callahan, if I were you, I'd sleep here tonight. Because when you try to leave . . ."

She walked off toward the doors. Nita stood where she was, still shaking, but with amazement and triumph as much as with fear. Kit came up beside her when Joanne was gone, and Fred appeared, a bright point between them.

"You were great!" Kit said.

"I'm gonna get killed tonight," Nita said, but she couldn't be terrified about it just yet. "Fred, have you got it?"

The point of light was flickering, and there was something about the way it did so that made Nita wonder if something was wrong. (Yes,) Fred said, the thought coming with a faint queasy feeling to it. (And that's the problem.)

"Are you okay?" Kit asked. "Where'd it go?"

(I swallowed it,) Fred said, sounding genuinely miserable now.

"But that was what you were going to do," Nita said, puzzled. "Catch it in your own energy field, you said, make a little pocket and hold it there."

(I know. But my fields aren't working the way they should. Maybe it's this gravity. I'm not used to any gravity but my own. I think it went down the wrong way.)

"Oh, brother," Kit said.

"Well," Nita said, "at least Joanne hasn't got it. When we go to the Advisories tonight, maybe they can help us get it out."

Fred made a small thought-noise somewhere between a burp and a squeak. Nita and Kit looked up at him, concerned—and then both jumped back hurriedly from something that went BANG! down by their feet.

They stared at the ground. Sitting there on the packed dirt was a small portable color TV, brand new.

"Uh, Fred—" Kit said.

Fred was looking down at the TV with embarrassment verging on shame. (I emitted it,) he said.

Nita stared at him. "But I thought white holes only emitted little things. Subatomic particles. Nothing so big—or so orderly."

(I wanted to visit an orderly place,) Fred said miserably. (See what it got me!)

"Hiccups," Kit muttered. "Fred, I think you'd better stay outside until we're finished for the day. We'll go straight to the Advisories' from here."

"Joanne permitting," Nita said. "Kit, we've got to go in."

(I'll meet you here,) Fred said. The mournful thought was followed by another burp/squeak, and another BANG! and four volumes of an encyclopedia were sitting on the ground next to the TV.

Kit and Nita hurried for the doors, sweating. Apparently wizardry had more drawbacks than the book had indicated....

Lunch wasn't calm, but it *was* interesting, due to the thirty teachers, assistant principal, principal, and school superintendent who were all out on the athletic field, along with most of the students. They were walking around looking at the furniture, vacuum cleaners, computer components, books, knickknacks, motorcycles, typewriters, art supplies, stoves, sculptures, lumber, and many other odd things that had since morning been appearing one after another in the field. No one knew what to make of any of it, or what to do; and though Kit and Nita felt sure they would be connected with the situation somehow, no one accused them of anything.

They met again at the schoolyard door at three, pausing just inside it while Nita peered out to see if Joanne was waiting. She was, and eight of her friends were with her, talking and laughing among themselves. "Kit," Nita said quietly, "we've got problems."

He looked. "And this is the only door we can use."

Something went BANG! out in the field, and Nita, looking out again, saw heads turn among Joanne's group. Without a moment's pause every one of the girls headed off toward the field in a hurry, leaving Joanne to glare at the school door for a moment. Then she took off after the others. Kit and Nita glanced at each other. "I get this feeling . . ." Kit said.

"Let's go."

They waited until Joanne was out of sight and then leaned cautiously out of the door, looking around. Fred was suddenly there, wobbling in the air. He made a feeling of greeting at them; he seemed tired, but cheerful, at least for the moment.

Nita glanced over her shoulder to see what had drawn the attention of Joanne and her group—and drew in a sharp breath at the sight of the shiny silver Learjet. "Fred," she said, "you did that on purpose!"

She felt him look back, too, and his cheerfulness drowned out his weariness and queasiness for a moment. (I felt you wondering whether to come out, so I exerted myself a little. What *was* that thing?)

"We'll explain later; right now we should run. Fred, thank you!"

(You're most welcome. Just help me *stop* this!)

"Can you hold it in for a few blocks?"

(What's a block?)

They ran down Rose Avenue, and Fred paced them. Every now and then a little of Fred's hiccup noise would squeak out, and he would fall behind them, controlling it while they ran on ahead. Then he would catch up again. The last time he did it, they paused and waited for him. Twenty-seven Hundred Rose had a high poplar hedge with one opening for the walk up to the house, and neither of them felt like going any farther without Fred.

(Well?) he said, when he caught up. (Now what?)

Nita and Kit looked at each other. "I don't care if they *are* wizards," Nita said, "I want to peek in and have a look before I just walk in there. I've heard too many stories about this place—"

(Look,) Fred said in great discomfort, (I've got to—)

Evidently there was a limit on how long a white hole in Fred's condition could hold it in. The sound of Fred's hiccup was so much louder than usual that Nita and Kit crowded back away from him in near panic. The BANG! sounded like the beginning of a fireworks display, and when its echoes faded, a powder blue Mercedes-Benz was sitting half on, half off the sidewalk.

(My gnaester hurts,) Fred said.

"Let's peek," Nita said, turned, and pushed a little way through the hedge. She wanted to be sure there were no monsters or skeletons hanging from trees or anything else uncanny going on in the yard before she went in. What she did *not* expect was the amiable face of an enormous black-and-white English sheepdog, which first slurped her face energetically, then grabbed her right arm in gentle but insistent teeth and pulled her straight through the hedge.

"Kit!" she almost screamed, and then remembered not to because Crazy Swale or whoever else lived here might hear her. Her cry came out as sort of a grunt. She heard Kit come right through the bushes behind her as the sheepdog dragged her along through the yard. There was nothing spooky about the place at all—the house was big, a two-story affair, but normal-looking, all warm wood and shingles. The yard was grassy, with a landscaped garden as pretty as one of her father's. One side of the house had wide glass patio doors open-ing on a roofed terrace. Potted plants hung down and there was even a big square masonry tank, a fishpond—Nita caught a glimpse of something coppery swimming as the sheepdog dragged her past it to the terrace doors. It was at that point that the dog let go of her arm and began barking noisily, and Nita began seriously thinking of running for it.

"All right, all right," said a man's voice, a humorous one, from inside the house, and it was *definitely* too late for running. Kit came up behind Nita, panting. "All *right*, Annie, let's see what you've got this time."

The screen door slid open, and Nita and Kit looked in slight surprise at the man who opened it. Somehow they had been expecting that any wizard not their age would be old, but this man was young, certainly no more than in his middle thirties. He had dark hair and was tall and broad-shouldered. He looked rather like someone out of a cigarette ad, except that he was smiling, which the men in cigarette ads rarely do. "Well," the man said, sounding not at all annoyed by three unexpected guests, "I see you've met Annie . . ."

"She, uh," Nita said, glancing down at the dog, who was smiling at her with the same bemused interest as her master. "She found me looking through your hedge."

"That's Annie for you," the man said, sounding a bit resigned. "She's good at finding things. I'm Tom Swale." And he held out his hand for Nita to shake.

"Nita Callahan," she said, taking it.

"Kit Rodriguez," Kit said from beside her, reaching out to shake hands, too.

"Good to meet you. Call me Tom. What can I do for you?"

"Are you the Advisory?" Kit said.

Tom's eyebrows went up. "You kids have a spelling problem?"

Nita grinned at the pun and glanced over her shoulder. "Fred?"

Fred bobbed up between her and Kit, regarding Tom, who looked back at the unsteady spark of light with only moderate surprise. "He's a white hole," Nita said. "He swallowed my space pen."

(T-*hup!*) Fred said, and BANG! went the air between Kit and Nita as they stepped hurriedly off to either side. Fourteen one-kilogram bricks of 999-fine Swiss gold fell clattering to the patio's brown tiles.

"I can see this is going to take some explaining," Tom said. "Come on in."

They followed him into the house. A big comfortable living room opened onto a den on one side and a bright kitchen-dining room on the other. "Carl, we've got company," Tom called as they entered the kitchen.

"Wha?" replied a muffled voice—muffled because the upper half of its owner was mostly in the cabinet under the double sink. The rest of him was sprawled across the kitchen floor. This by itself wasn't so odd; what *was* odd was the assortment of wrenches and other tools floating in the air just outside the cabinet doors. From under the sink came a sound like a wrench slipping off a pipe, and a sudden soft thump as it hit something else. Probably its user. "Nnngg!" said the voice under the sink, and all the tools fell clattering to the kitchen floor. The voice broke into some most creative swearing.

Tom frowned and smiled both at once. "Such language in front of guests! You ought to sleep outside with Annie. Come on out of there, we're needed for a consultation."

"You really are wizards!" Nita said, reassured but still surprised. She had rarely seen two more normal-looking people.

Tom chuckled. "Sure we are. Not that

we do too much freelancing these days—better to leave that to the younger practitioners, like you two."

The other man got out from under the sink, brushing himself off. He was at least as tall as Tom, and as broad-shouldered, but his dark hair was shorter and he had an impressive mustache. "Carl Romeo," he said in a voice with a pronounced Brooklyn accent. He shook hands with Kit and Nita. "Who's this?" he said, indicating Fred. Fred hiccuped; the resulting explosion produced six black star sapphires the size of tennis balls.

"Fred here," Tom said, "has a small problem."

"I wish *I* had problems like that," Carl remarked. "Something to drink, people? Soda?"

After a few minutes the four of them were settled around the kitchen table, with Fred hovering nearby. "It said in the book that you specialize in temporospatial claudications," Kit said.

"Carl does. Maintenance and repair; he keeps the worldgates at Grand Central

Station and Rockefeller Center working. You've come to the right place."

"His personal gate is acting up, huh?" Carl said. "I'd better get the books." He got up. "Fred, what're the entasis figures on your warp?"

Fred mentally rattled off a number of symbols in the Speech, as he had when Kit asked him what he was. "Right," Carl said, and went off to the den.

"What do you do?" Nita said to Tom.

"Research, mostly. Also we're something of a clearinghouse for news and gossip in the Business. If someone needs details on a rare spell, or wants to know how power balances are running in a particular place, I can usually find out for them."

"But you do other things, too." Kit looked around at the house.

"Oh, sure, we work. I write for a living—after all, some of the things I see in the Business make good stories. And Carl sells commercial time for WNXT in the city. As well as regular time, on the side."

Kit and Nita looked at each other,

puzzled. Tom chuckled. "Well, he does claudications, gatings, doesn't he? Temporo-spatial—time and space. If you can squeeze space—claudicate it—so that you pop out of one place and into another, why can't you squeeze time the same way? Haven't you heard the saying about 'buying time'? Carl's the one you buy it from. Want to buy a piece of next Thursday?"

"I can get it for you wholesale," Carl said as he came back into the room. In his arms he was carrying several hardbound books as thick as telephone directories. On his shoulder, more interesting, was a splendid scarlet-blue-and-yellow macaw, which regarded Kit and Nita and Fred out of beady black eyes. "Kit, Nita, Fred," Carl said, "Machu Picchu. Peach for short." He sat down, put the books on the table, and began riffling through the one on top of the stack; Tom pulled one out from lower in the pile and began doing the same.

"All right," Tom said, "the whole story, from the beginning."

They told him, and it took a while. When they got to Fred's part of the story, and the fact that the *Naming of Lights* was missing, Tom and Carl became very quiet and just looked at one another for a moment. "Damn," Tom said, "I *wondered* why the entry in the *Materia Magica* hadn't been updated in so long. This is news, all right. We'll have to call a regional Advisories' meeting."

Fred hiccuped again, and the explosion left behind it a year's back issues of *TV Guide*.

"Later," Carl said. "The situation here looks like it's deteriorating." He paused at one page of the book he was looking through, ran his finger down a column. The macaw peered over his shoulder as if interested. "Alpha-rai-entath-eight, you said?"

(Right.)

"I can fix you," Carl said. "Take about five minutes." He got up and headed for the den again.

"What *is* the *Naming of Lights?*" Kit said to Tom. "We tried to get Fred to tell us last night, but it kept coming out in symbols that weren't in our books."

"Well, this is a pretty advanced subject. A novice's manual wouldn't have much information on the *Naming of Lights* any more than the instruction manual for a rifle would have information on atomic bombs..." Tom took a drink. "It's a book. At least that's what it looks like when it's in or near this Universe. The *Book of Night with Moon*, it's called here, since in these parts you need moonlight to read it. It's always been most carefully accounted for; the Senior wizards keep an eye on it. If it's suddenly gone missing, we've got trouble..."

"Why?" Nita said.

"Well, if you've gotten even this far in wizardry, you know how the wizards' symbology, the Speech, affects the things you use it on. When you use it, you *define* what you're speaking about. That's why it's dangerous to use the Speech carelessly. You can accidentally redefine something, change its nature. Something, or some-*one*—" He paused, took another drink of his soda. "The *Book of Night with Moon* is written in the Speech. In it, every-thing's described. *Everything*. You, me, Fred, Carl, ... this house, this town, this world. This Universe and everything in it. *All* the Universes..."

Kit looked skeptical. "How could a book that big get lost?"

"Who said it was big? You'll notice something about your manuals after a while," Tom said. "They won't get any bigger, but there'll be more and more inside them as you learn more, or need to know more. Even in plain old math it's true that the inside can be bigger than the outside; it's definitely true in wizardry. But believe me, the *Book of Night with Moon* has everything described in it. It's one of the reasons we're all here—the power of those descriptions helps keep everything that *is* in existence." Tom looked worried. "And every now and then the Senior wizards have to go get the *Book* and read from it, to remind the worlds what they are, to preserve everything alive or inanimate."

"Have *you* read from it?" Nita said, made uneasy by the disturbed look on Tom's face.

Tom glanced at her in shock, then began to laugh. "Me? No, no. I hope I never have to."

"But if it's a good *Book*, if it preserves things—" Kit said.

"It's good—at least, yes, it preserves, or lets things grow the way they want to. But reading it, being the vessel for all that power—I wouldn't want to. Even good can be terribly dangerous. But this isn't anything you two need to worry about. The Advisories and the Senior wizards will handle it."

"But you *are* worried," Kit said.

"Yes, well—" Tom took another drink. "If it were just that the bright *Book* had gone missing, that wouldn't be so bad. A universe can go a long time without affirmation-by-reading. But the bright *Book* has an opposite number, a dark one; the *Book Which Is Not Named,* we call it. It's written in the Speech too, but its descriptions are ... skewed. And if the bright *Book* is missing, the dark one gains potential power. If someone should read from that one now, while the *Book of Night with Moon* isn't available to counteract the power of the dark one ..." Tom shook his head.

Carl came in then, the macaw still riding his shoulder. "Here we go," he said, and dumped several sticks of chalk, an enormous black claw, and a 1943 zinc penny on the table. Nita and Kit stared at each other, neither quite having the nerve to ask whose claw it had been. "Now you understand," Carl said as he picked up the chalk and began to draw a circle around the table, "that this is only going to stop the hiccups. You three are going to have to go to Manhattan and hook Fred into the Grand Central worldgate to get that pen out. Don't worry about being noticed. People use it all the time and no one's the wiser. *I* use it sometimes when the trains are late."

"Carl," Tom said, "doesn't it strike you as a little strange that the first wizardry these kids do produces Fred—who brings this news about the good *Book*—and they come straight to us—"

"Don't be silly," the macaw on Carl's shoulder said in a scratchy voice. "*You* know there are no accidents."

Nita and Kit stared.

"Wondered when you were going to say something useful," Carl said, sounding bored. "You think we keep you for your looks? OW!" he added, as the bird bit him on the ear. He hit it one on the beak, and while it was still shaking its head woozily, put it up on the table beside Tom.

Picchu sidled halfway up Tom's arm, stopped and looked at Nita and Kit. "Dos d'en agouni nikyn toude pheresthai," it muttered, and got all the way up on Tom's shoulder, and then glared at them again. "Well?"

"She only speaks in tongues to show off," Tom said. "Ignore her, or rap her one if she bites you. We just keep her around because she tells the future." Tom made as if to smack the bird again, and Picchu ducked back. "How about the stocks tomorrow, bird?" he said.

Picchu cleared her throat. " 'And that's the way it is,' " she said in a voice very much like that of a famous newscaster, " 'July eighteen, 1988. From New York, this is Walter—' "

Tom fisted the bird in the beak, *clunk!* Picchu shook her head again. " 'Issues were down in slow trading,' " she said resentfully. " 'The Dow-Jones average—' " and she called off some numbers. Tom grimaced.

"I should have gone into pork bellies," he muttered. "I ought to warn you two: If you have pets, look out. Practicing wizardry around them can cause some changes."

"There we go," Carl said, and stood up straight. "Fred, you ready? Hiccup for me again."

(I can't,) Fred said, sounding nervous. (You're all staring.)

"Never mind, I can start this in the meantime." Carl leaned over the table, glanced down at one of the books, and began reading in the Speech, a quick flow of syllables sharpened by his Brooklyn accent. In the middle of the third sentence Fred hiccuped, and without warning the wizardry took. Time didn't precisely stop, but it held still, and Nita became aware of what Carl's wizardry was doing to Fred, or rather had done already—subtly untangling forces that were knotted tight together. The half-finished hiccup and the wizardry came loose at the same time, leaving Fred looking bright and well for the first time since that morning. He still radiated uncertainty, though, like a person who isn't sure he's stopped hiccuping yet.

"You'll be all right," Carl said, scuffing away the chalk marks on the floor. "Though as I said, that pen is still in there with the rest of your mass, at the other end of your claudication, and you'll need Grand Central to get it out."

(Have you stopped my emissions entirely?) Fred said.

"No, of course not. I couldn't do that: you'll still emit from time to time. Mostly what you're used to, though. Radiation and such."

"Grand Central!" Kit was looking worried. "I don't think my mother and father are going to want me in the city alone. I could sneak in, I guess, but they'd want to know where I'd been all that while."

"Well," Tom said, looking thoughtful, "you've got school. You couldn't go before the weekend anyway, right? Carl could sell you a piece of Saturday or Sunday—"

Kit and Nita looked at each other, and then at the two men. "Uh, we don't have much money."

"Who said anything about money?" Carl said. "Wizards don't pay each other cash. They pay off in service—and some-times the services aren't done for years. But first let's see if there's any time available this weekend. Saturdays go fast, even though they're expensive, especially Satur-day mornings."

He picked up another book and began going through it. Like all the other books, it was printed in the same type as Nita's and Kit's manuals, though the print was much smaller and arranged differently. "This way," Tom said, "if you buy some time, you could be in the city all day, all week if you wanted—but once you activate the piece of time you're holding, you're back *then*. You have to pick a place to anchor the time to, of course, a twenty-foot radius. But after you've finished whatever you have to do, you bring your marked time to life, and there you are. Maybe five minutes before you started for the city, back at home. Or anywhere and anywhen else along the path you'll follow that day."

"Huh," Carl said suddenly. "Callahan, J., and Rodriguez, C., is that you two?" They nodded. "You have a credit already,"

Carl said, sounding a little surprised. "What have you two been doing to rate that?"

"Must have been for bringing Fred through," Tom said. "I didn't know that Upper Management had started giving out door prizes, though."

From her perch on Tom's shoulder, Picchu snorted. "Oh? What's that mean?" Tom said. "Come on, bird, be useful. Is there something you know that these kids ought to?"

"I want a raise," Picchu said, sounding sullen.

"You just had one. Talk!"

" 'Brush your teeth twice a day, and see your dentist regularly,' " the macaw began, in a commercial announcer's voice. Tom made a fist and stared at her. "All right, all right," Picchu muttered. She looked over at Kit and Nita, and though her voice when she spoke had the usual good-natured annoyance about it, her eyes didn't look angry or even teasing—they looked anxious. Nita got a sudden chill down her back. "Don't be afraid to make corrections," Picchu said. "Don't be afraid to lend a hand." She fell silent, seeming to think for a moment. "And don't look down."

Tom stared at the macaw. "Can't you be a little more specific?"

"Human lives," Picchu said irritably, "aren't much like the Dow-Jones average. No, I can't."

Tom sighed. "Sorry. Kids, if she says it, she has a reason for saying it—so remember."

"Here you go," Carl said. "Your piece of time is from 10:45 to 10:47 on this next Saturday morning. There aren't any weekend openings after that until sometime in July."

"We'll take this one," Kit said. "At least I can—Nita, will your folks let you go?"

She nodded. "I have some allowance saved up, and I'd been thinking about going into the city to get my dad a birthday present anyhow. I doubt there'll be any trouble."

Kit looked uncomfortable for a moment. "But there's something I'm not sure about. My spell—our spell brought Fred here. How are we going to get him back where he belongs?"

(Am I a problem?) Fred said, sounding concerned.

"Oh, no, no—it's just that, Fred, this isn't your home, and it seemed as if sooner or later you might want to go back where you came from."

"As far as that goes," Tom said, "if it's your spell that brought him here, you'll be able to send him back. The instructions are in your book, same as the instructions for opening the Grand Central worldgate."

"Stick to those instructions," Carl said. "Don't be tempted to improvise. That claudication is the oldest one in New York, and it's the trickiest because of all the people using it all the time. One false syllable in a spell and you may wind up in Schenectady."

(Is that another world?) Fred asked.

"Nearly." Carl laughed. "Is there anything else we can do for you?"

Nita and Kit shook their heads and got up to leave, thanking Tom and Carl and Picchu. "Let us know how things turn out," Tom said. "Not that we have any doubts—two wizards who can produce a white hole on the first try are obviously doing all right. But give us a call. We're in the book."

The two men saw Nita and Kit as far as the patio door, said their good-byes, and went back into the house. Nita started off across the lawn the way she had come, but Kit paused for a moment by the fishpond, staring down into it. He pulled a penny out of his pocket, dropped it in.

Nita saw the ripples spread—and then suddenly another set of ripples wavered away from the head of a very large goldfish, which spat the penny back at Kit and eyed him with distaste. "Do *I* throw money on *your* living-room floor?" it said, and then dived out of sight.

Kit picked up his penny and went after Nita and Fred as they pushed through the poplar hedge again. The blue Mercedes, which had been half in the street and half on the sidewalk, was now neatly parked by the curb. In front of it sat Annie, with her tongue hanging out and a satisfied look on her face. There were teeth marks deep in the car's front fender. Annie grinned at

them as Nita and Kit passed, and then trotted off down the street, probably to "find"
something else.

"If my dog starts doing things like
that," Kit muttered, "I don't know how
I'm going to explain it to my mother."

Nita looked down the street for signs
of Joanne. "If we can just get home without being killed, I wouldn't care *what* the
dog found. *Uh*-oh—" A good ways down
the street, four or five girls were heading
toward them, and Nita saw Joanne's blond
hair. "Kit, we'd better split up. No reason
for them to come after you too."

"Right. Give me a call tonight. I'm in
the book..." He took off down a side
street.

She looked around, considering the best
direction to run in—and then thought of
the book she was carrying. There wasn't
much time, though. She forced herself to
calm down even while she knew they were
coming for her, made herself turn the pages
slowly to the place Kit had shown her that
morning, the spell that made blows slide
off. She read through it slowly in the
Speech, sounding out the syllables, taking

the time to look up the pronunciation of the ones she wasn't sure of, even though they were getting close and she could hear Joanne's laugh.

Nita sat down on the curb to wait for them. They let her have it when they found her, as they had been intending to all day; and she rolled around on the ground and fell back from their punches and made what she hoped were horrible groaning noises. After a while Joanne and her four friends turned away to leave, satisfied that they had taught her a lesson. And Nita stood up and brushed herself off, uncut, unbruised, just a little dirty. "Joanne," she called after them. In what looked like amazement, Joanne turned around.

Nita laughed at her. "It won't work anymore," she said.

Joanne stood dumb.

"Never again," she said. She felt like turning her back on them, but instead she walked *toward* them, watching the confusion in their eyes. On a sudden urge, she jumped up in the air and waved her arms crazily. "BOO!" she shouted.

They broke and ran, all of them. Joanne

was the first, and then the rest followed her in a ragged tail down Rose Avenue. Not a word, not a taunt. They just ran.

Nita stopped short. The feeling of triumph that had been growing in her withered almost instantly. *Some victory,* she thought. *It took so little, so little to scare them. Maybe I could have done that at any time, without a shield. Maybe. And now I'll never know for sure.*

(Are you all right?) Fred said quietly, bobbing again by her shoulder. (They didn't hurt you this time.)

(No,) Nita said slowly. She was thinking of all the glorious plans she'd had to use her newfound wizardry on Joanne and her bunch, to shame them, confuse them, hurt them. And look what so small and inoffensive thing as a body shield had done to them. They would hate her worse than ever now.

I've got to be careful with this, she thought. *I thought it was going to be all fun.*

(Come on, Fred,) she said, (let's go home.)

Temporospatial Claudications:

USE AND ABUSE

THE WEEK WENT BY quickly for Nita. Though Carl had made the business of opening a worldgate sound fairly simple, she began to suspect that he'd been doing it so long that it actually seemed that way to him. It wasn't simple, as her book told her as soon as she opened to the pertinent chapter, which was forty pages long in small print.

Grand Central worldgate had its own special requirements: specific supplies and objects that had to be present at an opening so that space would be properly bent, spells that had to be learned just so. The phone calls flew between Nita's house and Kit's for a couple of days, and there was a lot of visiting back and forth as they divided up the work. Nita spent a lot of time keeping Fred from being noticed by her family, and also got to see a lot of Kit's mother and father and sisters, all of whom were very friendly and kept forgetting that Nita couldn't speak Spanish. She started to learn a little of it in self-defense. Kit's dog told her the brand of dog biscuits it could never get enough of; she began bringing them with her when she visited. The dog spoke the Speech with a Spanish accent, and would constantly interrupt Kit and Nita as they discussed who should do what in the spelling. Kit wound up with most of the spoken work, since he had been using the Speech longer and was better at it; Nita picked up supplies.

Late Friday afternoon, Nita was in a little antiques-and-junk store on Nassau Road, going through boxes of dusty odds and ends in search of a real silver fork. Fred was hanging over her shoulder, almost invisible, a faint red point lazily emitting heat. (You ever swallow anything accidentally before, Fred?) Nita said under her breath.

(Not for a long time,) he said, glancing curiously at a pressed-glass saltshaker Nita was holding. (Not since I was a black hole, certainly. Black holes swallow *everything*, but a white hole's business is emission. Within limits,) he added, and the air around him rippled with heat as he shuddered. (I don't ever again want to emit the way I did after your pen went down. Some of those things *hurt* on the way out. And anyway, all that emission makes me nervous. Too much of that kind of thing and I could blow my quanta.)

She looked up at him, worried. (Really? Have you emitted that much stuff that you're in danger of blowing up?)

(Oh, not really—I'd have to lose a lot more mass first. After all, before I was a black hole, I was a respectable-sized blue-white star, and even these days I massed a few hundred thousand times what your cute little yellow-dwarf Sun does. I wouldn't worry about it—I'm nowhere near the critical threshold yet.)

('Cute'?) Nita said.

(Well, it *is* . . . And I suppose there's no harm in getting better at emissions. I have been improving a lot. What's that?)

Nita looked farther down in the box, dug deep, and came up with a battered old fork. It was scratched and its tines were bent out of shape, but it was definitely silver, not stainless steel. (That's what I needed,) she said. (Thanks, Fred. Now all I need is that piece of rowan wood, and then tonight I go over my part of the spells again.)

(You sound worried.)

(Well, yeah, a little,) Nita said, getting up. All that week her ability to hear what the plants were saying had been getting stronger and surer; the better she got with the Speech, the more sense the bushes and trees made. (It's just—the rowan branch has to come off a live tree, Fred, and I can't just pick it—that'd be like walking up to someone and pulling one of their fingers off. I have to ask for it. And if the tree won't give it to me . . .)

(Then you don't get your pen back, at least not for a while.) Fred shimmered with colors and a feeling like a sigh. (I *am* a trouble to you.)

(Fred, no. Put your light out a moment so we can get out of here.) Nita interrupted the shopkeeper's intense concentration on a Gothic novel long enough to find out what the fork cost (a dollar) and buy it. A few steps outside the door, Fred was pacing her again. (If you're trouble, you're the best trouble that's happened around here for a while. You're good to talk to, you're good company—when you don't forget and start emitting cosmic rays...)

Fred blazed momentarily, blushing at Nita's teasing. In an excited moment the night before he had forgotten himself and emitted a brief blast of ultrashortwave radiation, which had heated up Nita's backyard a good deal, ionized the air for miles around, and produced a local but brilliant aurora. (Well, it's an old habit, and old habits die hard. I'm working on it.)

(Heat we don't mind so much. Or ultraviolet, the longwave kind that doesn't hurt people's eyes.)

(You fluoresce when I use that, though...)

Nita laughed. (I don't mind fluorescing. Though on second thought, don't do that where anyone but Kit can see. I doubt my mother'd understand.)

They walked home together, chatting alternately about life in the suburbs and life in a part of deep space close to the Great Galactic Rift. Nita felt more relaxed than she had for months. Joanne had been out of sight since Monday afternoon at Tom and Carl's. Even if she hadn't, Nita had been practicing with that body shield, so that now she could run through the syllables of the spell in a matter of seconds and nothing short of a bomb dropped on her could hurt her. She could even extend the spell to cover someone else, though it wasn't quite so effective; she had a harder time convincing the air to harden up. But even that lessened protection would come in handy if she and Kit should be in trouble together at some point and there was no time to cooperate in a spelling. Not that she was expecting any more trouble. The excitement of a trip into the city was already catching at her. And this wasn't just another shopping trip. Magic was loose in the world, and she was going to help work some. . . .

She ate supper and did her homework almost without thinking about either, and as a result had to do much of the math homework twice. By the time she was finished, the sun was down and the backyard was filling with a cool blue twilight. In the front of the house, her mother and father and Dairine were watching TV as Nita walked out the side door and stood on the step, letting her eyes get used to the dimness and looking east at the rising Moon. Canned laughter echoed inside the house as Fred appeared by her shoulder.

(My, that's bright for something that doesn't emit heat,) Fred said, looking at the Moon too.

(Reflected sunlight,) Nita said absently.

(You're going to talk to the tree now?)

(Uh-huh.)

(Then I'll go stay with the others and watch that funny box emit. Maybe I'll figure out what it's trying to get across.)

(Good luck,) Nita said as Fred winked out. She walked around into the backyard.

Spring stars were coming out as she

stood in the middle of the lawn and looked down the length of the yard at the rowan, a great round-crowned tree snowy with white flowers. Nita's stomach tightened slightly with nervousness. It had been a long time ago, according to her manual, that the trees had gone to war on human-kind's behalf, against the dark powers that wanted to keep human intelligence from happening at all. The war had been a ter-rible one, lasting thousands of centuries—the trees and other plants taking more and more land, turning barren stone to soil that would support them and the animals and men to follow; the dark powers breaking the soil with earthquake and mountain building, scouring it with glaciers, climate-changing good ground for desert, and burning away forests in firestorms far more terrible than the small brushfires any forest needs to stay healthy. But the trees and the other plants had won at last.

They had spent many more centuries readying the world for men—but when men came, they forgot the old debts and wasted the forests more terribly than even the old dark powers. Trees had no particular reason to be friendly to people these days. Nita found herself thinking of that first tree that had spoken to her, angry over the destruction of its friend's artwork. Even though the rowan tree had always been well tended, she wasn't certain how it was going to respond to her. With the other ash trees, rowans had been in the forefront of the Battle; and they had long memories.

Nita sighed and sat down under the tree, book in hand, her back against its trunk. There was no need to start right away, anyhow—she needed a little while to recover from her homework. The stars looked at her through the rowan's wind-stirred branches, getting brighter by the minute. There was that one pair of stars that always looked like eyes, they were so close together. It was one of the three little pairs associated with the Big Dipper. The Leaps of the Gazelle, the ancient Arabs had called them, seeing them as three sets of hoofprints left in the sky. "Kafza'at al Thiba," Nita murmured, the old Arabic name. Her eyes wandered down toward the horizon, finding a faint reddish gleam.

"Regulus." And a whiter gleam, higher: "Arcturus." And another, and another, old friends, with new names in the Speech, that she spoke silently, remembering Carl's warning: (Elthàthtë . . . ur'Senaahel . . .) The distant fires flickered among shadowy leaves. (Lahirien . . .)

(And Methchánë and Ysen and Cahadhwy and Rasaugéhil. . . . They *are* nice tonight.)

Nita looked up hurriedly. The tree above her was leaning back comfortably on its roots, finished with the stretching-upward of growth for the day, and gazing at the stars as she was. (I was hoping that haze would clear off,) it said as silently as Nita had spoken, in a slow, relaxed drawl. (This will be a good night for talking to the wind. And other such transient creatures. I was wondering when you were going to come out and pay your respects, wizard-ling.)

(Uh—) Nita was reassured: the rowan sounded friendly. (It's been a busy week.)

(You never used to be too busy for *me*,) the rowan said, its whispery voice sounding ever so slightly wounded. (Always up in my branches you were, and falling out of them again. Or swinging. But I suppose you outgrew me.)

Nita sat quiet for a moment, remembering how it had been when she was littler. She would swing for hours on end, talking to herself, pretending all kinds of things, talking to the tree and the world in general. And sometimes— (You talked *back!*) she said in shocked realization. (You *did*, I wasn't making it up.)

(Certainly I talked. You were talking to *me*, after all ... Don't be surprised. Small children look at things and *see* them, listen to things and hear them. Of course they understand the Speech. Most of them never realize it any more than you did. It's when they get older, and stop looking and listening, that they lose the Speech, and we lose them.) The rowan sighed, many leaves showing pale undersides as the wind moved them. (None of us are ever happy about losing our children. But every now and then we get one of you back.)

(All that in the book was true, then,) Nita said. (About the Battle of the Trees—)

(Certainly. Wasn't it written in the

Book of Night with Moon that this world's life would become free to roam among our friends there)—the rowan stretched upward toward the turning stars for a moment—(if we helped? After the world was green and ready, we waited for a long time. We started letting all sorts of strange creatures live in our branches after they came up out of the water. We watched them all; we never knew which of our guests would be the children we were promised. And then all of a sudden one odd-looking group of creatures went *down* out of our branches, and looked upward again, and called us by name in the Speech. Your kind...) The tree looked down musingly at Nita. (You're still an odd-looking lot,) it said.

Nita sat against the rowan and felt unhappy. (We weren't so kind to you,) she said. (And if it weren't for the plants, we wouldn't be here.)

(Don't be downcast, wizardling,) the tree said, gazing up at the sky again. (It isn't your fault. And in any case, we knew what fate was in store for us. It was written in the *Book*.)

(Wait a minute. You mean you knew we were going to start destroying your kind, and you got the world ready for us *anyway?*)

(How could we do otherwise? You *are* our children.)

(But ... we make our houses out of you, we—) Nita looked guiltily at the book she was holding. (We *kill* you and we write on your *bodies!*)

The rowan continued to gaze up at the night sky. (Well,) it said. (We are all in the *Book* together, after all. Don't you think that we wrote enough in the rock and the soil, in our day? And we still do. We have our own lives, our own feelings and goals. Some of them you may learn by your wizardry, but I doubt you'll ever come to know them all. We do what we have to, to live. Sometimes that means breaking a rock's heart, or pushing roots down into ground that screams against the intrusion. But we never forget what we're doing. As for you)—and its voice became very gentle—(how else should our children climb to the stars but up our branches? We made our peace with that fact a long time ago, that we would be used and maybe forgotten. So be it. What you learn in your climbing will make all the life on this planet greater, more precious. You have your own stories to write. And when it comes to that, who writes the things written in *your* body, *your* life? And who reads?) It breathed out, a long sigh of leaves in the wind. (Our cases aren't that much different.)

Nita sat back and tried to absorb what the tree was saying. (The *Book of Night with Moon*,) she said after a while. (Do you know who wrote it?)

The rowan was silent for a long time. (None of us are sure,) it said at last. (Our legends say it wasn't written. It's simply *been*, as long as life has been. Since they were kindled, and before.) It gazed upward at the stars.

(Then the other Book, the dark one—)

The whole tree shuddered. (*That* one was written, they say.) The rowan's voice dropped to a whisper. (By the Lone Power—the Witherer, the one who blights. The Kindler of Wildfires. Don't ask more. Even talking about that one or its works can lend it power.)

Nita sat quiet for a while, thinking. (You came to ask something,) the rowan said. (Wizards are always asking things of rowans.)

(Uh, yes.)

(Don't worry about it,) the rowan said. (When we decided to be trees of the Light, we knew we were going to be in demand.)

(Well—I need some live wood. Just enough for a stick, a little wand. We're going to open the Grand Central worldgate tomorrow morning.)

Above Nita's head there was a sharp cracking sound. She pressed back against the trunk, and a short straight branch about a foot and a half long bounced to the grass in front of her. (The Moon is almost full tonight,) the rowan said. (If I were you, I'd peel the leaves and bark off that twig and leave it out to soak up moonlight. I don't think it'll hurt the wood's usefulness for your spelling, and it may make it more valuable later on.)

(Thank you, yes,) Nita said. The book

had mentioned something of the sort—a rowan rod with a night's moonlight in it could be used for some kind of defense. She would look up the reference later. (I guess I should go in and check my spells over one more time. I'm awfully new at this.)

(Go on,) the tree said, with affection. Nita picked up the stick that the rowan had dropped for her, got up and stretched, looking up at the stars through the branches. On impulse she reached up, hooked an arm around the branch that had had the swing on it.

(I guess I could still come and climb sometimes,) she said.

She felt the tree looking at her. (My name in the Speech is Liused,) it said in leafrustle and starflicker. (If there's need, remember me to the trees in Manhattan. You won't be without help if you need it.)

"*I'm Nita,*" she said in the Speech, aloud for this once. The syllables didn't sound strange: they·sounded like a native language and made English feel like a foreign tongue. For a moment every leaf on the tree quivered with her name, speaking it in a whispery echo.

(Go,) the rowan said again. (Rest well.) It turned its calm regard to the stars again.

Nita went back inside.

Saturday morning about eight, Kit and Nita and Fred took the bus down to the Long Island Railroad station and caught a shiny silver train for Manhattan. The train was full of the usual cargo of Saturday travelers and shoppers, none of whom paid any particular attention to the boy and girl sitting by one window, going over the odd contents of their backpacks with great care. Also apparently unnoticed was a faint spark of white light hanging in the center of the window between the two, gazing out in fascination at the backyards and parking lots and stores the train passed.

(What are all those dead hunks of metal there? All piled up?)

(Cars, Fred.)

(I thought cars moved.)

(They did, once.)

(They all went there to die?)

(They were dead when they got there, probably.)

(But they've all climbed on top of each other! When they were dead?)

(No, Fred. They have machines—)

Nita sighed out loud. "Where were we?" she said to Kit.

"The battery."

"Right. Well, here it is."

"Lithium-cadmium?"

"Right. Heavy thing, it weighs more than anything else we've got. That's the last thing for activating the piece of time, isn't it?"

"One more. The eight and a half sugar cubes."

"Here." Nita held up a little plastic bag.

"Okay. Now the worldgate stuff. The pinecone—"

"Bristlecone pine." Nita held it up, then dropped it in her backpack.

"The aspirin."

"Uh-huh."

"The fork."

"Here."

"The rowan branch."

"Yup." She held it up. Cut down and

peeled, it was about a foot long, a greenish white wand.

"Great. Then we're set. You've got all that other stuff, why don't you give me the battery?"

"Here." Nita handed it to him, watched as he found a good spot for it in his backpack, under the sandwiches. "What's that?" she said, spotting something that hadn't been accounted for in the equipment tally.

"Huh? Oh, this." He reached in and brought out a slim piece of metal like a slender rod, with a small knob at one end and broken off jaggedly at the other.

"What is it?"

"A piece of junk. A busted-off car antenna. Well," Kit amended, "it was, anyway. I was sitting out behind the garage yesterday afternoon, reading, and I started talking to my dad's old car. He has this ancient Edsel. He's always talking about getting it reconditioned, but I don't think he's really going to—there's never enough money. Anyway he goes out every now and then to work on the engine, usually when he's tired or mad about something. I don't know if he ever really gets any work done, but he always comes inside greasy all over and feeling a lot better. But I was going over the spells in my head, and the car spoke to me in the Speech—"

"Out loud?"

"No, inside, like Fred does. Kind of a grindy noise, like its voice needed a lube job. I wasn't too surprised; that kind of thing has been happening since I picked the book up. First it was rocks, and then *things* started to talk to me when I picked them up. They would tell me where they'd been and who'd handled them. Anyway, the car and I started talking." Kit paused, looking a touch guilty. "They don't see things the way we do. We made them, and they don't understand why most of the time we make things and then just let them wear out and throw them away afterward . . ."

Nita nodded, wondering briefly whether the train was alive too. Certainly it was as complex as a car. "What about this antenna thing, though?" she said after a moment.

"Oh. The car said to take it for luck. It was just lying there on the ground, rusting.

Dad replaced the antenna a long time ago. So I took it inside and cleaned it up, and there are some wizardries you can do with metal, to remind it of the different forces it felt when it was being made. I did a couple of those. Partly just practicing, partly . . ."

"You thought there might be trouble," Nita said.

Kit looked at her, surprised. "I don't know," he said. "I'm going to be careful, anyway. Carl was pretty definite about not messing around with the worldgate; I wasn't thinking about anything like that. But it occurred to me that it'd be easy to carry the antenna to school if I wanted to. And if anyone started bothering me—" He shrugged, then laughed. "Well, that's their problem. Hey, look, we're getting close to that big curve where you can see the city before you go under the river. Come on, these trains have a window in the very front of the first car. (Fred! Want to see where we're going?)

(Why not? Maybe I'll understand it better than where we've been . . .)

Kit and Nita wriggled into their backpacks and made their way up through a couple of cars, hanging on carefully as they crossed the chained walkways between them. Treetops and housetops flashed by in a rush of wind and clatter of rails. Each time Nita touched the bare metal of the outside of the train, she jumped a little, feeling something, she wasn't quite sure what. *The train?* she thought. *Thinking? And now that I'm aware that it does, I can feel it a little?—though not as clearly as the trees. Maybe my specialty is going to be things that grow and Kit's is going to be things that run. But how many other kinds of life are there that I could learn to feel? Who knows where thought is hiding? . . .*

They went into the first car and made their way up to the front window, carefully hanging on to the seats of oblivious riders to keep the swaying of the train from knocking them over. There were no more stops between there and Penn Station, and the train was plunging along, the rails roaring beneath it. Those rails climbed gradually as the already elevated track went higher still to avoid a triple-stacked freeway. Then the rails bent away to the left in a long graceful curve, still climbing slightly;

and little by little, over the low brown cityscape of Brooklyn, the towers of Manhattan rose glittering in the early sunlight. Gray and crystal for the Empire State Building, silver-blue for the odd sheared-off Citibank building, silver-gold for the twin square pillars of the World Trade Center, and steely white fire for the scalloped tower of the Chrysler Building as it caught the Sun. The place looked magical enough in the bright morning. Nita grinned to herself, looking at the view and realizing that there *was* magic there. That forest of towers opened onto other worlds. One day she would open that worldgate by herself and *go* somewhere.

Fred stared at the towers, amazed. (This is *more* life? More even than the place where you two live?)

(Ten million lives in the city, Fred. Maybe four or five million on that island alone.)

(Doesn't it worry you, packing all that life together? What if a meteor hits it? What if there's a starflare? If something should happen to all that life—how terrible!)

Nita laughed to herself. (It doesn't seem to worry *them*...) Beside her, Kit was hanging on to a seat, being rocked back and forth by the train's speed. Very faintly Nita could hear what Kit heard and felt more strongly; the train's aliveness, its wild rushing joy at doing what it was made to do— its dangerous pleasure in its speed, the wind it fought with, the rails it rode. Nita shook her head in happy wonder. *And I wanted to see the life on other planets. There's more life in* this *world than I expected.*

(It's beautiful,) Fred said from his vantage point just above Kit's shoulder.

"It really is," Nita said, very quiet.

The train howled defiant joy and plunged into the darkness under the river.

Penn Station was thick with people when they got there, but even so it took them only a few minutes to get down to the Seventh Avenue subway station and from there up to Times Square and the shuttle to Grand Central. The shuttle ride was short and crowded. Nita and Kit and Fred were packed tight together in a corner, where they braced themselves against walls and seats and other people while the train shouted along through the echoing underground darkness.

(I can't feel the Sun,) Fred said, sounding worried.

(We're ten or twenty feet underground,) Nita said silently. (We'll get you some Sun as soon as we get off.)

Kit looked at Fred with concern. (You've been twitchy ever since we went into the tunnel, haven't you?)

Fred didn't speak for a moment. (I miss the openness,) he said then. (But worse I miss the feeling of your star on me. Where I come from no one is sealed away from the surrounding emissions.) He trailed off, his thoughts full of the strange hiss and crackle of interstellar radiation—subtly patterned sound, rushing and dying away and swelling up again—the Speech in yet another of its forms. *Starsong*, Nita thought. (You said you *heard* about the *Book of Night with Moon*,) she said. (Was that how? Your...friends, your people, they actually talk to each other over all those distances—millions of light-years?)

(That's right. Not that we use light to do it, of course. But the words, the song, they never stop. Except now. I can hardly hear anything but neutrinos ...)

Kit and Nita glanced at each other. (The worldgate is underground, Fred,) Kit said. (In back of a deli, a little store. We'll have to be there for at least a few minutes to get Nita's pen out.)

(We could go out first and look around,) Nita said. (We're early—it's only nine thirty. We don't even have to think about anchoring the timeslide for a little bit yet.)

The subway cars screeched to a halt, doors rolled open, and the crush loosened as people piled out. Nita got off gladly, looking around for directional signs to point the way toward the concourse level of Grand Central—it had been a while since she'd been there.

"Are you sure you know your way around this place?" Kit asked as Nita headed down a torn-up looking corridor.

"Uh-huh. They're always doing construction in here. C'mon."

She led them up a flight of stairs into

the lower Grand Central concourse—all beige tiles, gray floor, signs pointing to fifty different trains, and small stores packed together. "The deli's down there," she said as she went, waving a hand at a crowd of hurrying people and the wide hall past them. "We go up here." And another flight of stairs, wider and prettier, let them out on the upper concourse, a huge stretch of cream-colored marble under a great blue dome painted with constellations and starred with lights.

They headed across the marble floor, up a short ramp, and out one of many brassy yellow doors, onto the street. Immediately the three of them were assailed by noise, exhaust fumes, people hurrying in all directions, a flood of cabs and buses and cars. But there was also sunlight, and Kit and Nita stood against the wall by the Grand Central doors, letting Fred soak it up and get his composure back. He did so totally oblivious to the six men and three jackhammers working just across the street behind a barrier of sawhorses and orange plastic cones. (That's much better,) he said.

(It was quieter inside, though,) Kit said,

and Nita was inclined to agree with him. The rattling clamor of the jackhammers was climbing down her ears into her bones and making her teeth jitter. The men, two burly ones and one skinny one, all three broad-shouldered and tan, all in helmets and jeans and boots, appeared to be trying to dig to China. One of them hopped down into the excavation for a moment to check its progress, and vanished up to his neck. Then the hammering started again. "How can they stand it?" Nita muttered.

(Stand what? It's lovely out here.) Fred danced about a little in the air, brightening out of invisibility for a few moments and looking like a long-lived remnant of a fireworks display.

(Fred, put it out!) Kit said. (If somebody sees you—)

(They didn't see me in the field the other day,) Fred replied, (though Artificer knows they *looked.*)

(Probably the Learjet distracted them. Fred, come on, tone it down a little,) Nita said. (Let's go back inside and do what we have to. Then we can set the timeslide and have fun in the city for the rest of the day.)

They went back inside and down the stairs again, accompanied by the quiet inward sound of Fred's grumbling. There was no trouble finding the little deli where the worldgate was situated, and Nita and Kit paused outside it. (You have everything ready?) Nita said.

(All in here.) Kit tapped his head. (The spells are all set except for one or two syllables—it's like dialing almost all of a phone number. When I call for you, just come on back. All we need is for the supplies to be in range of the spell; there's nothing special that has to be done with them. Fred, you stay with Nita.)

(As you say.)

They went in. Nita lingered by the front counter, staring at dill pickles and sandwich makings, trying to look normal while she waited for Kit to call her. Fred hung over her shoulder, looking with great interest at bologna and salami and mayonnaise and cream cheese. (You people certainly have enough ways to internalize energy,) he said. (Is there really that much difference between one brand of matter and another?)

(Well, wasn't there any difference when you were a black hole? Didn't a rock, say, taste different from a ray of light, when you soaked one or the other up?)

(Now that you mention it, yes. But appreciating differences like that was something you had to work at for a long time. I wouldn't expect someone as young as you to—)

(Nita,) Kit's thought came abruptly. (We've got trouble. It's not here.)

(What? It has to be!)

(It's *gone*, Nita.)

"Girlie," said the man behind the deli counter in a no-nonsense growl, "you gonna buy anything?"

"Uh," Nita said, and by reflex more than anything else picked up a can of soda from the nearby cooler and fished around in her pocket for the change. "Kit—" she called.

"Coming."

Nita paid for the soda. Kit joined her, carrying a small bag of potato chips, which he paid for in turn. Together they went back out into the corridor, and Kit knelt down by the window of a store across the way, a window full of shiny cutlery. He got his wizards' manual out of his pack and began going through the pages in a hurry. "I don't get it," he said. "I even checked this morning to make sure there hadn't been any change in the worldgate status. It said, right here, 'patent and operative.'"

"Were the spells all right?"

Kit glared up at Nita, and she was instantly sorry she'd asked. "The spells were fine," Kit said. "But they got caught like that first one I did, when you came along. Oh, damn..." He trailed off, and Nita edged around beside him to look at the page. "Something's changed," Kit said, and indeed the page didn't look as it had when Nita had checked it herself in her own manual the night before. The listings for the other Manhattan worldgates were the same—the World Trade Center gate was still listed as "under construction" and the Rockefeller Center gate as "closed for routine maintenance." But under the Grand Central gate listing was a small red box that said in boldface type, *Claudication temporarily dislocated due to unscheduled spatial interruption*, followed by a string of numbers and symbols in the Speech, a description of the gate's new location. Kit glanced up at the roof, through which the sound of jackhammers could plainly be heard. "The construction," he said. "It must have screwed up the worldgate's interruption of space somehow."

Nita was puzzling over the symbols for the new location. "Isn't that term there the one for height above the ground?" she asked.

"Uh-huh. Look at it, it must be sixty, seventy stories straight up from here." Kit slapped the book shut in great annoyance, shoved it back in his backpack. "*Now* what do we do?"

(We go back outside?) Fred asked, very hopefully.

It seemed the best suggestion. The three of them walked out again, and Fred bobbed and danced some more in the sunlight while Nita and Kit walked slowly east along Forty-second Street, toward the Park Avenue overpass. "Dislocated," Kit muttered. "And who knows how long it'll take to come *un*dislocated? A perfectly good piece of time wasted."

Nita stopped and turned, looking up into the air and trying to estimate where the deli lay under the Grand Central complex. She picked a spot that seemed about right, let her eye travel up and up, sixty, maybe seventy stories. "Kit," she said. "Kit! Look what's seventy stories high, and right next door."

Kit looked. Dark blue and silver, with its big stylized globe logo on one side, the Pan Am Building reared its oblong self up at least seventy stories high, right there— not only right behind Grand Central, but part of it. "Yeah," Kit said, his voice still heavy with annoyance. "So?"

"So you remember that shield spell you showed me? The one that makes the air solid? If you change the quantities in the spell a little, you can use it for something else. To walk on, even. You just keep the air hard."

She couldn't keep from grinning. Kit stared at Nita as if she'd gone crazy. "Are you suggesting that we *walk out* to the worldgate and—" He laughed. "How are we going to get up there?"

"There's a heliport on top of the building," Nita said promptly. "They don't use it for big helicopters anymore, but the little ones still land, and there's an elevator in the building that goes right to the top. There's a restaurant up there, too; my father had lunch with someone up there once. I bet we could do it."

Kit stared at her. "If you talk the air solid, *you're* going to walk on it first! I saw that spell; it's not that easy."

"I practiced it some. Come on, Kit, you want to waste the timeslide? It's almost ten now! It'll probably be years before these guys are finished digging. Let's do it!"

"They'll never let us up there," Kit said with conviction.

"Oh yes, they will. They won't have a choice, because Fred'll make a diversion for us. We don't even need anything as big as a Learjet this time. How about it, Fred?"

Fred looked at them reluctantly. (I must admit I *have* been feeling an urge to burp . . .)

Kit still looked uncertain. "And when we get up there," he said, "all those stories up, and looking as if we're walking on nothing—what if somebody sees us?"

Nita laughed. "Who are they going to tell? And who's going to believe them?"

Kit nodded and then began to grin slowly, too. "Yeah," he said. "Yeah! Let's go, it's getting late."

Back they went into Grand Central, straight across the main concourse this time and up one of the six escalators that led up to the lobby of the Pan Am Building. They paused just outside the revolving doors at the end of the escalators. The Pan Am lobby was a big place, pillared and walled and paved in dark granite, echoing with the sound of people hurrying in and out of the station. They went up the escalator to the next floor, and Nita pointed off to one side, indicating an elevator bank. One elevator had a sign standing by it: COPTER CLUB— HELIPAD LEVEL—EXPRESS. Also standing by it was a bored-looking uniformed security guard.

"That's it," Nita said.

"So if we can just get him away from there..."

"It's not that simple." She pointed down at the end of the hall between two more banks of elevators. Another guard sat behind a large semicircular desk, watching a row of TV monitors. "They've got cameras all over the place. We've got to get that guy out of there, too. Fred, if you're going to do something, do it right between them. Out in front of that desk."

(Well,) Fred said, sounding interested, (let's see, let's see . . .) He damped his light down and floated off toward the elevators, looking like an unusually large speck of dust, nothing more. The dust mote stopped just between the desk and the elevator guard, hung in midair, and concentrated so fiercely that Nita and Kit could both feel it thirty feet away.

(T-*hup!*)

BANG!

"That'll get their attention," Kit muttered. It did; both the guards started at the noise, began looking around for the source of it—then both went very very slowly over to examine the large barrel cactus in a brass pot that had suddenly appeared in the middle of the shiny floor.

"Now," Kit said, and took off toward the elevator with Nita close behind. Both the guards had their backs turned, and Nita, passing them, saw the elevator keys hanging off one guard's belt. (Fred,) she said hurriedly, (can you grab those real fast, the way you grabbed my pen? Don't swallow them!)

(I might make that mistake once,) Fred said, (but not twice.) As they slipped into the elevator Fred paused by the guard's belt, and the keys vanished without so much as a jingle. He sailed in to them. (How was that?)

(Great. Quick, Nita, close the door!)

She punched one of the elevator buttons and the doors slid shut; the keys appeared again, and Kit caught them in midair before they fell. "It's always one of these round ones, like they use on coin phones," he said, going through the keys. "Fred, I didn't know you could make *live* things!"

(I didn't know either,) Fred said, sounding unsettled, (and I'm not sure I like it!)

"Here we go," Kit said, and put one key into the elevator lock, turning it to

RUN, and then pressed the button marked 73—RESTAURANT—HELIPAD. The elevator took off in a hurry.

Nita swallowed repeatedly to pop her ears. "Aren't you going to have to change the spells a little to compensate for the gate being up high now?" she said after a moment.

"A little. You just put in the new height coordinate. Oops!"

The elevator began to slow down quickly, and Nita's stomach churned for a moment. She and Kit both pressed themselves against the sides of the elevator, so they wouldn't be immediately visible to anyone who might happen to be standing right outside the door. But when the doors slid open, no one was there. They peered out and saw a long carpeted corridor with a plate-glass door at one end. Through it they saw tables and chairs and, more dimly, through a window, a hazy view of the East Side skyline. A muffled sound of plates and silverware being handled came down the hall to them.

(It's early for lunch,) Nita said, relieved. (Let's go before someone sees us.)

(What about these keys?)

(Hmm . . .)

(Look, let's leave them in the elevator lock. That way the guard downstairs'll just think he left them there. If they discover they're missing, they'll start looking for whoever took them—and this would be the first place they'd look.)

(Yeah, but how are we going to get down?)

(We'll walk on air,) Kit said, his voice teasing. Nita rolled her eyes at the ceiling. (Or we'll go down with the people coming out from lunch, if that doesn't work. Let's just get out of *here* first, okay? Which way do we go to get up on the heliport?)

(Left. There are stairs.)

They slipped out of the elevator just as it chimed and its doors shut again—probably the guard had called it from downstairs. The corridor off to the left was featureless except for one door at its very end. HELIPAD ACCESS, the door said in large red letters. Nita tried the knob, then let her hand fall in exasperation. (Locked. Crud!)

(Well, wait a moment,) Kit said, and tried the knob himself. *"You don't really want to be locked, do you?"* he said aloud in the Speech, very quietly. Again Nita was amazed by how natural the wizards' language sounded when you heard it, and how nice it was to hear—as if, after being lost in a foreign country for a long time, someone should suddenly speak warmly to you in English. *"You've been locked for a couple of days now,"* Kit went on, his voice friendly and persuasive, not casting a spell, just talking—though in the Speech, the two were often dangerously close. *"It must be pretty dull being locked, no one using you, no one paying any attention. Now we need to use you at least a couple of times this morning, so we thought we'd ask—"*

Kt-chk! said the lock, and the knob turned in Kit's hand. *"Thank you,"* he said. *"We'll be back later."* He went through the door into the stairwell, Nita and Fred following, and as the door swung to behind them and locked itself again, there was a decidedly friendly sound to the click. Kit grinned triumphantly at Nita as they climbed the stairs. "How about *that?*"

"Not bad," Nita said, determined to

learn how to do it herself, if possible. "You've been practicing, too."

"Not really—some of this stuff just seems to come naturally as you work with it more. My mother locked herself out of the car at the supermarket last week and I was pulling on the car door and talking at it—you know how you do when you're trying to get something to work. And then it worked. I almost fell over, the door came open so fast. It's the Speech that does it, I think. Everything loves to hear it."

"Remember what Carl said, though."

"I know. I won't overdo it. You think we ought to call him later, let him know what happened to the gate?"

They came to the top of the stairs, paused before the next closed door, breathing hard from the exertion of climbing the stairs fast. "Probably he knows, if he's looked at his book this morning," Nita said. "Look, before we do anything else, let's set the timeslide. This is a good place for it; we're out of sight. When we're tired of running around the city, we can just activate it and we'll be back here at quarter of eleven. Then we just go downstairs, into Grand Central and downstairs to the shuttle, and then home in time for lunch."

"Sounds good." They began rummaging in their backpacks, and before too long had produced the eight and a half sugar cubes, the lithium-cadmium battery—a fat one, bigger than a D cell and far heavier—a specific integrated-circuit chip salvaged from the innards of a dead pocket calculator, and the handle of a broken glass teacup. "You might want to back away a little, Fred, so your emissions don't interfere with the spell," Kit said.

(Right.) Fred retreated high up into one ceiling-corner of the stairwell, flaring bright with interest.

"All right," Kit said, thumbing through his manual to a page marked with a bit of ripped-up newspaper, "here we go. *This is a timeslide inauguration,*" he said aloud in the Speech. *"Claudication type mesarrh-gimel-veignt-six, authorization group—"* Nita swallowed, feeling the strangeness set in as it had during their first spell together, feeling the walls lean in to listen. But it was not a silence that fell this time. As Kit spoke, Nita became aware of a roaring away at the edge of her hearing and a blurring at the limits of her vision. Both effects grew and strengthened to the overwhelming point almost before she realized what was happening. And then it was too late. She was seeing and hearing everything that would happen for miles and miles around at quarter to eleven, as if the building were transparent, as if she had eyes that could pierce stone and ears that could hear a leaf fall blocks away. The words and thoughts of a million minds poured down on her in a roaring onslaught like a wave crashing down on a swimmer, and she was washed away, helpless. Too many sights, commonplace and strange, glad and frightening, jostled and crowded all around her, and squeezing her eyes shut made no difference—the sights were in her mind. *I'll go crazy, I'll go crazy, stop it!* But she was caught in the spell and couldn't budge. *Stop it, oh, let it stop—*

It stopped. She was staring at the floor between her and Kit as she had been doing when the flood of feelings swept over her. Everything was the same as it had been, except that the sugar was gone. Kit was looking at her in concern. "You all right?" he said. "You look a little green."

"Uh, yeah." Nita rubbed her head, which ached slightly as if with the memory of a very loud sound.

"What happened to the sugar?"

"It went away. That means the spell took." Kit began gathering up the rest of the materials and stowing them. He looked at her again. "Are you *sure* you're okay?"

"Yeah, I'm fine." She got up, looked around restlessly. "C'mon, let's go."

Kit got up too, shrugging into his backpack. "Yeah. Which way is the—"

CRACK! went something against the door outside, and Nita's insides constricted. She and Kit both threw themselves against the wall behind the door, where they would be hidden if it opened. For a few seconds neither of them dared to breathe.

Nothing happened.

(What was that?) Kit asked.

(I don't know. It sounded like a shot. Lord, Kit, what if there's somebody up here with a gun or something—)

(What's a gun?) Fred said.

(You don't want to know,) Kit said. (Then again, if there *was* somebody out there with a gun, I doubt they could hurt you. Fred, would you go out there and have a quick look around? See who's there?)

(Why not?) Fred floated down from the ceiling, looked the door over, put his light out, and slipped through the keyhole. For a little while there was silence, broken only by the faint faraway rattle of a helicopter going by, blocks away.

Then the lock glowed a little from inside, and Fred popped back in. (I don't see anyone out there,) he said.

Kit looked at Nita. (Then what made that noise?)

She was as puzzled as he was. She shrugged. (Well, if Fred says there's nothing out there—)

(I suppose. But let's keep our eyes open.)

Kit coaxed the door open as he had the first one, and the three of them stepped cautiously out onto the roof.

Most of it was occupied by the helipad

proper, the long wide expanse of bare tarmac ornamented with its big yellow square-and-H symbol and surrounded by blue low-intensity landing lights. At one end of the oblong pad was a small glass-walled building decorated with the Pan Am logo, a distended orange wind sock, and an anemometer, its three little cups spinning energetically in the brisk morning wind. Beyond the helipad, the roof was graveled, and various low-set ventilator stacks poked up here and there. A yard-high guardrail edged the roof. Rising up on all sides was Manhattan, a stony forest of buildings in all shapes and heights. To the west glimmered the Hudson River and the Palisades on the New Jersey side; on the other side of the building lay the East River and Brooklyn and Queens, veiled in mist and pinkish smog. The Sun would have felt warm if the wind had stopped blowing. No one was up there at all.

Nita took a few steps off the paved walkway that led to the little glass building and scuffed at the gravel suspiciously. "This wind is pretty stiff," she said. "Maybe a good gust of it caught some of this gravel and threw it at the door." But even as she said it, she didn't believe it.

"Maybe," Kit said. His voice made it plain that he didn't believe it either. "Come on, let's find the gate."

"That side," Nita said, pointing south, where the building was wider. They headed toward the railing together, crunching across the gravel. Fred perched on Nita's shoulder; she looked at him with affection. (Worried?)

(No. But you are.)

(A little. That sound shook me up.) She paused again, wondering if she heard something behind her. She turned. Nothing; the roof was bare. *But still*... Nita turned back and hurried to catch up with Kit, who was looking back at her.

"Something?"

"I don't know. I doubt it. You know how you see things out of the corner of your eye, movements that aren't there? I thought maybe the door moved a little."

"I don't know about you," Kit said, "but I'm not going to turn my back on anything while I'm up here. Fred, keep your eyes open." Kit paused by the railing, examining the ledge below it, maybe six feet wide, then looked up again. (On second thought, do you *have* eyes?)

(I don't know,) Fred said, confused but courteous as always. (Do you have chelicerae?)

"Good question," Nita said, a touch nervously. "Kit, let's do this and get out of here."

He nodded, unslung his pack, and laid the aspirin, pinecone, and fork on the gravel by the railing. Nita got out the rowan wand and dropped it with the other materials, while Kit went through his book again, stopping at another marked spot. "Okay," he said after a moment. *"This is an imaging-and-patency spell for a temporospatial claudication, asdekh class. Purpose: retrieval of an accidentally internalized object, matter-energy quotient..."* Kit read a long string of syllables, a description of Nita's pen in the Speech, followed by another symbol group that meant Fred and described the properties of the little personal worldgate that kept his great mass at a great distance.

Nita held her breath, waiting for another onslaught of uncanny feelings, but none ensued. When Kit stopped reading and the spell turned her loose, it was almost a surprise to see, hanging there in the air, the thing they had been looking for. Puckered, roughly oblong, vaguely radiant, an eight-foot scar on the sky; the worldgate, about a hundred feet out from the edge where they stood and maybe thirty feet below the heliport level.

"Well," Kit said then, sounding very pleased with himself. "There we are. And it looks all right, not much different from the description in the book."

"Now all we have to do is get to it." Nita picked up the rowan wand, which for the second part of the spell would serve as a key to get the pen through the worldgate and out of Fred. She tucked the wand into her belt, leaned on the railing, and looked out at the air.

According to the wizards' manual, air, like the other elements, had a memory and could be convinced in the Speech to revert to something it had been before. It was this memory of being locked in stone as oxides or nitrates, or frozen solid in the deeps of space, that made the air harden briefly for the shielding spell. Nita started that spell in its simplest form and then went on into a more formal one, as much a reminiscence as a convincing—she talked to the air about the old days when starlight wouldn't twinkle because there was nothing to make it do so, and when every shadow was sharp as a razor, and distances didn't look distant because there was no air to soften them. The immobility came down around her as the spell began to say itself along with Nita, matching her cadence. She kept her eyes closed, not looking, for fear something that should be happening might not be. Slowly with her words she began to shape the hardening air into an oblong, pushing it out through the other, thinner air she wasn't including in the spell. *It's working better than usual, faster,* she thought. *Maybe it's all the smog here—this air's half-solid already.* She kept talking.

Kit whispered something, but she couldn't make out what and didn't want to try. *"I know it's a strain, being solid these days,"* she whispered in the Speech, *"but just for a little while. Just to make a walk-*

*way out to that puckered place in the sky,
then you can relax. Nothing too thick, just
strong enough to walk on—"*

"Nita. *Nita!*"

The sound of her name in the Speech
caught her attention. She opened her eyes.
Arrow-straight, sloping down from the
lower curb of the railing between her and
Kit, the air had gone hard. There was dirt
and smog trapped in it, making the sudden walkway more translucent than transparent—but there was no mistaking it for
anything but air. It had a more delicate,
fragile look than any glass ever could, no
matter how thin. The walkway ran smooth
and even all the way out to the worldgate,
widening beneath it into room enough for
two to stand.

"Wow!" Nita said, sagging against the
railing and rubbing at her eyes as she let
the spell go. She was tired; the spelling was
a strain—and that feeling of nervousness
left over from the loud noise outside the
stairwell came back. She glanced over her
shoulder again, wondering just what she
was looking for.

Kit peered over the railing at the walkway. "This better be some pen," he said, and turned his back to the worldgate, watching the roof. "Go ahead."

Nita made sure her backpack was slung properly, checked the rowan wand again, and slowly swung over the guardrail, balancing on the stone in which it was rooted. She was shaking, and her hands were wet. *If I don't just do this,* she thought, *I never will. Just one step down, Callahan, and then a nice solid walkway straight across. Really. Believe. Believe. Ouch!*

The air was so transparent that she misjudged the distance down to it—her foot hit before she thought it would, and the jolt went right up her spine. Still holding the railing, Nita lifted that foot a bit, then stomped down hard on the walkway. It was no different from stomping on a sidewalk. She let her weight down on that foot, brought the second down, and stomped with that, too. It *was* solid.

"Like rock, Kit!" she said, looking up at him, still holding the rail. "C'mon!"

"Sure," Kit said, skeptical. "Let go of the rail first."

Nita made a face at Kit and let go. She

held both arms out at first, as she might have on a balance beam in gym, and then waved them experimentally. "See? It works. Fred?"

Fred bobbed down beside her, looking with interest at the hardened air of the walkway. (And it will stay this way?)

(Until I turn it loose. Well?) She took a step backward, farther onto the walkway, and looked up challengingly. "How about it?"

Kit said nothing, just slung his own backpack over his shoulders and swung over the railing as Nita had done, coming down cautiously on the hardened air. He held on to the rail for a moment while conducting his own tests of the air's solidity. "Come on," Nita said. "The wind's not too bad."

"Lead the way."

Nita turned around, still holding her arms a little away from her to be sure of her balance, and started for the worldgate as quickly as she dared, with Fred pacing her cheerfully to the left. Eight or ten steps more and it was becoming almost easy. She even glanced down toward the walkway—

and there she stopped very suddenly, her stomach turning right over in her at the sight of the dirty, graveled roof of Grand Central, a long, long, *long* fall below. "Don't look down," a memory said to her in Machu Picchu's scratchy voice. She swallowed, shaking all over, wishing she had remembered the advice earlier.

"Nita, what's the—"

Something went *whack!* into the walkway. Nita jumped, lost her balance, and staggered back into Kit. For a few awful seconds they teetered back and forth in wind that gusted suddenly, pushing them toward the edge together—and then Kit sat down hard on the walkway, and Nita half fell on top of him, and they held very still for a few gasps.

"Wh-what—"

"I think it was a pigeon," Nita said, not caring whether Kit heard the tremulousness of her voice. "You okay?"

"Sure," Kit said, just as shakily. "I try to have a heart attack every day whether I need one or not. Get off my knee, huh?"

They picked each other up and headed for the gate again. (Even you have trouble with gravity,) Fred said wonderingly as he paced them. (I'm glad I left my mass elsewhere.)

(So are we,) Nita said. She hurried the last twenty steps or so to the widened place at the end of the walkway, with Kit following close.

She knelt down in a hurry, to make sure the wind wouldn't push her over again, and looked up at the worldgate. Seen this close it was about four feet by eight, the shape of a tear in a piece of cloth. It shone with a palely glowing, shifting, soap-bubble iridescence. *Finally, finally, my pen!* she thought—but somehow the thought didn't make Nita as happy as it should have. The uneasy feeling that had started in the stairwell was still growing. She glanced over her shoulder at Kit. He was kneeling too, with his back to her, watching the walkway and the rooftop intently. Beside her, Fred hung quietly waiting.

(Now what?) he asked.

Nita sighed, pulled the rowan rod out of her belt, and inserted one end of it delicately into the shimmering veil that was the surface of the worldgate. Though the city skyline could be seen very clearly through the shimmer, the inch or so of the wand that went through it appeared to vanish. (Just perch yourself on the free end here,) Nita said, holding the wand by its middle. (Make contact with it the same way you did with those keys. Okay?)

(Simple enough.) Fred floated to the end of the rod and lit there, a bright, still spark. (All right, I'm ready.)

Nita nodded. *"This is a retrieval,"* she said in the Speech. *"Involvement confined to a pen with the following characteristics: m'sedh-zayin six point three—"*

(Nita!)

The note of pure terror in Kit's mind-voice caused Nita to do the unforgivable— break off in the middle of a spell and look over her shoulder. Shapes were pouring out of the little glass shelter building, which had been empty, and was still somehow empty even as Nita looked. She got a first impression of grizzled coats, red tongues that lolled and slavered, fangs that gleamed in the sunlight, and she thought, *Wolves!*

But their eyes changed her mind as ten or twelve of the creatures loped across the roof toward the transparent walkway, giving tongue in an awful mindless cacophony of snarls and barks and shuddering howls. The eyes. *People's* eyes, blue, brown, green, but with almost all the intelligence gone out of them, nothing left but a hot deadly cunning and an awful desire for the taste of blood. From her reading in the wizards' manual, she knew what they were: perytons. Wolves would have been preferable—wolves were sociable creatures. *These* had been people once, people so used to hating that at the end of life they'd found a way to keep doing it, by hunting the souls of others through their nightmares. And once a peryton caught you . . .

Nita started to hitch backward in total panic and then froze, realizing that there was nowhere to go. She and Kit were trapped. Another second and the perytons would be on the bridge, and at their throats, for eternity. Kit whipped his head around toward Nita and the worldgate. "Jump through and break the spell!" he yelled.

"But—" And she grabbed his arm, pushed the rowan wand through her belt, and yelled, "Come on, Fred!" The first three perytons leaped the guardrail and landed on the bridge, running. Nita threw herself and Kit at the worldgate, being careful of the edges, as she knew she must, while screaming in absolute terror the word that would dissolve the walkway proper.

For a fraction of a second she caught the sound of screams other than her own, howls of creatures unseen but falling. Then the shimmer broke against her face like water, shutting out sound, and light, and finally thought. Blinded, deafened, and alone, she fell forever....

Exocontinual Protocols

SHE LAY WITH HER face pressed against the cold harsh gravel, feeling the grit of it against her cheek, the hot tears as they leaked between her lashes, and that awful chill wind that wouldn't stop tugging at her clothes. Very slowly Nita opened her eyes, blinked, and gradually realized that the problem with the place where she lay was not her blurred vision. It was just very dim there. She leaned on her skinned hands, pushed herself up, and looked to see where she was.

Dark gray gravel was all around. Farther off, something smooth and dark, with navy blue bumps. The helipad. Farther still, the railing, and beyond it the sky, dark. That was odd—it had been morning. The sound of a moan made Nita turn her head. Kit was close by, lying on his side with his hands over his face. Sitting on his shoulder, looking faint as a spark about to go out, was Fred.

Nita sat up straighter, even though it made her head spin. She had fallen a long way; she didn't want to remember how far.... "Kit," she whispered. "You okay? Fred?"

Kit turned over, pushed himself up on his hands to a sitting position, and groaned again. Fred clung to him. "I don't think I busted anything," Kit said, slow and uncertain. "I hurt all over. Fred, what about you?"

(The Sun is gone,) Fred said, sounding absolutely horrified.

Kit looked out across the helipad into the darkness and rubbed his eyes. "Me and my bright ideas. What have I got us into?"

"As much my bright idea as yours," Nita said. "If it weren't for me, we wouldn't have been out by that worldgate in the first place. Anyway, Kit, where else could we have gone? Those perytons—"

Kit shuddered. "Don't even talk about them. I'd sooner be here than have *them* get me." He got to his knees, then stood up, swaying for a moment. "Oooh. C'mon, let's see where the worldgate went."

He headed off across the gravel. Nita got up on her knees too, then caught sight of a bit of glitter lying a few feet away and grabbed at it happily. Her pen, none the worse for wear. She clipped it securely to the pocket of her shirt and went after Kit and Fred.

Kit was heading for the south-facing railing. "I guess since you only called for a retrieval, the gate dumped us back on top of the ..."

His voice trailed off suddenly as he reached the railing. Nita came up beside him and saw why.

The city was changed. A shiver ran all through Nita, like the odd feeling that comes with an attack of *déjà vu*—but this was true memory, not the illusion of it. She recognized the place from her first spell with Kit—the lowering, sullen-feeling gloom, the shadowed island held prisoner between its dark, icy rivers. Frowning buildings hunched themselves against the oppressive, slaty sky. Traffic moved, but very little of it, and it did so in the dark. Few headlights or taillights showed anywhere. The usual bright stream of cars and trucks and buses was here only dimly seen motion and a faint sound of snarling engines. And the sky! It wasn't clouded over; it wasn't night. It was *empty*. Just a featureless grayness, hanging too low, like a ceiling. Simply by looking at it Nita knew that Fred was right. There was no Sun behind it, and there were no stars—only this wall of gloom, shutting them in, imprisoning them with the presence Nita remembered from the spell, that she could feel faintly even now. It wasn't aware of her, but . . . She pushed back away from the rail, remembering the rowan's words. (The Other. The Witherer, the Kindler of Wildfires—)

"Kit," she said, whispering, this time doing it to keep from perhaps being overheard by *that*. "I think we better get out of here."

He backed away from the rail too, a

step at a time. "Well," he said, very low, "now we know what your pen was doing in New York City..."

"The sooner it's out of here, the happier I'll be. Kit—*where did the worldgate go?*"

He shook his head, came back to stand beside her. "Wherever it went, it's not out *there* now."

Nita let out an unhappy breath. "Why should it be? Everything else is changed." She looked back at the helipad. The stairwell was still there, but its door had been ripped away and lay buckled on the gravel. The helipad itself had no design painted on it for a helicopter to center on when landing. The glass of the small building by the pad was smashed in some places and filmed all around; the building was full of rubble and trash, a ruin. "Where *are* we?" Nita said.

"The place we saw in the spell. Manhattan—"

"But different." Nita chewed her lip nervously. "Is this an alternate world, maybe? The next universe over? The worldgate *was* just set for a retrieval, but we jumped through; maybe we messed up its workings. Carl said this one was easy to mess up."

"I wonder how much trouble you get in for busting a worldgate," Kit muttered.

"I think we're in enough trouble right now. We have to *find* the thing."

(See if you can find me the Sun and the stars and the rest of the Universe while you're at it,) Fred said. He sounded truly miserable, much worse than when he had swallowed the pen. (I don't know how long I can bear this silence.)

Kit stood silent for a moment, staring out at that grim cold cityscape. "There *is* a spell we can use to find it that doesn't need anything but words," he said. "Good thing. We don't have much in the way of supplies. We'll need your help, though, Fred. Your claudication was connected to the worldgate's when we went through. You can be used to trace it."

(Anything to get us out of this place,) Fred said.

"Well," Nita said, "let's find a place to get set up."

The faint rattling noise of helicopter rotors interrupted her. She looked westward along the long axis of the roof, toward the dark half-hidden blot that was Central Park, or another version of it.

A small flying shape came wheeling around the corner of a skyscraper a few blocks away and cruised steadily toward the roof where they stood, the sharp chatter of its blades ricocheting more and more loudly off the blank dark faces of neighboring skyscrapers. "We better get under cover," Kit said. Nita started for the stairwell, and Kit headed after her, but a bit more slowly. He kept throwing glances over his shoulder at the approaching chopper, both worried by it and interested in it. Nita looked over her shoulder too, to tell him to hurry—and then realized how close the chopper was, how fast it was coming. A standard two-seat helicopter, wiry skeleton, glass bubble protecting the seats, oval doors on each side. But the bubble's glass was filmed over except for the doors, which glittered oddly. They had a faceted look. *No pilot could see out of that,* Nita thought, confused. *And the skids, the landing skids are wrong somehow.* The helicopter came sweeping over their heads, low, too low.

"KIT!" Nita yelled. She spun around and tackled him, knocking him flat, as the skids made a lightning jab at the place where he had been a moment before, and hit the gravel with a screech of metal. The helicopter soared on past them, refolding its skids, not yet able to slow down from the speed of its first attack. The thunderous rattling of its rotors mixed with another sound, a high frustrated shriek like that of a predator that has missed its kill—and almost immediately they heard something else too, an even higher pitched squealing, ratchety and metallic, produced by several sources and seeming to come from inside the ruined glass shelter.

Kit and Nita clutched at each other, getting a better look at the helicopter from behind as it swung around for another pass. The "skids" were doubled-back limbs of metal like those of a praying mantis, cruelly clawed. Under what should have been the helicopter's "bubble," sharp dark mandibles worked hungrily—and as the chopper heeled over and came about, those faceted eyes *looked* at Kit and Nita with the cold, businesslike glare reserved for helpless prey.

"We're dead," Nita whispered.

"Not yet." Kit gasped, staggering up again. "The stairwell—" Together he and Nita ran for the stairs as the chopper-creature arrowed across the rooftop at them. Nita was almost blind with terror; she knew now what had torn the door off the stairwell and doubted there was any way to keep that thing from getting them. They fell into the stairwell together. The chopper roared past again, not losing so much time in its turn this time, coming about to hover like a deadly dragonfly while positioning itself for another jab with those steel claws. Kit fell farther down the stairs than Nita did, hit his head against a wall, and lay moaning. Nita slid and scrabbled to a stop, then turned to see that huge, horrible face glaring into the stairwell, sighting on her for the jab. It was unreal. None of it could possibly be real; it was all a dream; and with the inane desperation of a dreamer in a nightmare, Nita felt for the only thing at hand, the rowan rod, and slashed at the looming face with it.

She was completely unprepared for the result. A whip of silver fire the color of the full Moon cracked across the bubble-face from the rod, which glowed in her hand. Screaming in pain and rage, the chopper-creature backed up and away, but only a little. The razor-combed claws shot down at her. She slashed at them too, and when the moonfire curled around them, the creature screamed again and pulled them back.

"Kit!" she yelled, not daring to turn her back on those raging, ravenous eyes. "Kit! The antenna!"

She heard him fumbling around in his pack as the hungry helicopter took another jab at her, and she whipped it again with fire. Quite suddenly something fired past her ear—a bright, narrow line of blazing red light the color of metal in the forge. The molten light struck the helicopter in the underbelly, splattering in bright hot drops, and the answering scream was much more terrible this time.

"It's a machine," Nita said, gasping. "Your department."

"Great," Kit said, crawling up the stairs beside her. "How do you kill a helicopter?" But he braced one arm on the step just above his face, laid the antenna over it, and fired again. The chopper-creature screeched again and swung away.

Kit scrambled up to his feet, pressed himself flat against what remained of the crumbling doorway, pointed the antenna again. Red fire lanced out, followed by Nita's white as she dove back out into the stinging wind and thunder of rotors and slashed at the horror that hung and grabbed from midair. Gravel flew and stung, the wind lashed her face with her hair, the air was full of that ear-tearing metallic scream, but she kept slashing. White fire snapped and curled—and then from around the other side of the chopper-creature there came a sharp *crack!* as a bolt of Kit's hot light fired upward. The scream that followed made all the preceding ones sound faint. Nita wished she could drop the wand and cover her ears, but she didn't dare—and anyway she was too puzzled by the creature's reaction. That shot hadn't hit anywhere on its body that she could see. Still screaming, it began to spin helplessly in a circle like a toy pinwheel. Kit had shattered the helicopter's tail rotor. It might still be airborne, but it couldn't fly straight, or steer. Nita danced back from another jab of those legs, whipped the eyes again with the silver fire of the rowan wand as they spun past her. From the other side there was another *crack!* and a shattering sound, and the bubble-head spinning past her again showed one faceted eye now opaque, spiderwebbed with cracks. The helicopter lurched and rose, trying to gain altitude and get away.

Across the roof Kit looked up, laid the antenna across his forearm again, took careful aim, fired. This time the molten line of light struck through the blurring main rotors. With a high, anguished, ringing snap, one rotor flew off and pinwheeled away almost too fast to see. The helicopter gave one last wild screech, bobbled up, then sideways, as if staggering through the air. "Get down!" Kit screamed at Nita, throwing himself on the ground. She did the same, covering her head with her arms and frantically gasping the syllables of the defense-shield spell.

The explosion shook everything and sent gravel flying to bounce off the hardened air around her like hail off a car roof. Jagged blade shards snapped and rang and shot in all directions. Only when the roaring and the wash of heat that followed it died down to quiet and flickering light did Nita dare to raise her head. The helicopter-creature was a broken-backed wreck with oily flame licking through it. The eye that Kit had shattered stared blindly up at the dark sky from the edge of the helipad; the tail assembly, twisted and bent, lay half under the creature's body. The only sounds left were the wind and that shrill keening from the little glass building, now much muted. Nita rid herself of the shielding spell and got slowly to her feet. "Fred?" she whispered.

A pale spark floated shakily through the air to perch on her shoulder. (Here,) he said, sounding as tremulous as Nita felt. (Are you well?)

She nodded, walked toward the wreck.

Kit stood on the other side of it, his fist clenched on the antenna. He was shaking visibly. The sight of his terror made Nita's worse as she came to stand by him. "Kit," she said, fighting the urge to cry and losing—tears spilled out anyway. "This is *not* a nice place," she said.

He gulped, leaking tears himself. "No," he said, trying to keep his voice steady, "it sure isn't." He looked over at the glass-walled building.

"Yeah," Nita said, scrubbing at her face. "We better have a look."

Slowly and carefully they approached the building, came to one collapsed wall, peered in. Nita held her wand high, so they could see by its glow. Inside, hidden amid the trash and broken glass, was what seemed to be a rude nest built of scraps of metal and wire. In the nest were three baby helicopters, none more than two feet long. They stared fiercely at Kit and Nita from tiny faceted eyes like their parent's, and threatened with little jabbing forelegs, whirring with rotors too small to lift them yet. Sharing the nest with the fledglings was the partially stripped skeleton of a dog.

Kit and Nita turned away together. "I think maybe we should go downstairs a little ways before we do that finding spell," Kit said, his voice still shaking. "If there's another of those things—"

"Yeah." They headed down the stairwell, to the door that in their own world had opened onto the elevator corridor. The two of them sat down, and Nita laid the rowan wand in her lap so there would be light—the ceiling lights in the stairwell were out, and the place felt like the bottom of a hole.

"Fred," Kit said, "how're you holding up?"

Fred hung between them, his light flickering. (A little better than before. The silence is still very terrible. But at least you two are here.)

"We'll find you the Sun, Fred," Nita said, wishing she was as sure as she was trying to sound. "Kit, which spell was it you were going to use?"

Kit had his manual out. "At the bottom of page 318. It's a double, we read together."

Nita got out her own book, paged

through it. "McKillip's Stricture? That's for keeping grass short!"

"No, no!" Kit leaned over to look at Nita's manual. "Huh. How about that, our pages are different. Look under 'Eisodics and Diascheses.' The fourth one after the general introduction. Davidson's Minor Enthalpy."

Nita riffled through some more pages. Evidently her book had more information than Kit's on the spells relating to growing things. Her suspicion about what their specialties were grew stronger. "Got it." She glanced through the spell. "Fred, you don't have to do anything actually. But this is one of those spells that'll leave us blind to what's happening around here. Watch for us?"

(Absolutely!)

"Okay," Kit said. "Ready? One—two—three—"

They spoke together, slowly and carefully, matching cadence as they described the worldgate, and their own needs, in the Speech.

The shadowy stairwell grew darker still, though this darkness seemed less hostile than what hung overhead; and in the deepening dimness, the walls around them slowly melted away. It seemed to Nita that she and Kit and the small bright point between them hung at a great height, unsupported, over a city built of ghosts and dreams. The buildings that had looked real and solid from the roof now seemed transparent skeletons, rearing up into the gloom of this place. Stone and steel and concrete were shadows—and gazing through them, down the length of the island, Nita saw again the two points of light that she and Kit had seen in the first spell.

The closer one, perhaps ten blocks north in the east Fifties, still pulsed with its irregular, distressing light. Compelled by the spell's working, Nita looked closely at it, though that was the last thing she wanted to do—that bit of angry brightness seemed to be looking back at her. But she had no choice. She examined the light, and into her mind, poured there by the spell, came a description of the light's nature in the Speech. She would have backed away, as she had from the perytons, except that again there was nowhere to go. A catalogue of sorts, that light was—a listing, a set of descriptions. But all wrong, all twisted, angry as the light looked, hungry as the helicopter-creature had been, hating as the surrounding darkness was, full of the horrors that everything in existence could become. The *Book Which Is Not Named...*

Nita struggled, though unable to move or cry out; her mind beat at the spell like a bird in a cage, and finally the spell released her. But only to look in the other direction, downtown toward the Wall Street end of the island. There in the illogical-looking tangle of streets built before the regular gridwork of Manhattan was laid down, buried amid the ghosts of buildings, another light throbbed, regular, powerful, unafraid. It flared, it dazzled with white silver fire, and Nita thought of the moonlight radiance of the rowan wand.

In a way, the spell said, this second light was the source of the wand's power, even though here and now the source was bound and limited. This time the syllables of the Speech were no crushing weight of horror. They were a song, one Nita wished would never stop. Courage, merriment, an invitation to everything in existence to be what it was, be the best it could be, grow, *live*—description, affirmation, encouragement, all embodied in one place, one source, buried in the shadows. The *Book of Night with Moon*.

A feeling of urgency came over Nita, and the spell told her that without the protection of the bright *Book*, she and Kit and Fred would never survive the hungry malevolence of this place long enough to find the worldgate and escape. Nor, for that matter, would they be able to find the worldgate at all; it was being held against them by powers adept in wizardries more potent than anything the two of them could manage. It would be folly to try matching wizardries with the Lone Power on its own ground, this outworld long given over to its rule. Their best chance was to find the bright *Book* and free it of the constraint that held its power helpless. Then there might be a chance.

The spell shut itself off, finished. Walls and physical darkness curdled around them again. Kit and Nita looked at each other, uncertain.

"We've been had," Kit said.

Nita shook her head, not following him.

"Remember Tom saying it was odd that our first spell turned up Fred and the news that the bright *Book* was missing? And what Picchu said then?"

"There are no accidents," Nita murmured.

"Uh-huh. How likely do you think it is that all *this* is an accident? Something *wanted* us here, I bet." Kit scowled. "They might have asked *us!* It's not fair!"

Nita held still for a moment, considering this. "Well, maybe they did ask us."

"Huh? Not *me*, I—"

"The Oath."

Kit got quiet quickly. "Well," he admitted after a while, "it did have all kinds of warnings in front of it. And I went ahead and read it anyway."

"So did I." Nita closed her eyes for a second, breathing out, and heard something in the back of her head, a thread of memory: *Did I do right? Go find out . . .*

"Look," she said, opening her eyes again, "maybe we're not as bad off as we think.

Tom did say that younger wizards have more power. We don't have a lot of supplies, but we're both pretty good with the Speech by now, and Fred is here to help. We're armed—" She glanced down at the rowan wand, still lying moon bright in her lap.

"For how long?" Kit said. He sighed too. "Then again, I guess it doesn't matter much—if we're going to find the bright *Book*, the only way to do it is to hurry. Somebody knows we're here. That thing showed up awful fast—" He nodded at the roof.

"Yeah." Nita got up, took a moment to stretch, then glanced down at Kit. He wasn't moving. "What's the matter?"

Kit stared at the antenna in his hands. "When I was talking to the Edsel it told me some things about the Powers that didn't want intelligence to happen in machines. They knew that people would start talking to them, make friends with them. Everybody would be happier as a result. Those Powers—" He looked up. "If I understood that spell right, the one running this place is the chief of them all, the worst of them. The Destroyer, the engenderer of rust—"

"Kit!"

"I know, you shouldn't name it—" He got up, held out a hand to Fred, who bobbled over to Kit and came to rest on his palm. "But that's who we're up against. Or what. Fred, do you know what we're talking about?"

Fred's thought was frightened but steady. (The Starsnuffer,) he said. (The one who saw light come to be and could not make it in turn—and so rebelled against it, and declared a war of darkness. Though the rebellion didn't work as well as it might have, for darkness only made the light seem brighter.)

Kit nodded. "That's the one. If we do get the bright *Book,* that's who'll come after us."

Fred shuddered a flicker of light so like a spark about to go out in the wind that Kit hurriedly tucked the antenna under his arm and cupped his other hand around Fred protectively. (I've lost enough friends to that one,) Fred said, (heard enough songs stilled. People gone nova before their time, or fallen through naked singularities into places where you burn forever but don't learn anything from it.)

For a moment neither of them could follow Fred's thought. Though he was using the Speech, as always, they couldn't follow what other things he was describing, only that those things were as terrible a warped thing as the helicopter-creature was to them. (No matter,) he said at last. (You two are part of the answer to stopping that kind of thing. Otherwise my search for an Advisory nexus wouldn't have brought me to you. Let's do what we can.)

Kit nodded. "Whatever that is. I wish I knew where to begin."

Nita leaned back against the wall. "Didn't Tom say something about the two Books being tied together? So that you could use one to guide you to the other?"

"Yeah."

"Well. We're not too far from the dark one." Nita swallowed. "If we could get hold of that—and use it to lead us to the bright one. That vision only gave a general idea of where the *Book of Night with Moon* was. Probably because of its being restrained, or guarded, or whatever—"

"Steal the dark Book?" Kit looked at Nita as if she had taken leave of her senses. "Sure! And then have—," he waved his hand at the northward wall, not wanting to say any name, "—and Lord knows what else come chasing after us?"

"Why not?" Nita retorted. "It's a better chance than going straight for the bright one, which we *know* is guarded somehow. We'd go fumbling around down there in the financial district and probably get caught right away. But why would they guard the dark Book? They're the only ones who would want it! I bet you we could get at the dark one a lot more easily than the other."

Kit chewed his lip briefly. "Well?" Nita said. "What do you think?"

"I think you're probably nuts. But we can't just sit here, and it wouldn't hurt to go see what the situation is—Fred?"

(Lead,) Fred said, (I'll follow.)

Kit gently tossed Fred back into the air and paused long enough to put his book away. He didn't put the antenna away, though. The rowan wand glowed steadily and brilliantly. "Can't you damp that down a little?" Kit said. "If somebody sees us—"

"No, I can't. I tried." Nita cast about for ways to hide it, finally settled on sticking it in her back jeans pocket and settling her down vest over it. "Better?"

"Yeah." Kit had turned his attention to the doorknob. He touched it, spoke softly to it in the Speech, turned it. Nothing happened. "Not listening?" he wondered out loud, and bent to touch the keyhole. "Now why— Ow!" He jumped back, almost knocking Nita over.

"What's the matter?"

Kit was sucking on his finger, looking pained. "Bit me!" he said, removing the finger to examine it. It bled.

"I get the feeling," Nita said slowly, "that there's not much here that's friendly."

"Yeah." Kit looked glumly at the doorknob. "I guess we'd better consider everything we see potentially dangerous." He lifted the antenna, bent down by the lock again, and touched the keyhole delicately with the knob at the antenna's end. A brief red spark spat from the antenna; the innards of the lock clicked. This time when Kit turned the knob, the door came open a crack.

With great caution he opened the door a bit more, peered out, then opened it all the way and motioned Nita to follow him. Together they stepped out into a hall much like the elevator corridor in their own world, but dark and silent. (The elevator?) Kit said inwardly, not wanting to break that ominous quiet.

(Do you trust it?)

(No. Know where the stairs are?)

(Down the way we came. Past the elevator.)

The door to the main stairway had to be coerced into opening by the same method as the door to the roof. When they were through it Kit spent another moment getting it to lock again, then stepped over to the banister and looked down at story after story of switchback stairs. (It could be worse,) Nita said. (We could be going up.)

(It *will* be worse,) Kit said. (If the worldgate stays at this level, we're going to *have* to come back up . . .)

They headed down. It took a long time. The few times they dared stop to rest, Kit and Nita heard odd muffled noises through the walls—vaguely threatening scrapes and groans and rumbles, the kind of sounds heard in nightmares. The stairs were as dark as the corridor had been, and it was hard to sit in the corner of a landing, rubbing aching legs, with only the light of Nita's wand to argue with the blackness that towered above and yawned below, as those sounds got louder.

They quickly lost count of how many stories downward they'd gone. All the landings looked the same, and all the doors from them opened off into the same pitch blackness—until finally Kit eased one open as he had eased open scores of others and abruptly stood very still. He put his hand out behind him. (Nita! The wand.)

She passed it to him. It dimmed in his hand from moonfire to foxfire, a faint silver glimmer that he held out the door as he looked around. (It's all that shiny stone, like the other lobby. There should be a way down into the station, then—)

Nita's hair stood up on end at the thought. (Kit, you saw what happened to helicopters. Do you really want to meet a *train?* Let's go out on the street level, okay?)

He gulped and nodded. (Which way?)

(There's a door out onto Forty-fifth Street. C'mon.)

She slipped out, and Kit followed with the wand. Its pale light reached just far enough ahead to gleam off the glass wall at the end of the corridor. Near it was the down escalator, frozen dead. They made their way softly down it, then across the slick floor and out the glass doors to the street.

It was nearly as dark outside as it had been inside; a night without a hint of Moon or stars. The air down there wasn't as chill as it had been on the building's roof, but it stank of dark city smells—exhaust, spilled gasoline, garbage, and soot. The gutter was clogged with trash. They stepped out to cross Forty-fifth.

"No," Nita hissed, startled into speech, and dragged Kit back into the dark of the doorway. Pale yellow-brown light flickered down the street, got brighter. A second later, with a snarl of its engine, a big yellow Checker Cab hurled itself past them, staring in front of it with headlight-eyes burned down to yellow threads of filament—eyes that looked somehow as if they could see. But the cab seemed not to notice them. Its snarl diminished as it plunged down the street, leaving a whirl of dirty paper and dead leaves in its wake. Kit coughed as its exhaust hit them.

(That was alive,) he said when he got his breath back. (The same way the helicopter was.)

Nita made a miserable face. (Let's get outta here,) she said.

Kit nodded. She led him off to their left, through the Helmsley-Spear Building, which should have been bright with gold-leafed statuary. Here it was gray with soot, and the carvings stared down with such looks of silent malice that Nita refused to glance up more than that once.

She hoped for some more encouraging

sight as they came onto Forty-sixth Street and looked up Park Avenue. The hope was vain. The avenue stretched away and slightly upward for blocks as it did in their own world, vanishing in the murk. But the divider between the uptown and downtown lanes, usually green with shrubbery, had become one long tangle of barren thornbushes. The old-fashioned red-and-green traffic lights burned low and dark as if short on power; and no matter how long one watched, they never changed from red. The shining glass-and-steel office buildings that had lined the avenue in their Manhattan were grimy shells here, the broad sidewalks before them cluttered with rubbish. Nothing moved anywhere, except far up Park, where another pair of yellow eyes waited at a corner.

Those eyes made Nita nervous. (This way,) she said. She hurried past a dirty granite facade full of still doors and silent windows. Kit followed close, and Fred with him, both looking worriedly at everything they passed.

Nita was doing her best to keep herself calm as they turned the corner onto Forty-seventh. *It can't all be as bad as the helicopter,* she told herself. *And nothing really bad has happened to us yet. It was just the shock of the—*

She jumped back into the shadow of a building on hearing a clapping sound so loud she felt sure the helicopter's mate was coming for them. Fred and Kit huddled terrified into that shadow, too, and it took a few seconds for any of them to find the source of the sound. Not more than five or six feet from them, a pigeon had landed— a sooty dark one, cooing and strutting and head bobbing in a perfectly normal fashion. It walked away from them, muttering absently, intent on its own pursuits. Kit poked Nita from behind—not a warning: a teasing poke. (Getting jumpy, huh?)

(Yeah, well, *you* were the one who said—)

The lightning stroke of motion not six feet away knocked the merriment right out of them. What had seemed a perfectly ordinary fire hydrant, dull yellow, with rust stains and peeling paint, suddenly cracked open and shot out a long, pale, ropy tongue like a toad's. The pigeon never had a chance. Hit side on, the bird made just one strangled gobbling noise before the tongue was gone again, too fast to follow, and the wide horizontal mouth it came from was closed again. All that remained to show that anything had happened was a slight bulge under the metallic-looking skin of the fire hydrant. The bulge heaved once and was still.

Nita bit her lip. Behind her she could feel Kit start shaking again. (I feel sorry for the next dog that comes along,) he said. (I hope you don't mind if I cross the street.) Kit headed out of the shadow.

(I think I'll join you,) Nita said. She backed out of range of that tongue before she started across the street herself.

There was no time to move, to scream, even to think. Kit was halfway across the street, with his eye on that fire hydrant, his head turned away from the big yellow Checker Cab that was maybe six feet away and leaping straight at him.

A flash of brilliance struck Nita like a blow, and did the same for the cab, so that it swerved to its left and knocked Kit sideways and down. The cab roared on by, engine racing in frustration, evidently too angry to try for another pass. But something about it, maybe the savage sidelong look it threw Nita out of its burned-down eyes as it squealed around the corner of Forty-sixth and Madison—something made Nita suspect that it would not forget them. She ran out into the street and bent over Kit, not sure whether she should try to move him.

" 'S awright," Kit said, groaning softly as he worked at getting up. Nita slipped hands under his arms to help. "Fred did it."

(Are you all right?) came the frantic thought, as Fred appeared in front of Kit's face. (Did I hurt you? Did I emit anything you can't take? I took out all the ultraviolet. Oh no! I forgot the cosmic rays again.)

Kit managed a smile, though not much of one; his face was skinned and bruised where one cheekbone had hit the pavement. (Don't worry about it, Fred. That thing would have done a lot worse to me than a few cosmic rays if it'd hit me the way it wanted to.) He stood up, wincing. (It got my leg some, I think.)

Nita bent down to look at Kit's left leg and sucked in her breath. His jeans were torn, and he had a straight horizontal gash six inches or so below the knee, which was bleeding freely. (Does it feel deep?)

(No. It just hurts a lot. I think it was the cab's fender, there was a jagged piece sticking out of the chrome. Listen, Fred, thanks—)

(You're sure I didn't hurt you? You people are so fragile. A little gamma radiation will ruin your whole day, it seems.)

(I'm fine. But I've gotta do something about this leg. And then we've got to get moving again and get to the dark Book.)

Nita looked over at the fire hydrant, fear boiling in her. Casually, as if this was something it did many times a day, the hydrant cracked open and spat something out onto the sidewalk—a dessicated-looking little lump of bones and feathers. Then it got up and waddled heavily down to a spot about fifty feet farther down the block, and sat down again.

And I thought it couldn't all be bad.

Together, as quickly as they could, two small, frightened-looking figures and a spark like a lost star hurried into the shadows and vanished there.

Entropics:

DETECTION
AND AVOIDANCE

(HOW CLOSE ARE WE?)

(Uh...this is Madison and Forty-ninth. Three blocks north and a long one east.)

(Can we rest? This air burns to breathe. And we've been going fast.)

(Yeah, let's.)

They crouched together in the shadow of a doorway, two wary darknesses and a dim light, watching the traffic that went by. Mostly cabs prowled past, wearing the same hungry look as the one that had wounded Kit. Or a sullen truck might lumber by, or a passenger car, looking uneasy and dingy and bitter. None of the cars or trucks had drivers, or looked like they wanted them. They ignored the traffic lights, and their engines growled.

Nita's eyes burned in the dark air. She rubbed them and glanced down at Kit's leg, bound now with a torn-off piece of her shirt. (How is it?)

(Not too bad. It feels stiff. I guess it stopped bleeding.) He looked down, felt the makeshift bandage, winced. (Yeah... I'm hungry.)

Nita's stomach turned over—she was too nervous to even consider eating—as Kit came up with a ham sandwich and offered her half. (You go ahead,) she said. She leaned against the hard cold wall, and on a sudden thought pulled her pen out of her pocket and looked at it. It seemed all right, but as she held it she could feel a sort of odd tingling in its metal that hadn't been there before.

(Uh, Fred—)

He hung beside her at eye level, making worried feelings that matched the dimness of his light. (Are you *sure* that light didn't hurt you?)

(Yeah. It's not that.) She held out the

pen to him. Fred backed away a little, as if afraid he might swallow it again. (Is this radioactive or anything?) Nita said.

He drifted close to it, bobbed up and down to look at it from several angles. (You mean beta and gamma and those other emissions you have trouble with? No.)

Nita still felt suspicious about the pen. She dug into her backpack for a piece of scrap paper, laid it on her wizards' manual, clicked the point out, and scribbled on the paper. Then she breathed out, perplexed. (Come *on*, Fred! Look at that!)

He floated down to look. The pen's blue-black ink would normally have been hard to see in that dimness, no matter how white the paper. But the scrawl had a subtle glimmer about it, a luminosity just bright enough to make out. (I don't think it's anything harmful to you,) Fred said. (Are you sure it didn't do that before?)

(Yes!)

(Well, look at it this way. Now you can see what you're writing when it's dark. Surprising you people hadn't come up with something like that already.)

Nita shook her head, put the paper away, and clipped the pen back in her pocket. Kit, finishing the first half of his sandwich, looked over at the scribble with interest. (Comes of being inside Fred, I guess. With him having his own claudication, and all the energy boiling around inside him, you might have expected something like that to happen.)

(Yeah, well, I don't like it. The pen was fine the way it was.)

(Considering where it's been,) Kit said, (you're lucky to get it back in the same shape, instead of crushed into a little lump.) He wrapped up the other half of his sandwich and shoved it into his backpack. (Should we go?)

(Yeah.)

They got up, checked their surroundings as usual to make sure that no cabs or cars were anywhere close, and started up Madison again, ducking into doorways or between buildings whenever they saw or heard traffic coming.

(No people,) Kit said, as if trying to work it out. (Just things—all dark and ruined—and machines, all twisted. Alive—

but they seem to hate everything. And pigeons—)

(Dogs, too,) Nita said.

(Where?) Kit looked hurriedly around him.

(Check the sidewalk and the gutter. They're here. And remember that nest.) Nita shrugged uneasily, setting her pack higher. (I don't know. Maybe people just can't live here.)

(*We're* here,) Kit said unhappily. (And maybe not for long.)

A sudden grinding sound like tortured metal made them dive for another shadowy doorway close to the corner of Madison and Fiftieth. No traffic was in sight; nothing showed but the glowering eye of the traffic light and the unchanging DON'T WALK signs. The grinding sound came again—metal scraping on concrete, somewhere across Madison, down Fiftieth, to their left. Kit edged a bit forward in the doorway.

(What are you—)

(I want to see.) He reached around behind him, taking the antenna in hand.

(But if—)

(If that's something that might chase us later, I at least want a look at it. Fred? Take a peek for us?)

(Right.) Fred sailed ahead of them, keeping low and close to the building walls, his light dimmed to the faintest glimmer. By the lamppost at Madison and Fiftieth he paused, then shot low across the street and down Fiftieth between Madison and Fifth, vanishing past the corner. Nita and Kit waited, sweating.

From around the corner Fred radiated feelings of uncertainty and curiosity. (These are like the other things that run these streets. But these aren't moving. Maybe they were dangerous once. I don't know about now.)

(Come on,) Kit said. He put his head out of the doorway. (It's clear.)

With utmost caution they crossed the street and slipped around the corner, flattening to the wall. Here stores and dingy four-story brownstones with long flights of railed stairs lined the street. Halfway down the block, jagged and bizarre in the dimness and the feeble yellow glow of a flickering sodium-vapor streetlight, was the remains of an accident. One car, a heavy two-door sedan, lay crumpled against the pole of another nearby streetlight, its right-hand door ripped away and the whole right side of it laid open. A little distance away, in the middle of the street, lay the car that had hit the sedan, resting on its back and skewed right around so that its front end was pointed at Kit and Nita. It was a sports car of some kind, so dark a brown that it was almost black. Its windshield had been cracked when it overturned, and it had many other dents and scrapes, some quite deep. From its front right wheel well jutted a long jagged strip of chrome, part of the other car's fender, now wound into the sports car's wheel.

(I don't get it,) Nita said silently. (If that dark one hit the other, why isn't its front all smashed in?)

She broke off as with a terrible metallic groan the sports car suddenly rocked back and forth, like a turtle on its back trying to right itself. Kit sucked in a long breath and didn't move. The car stopped rocking for a moment, then with another scrape of metal started again, rocking more energetically this time. Each time the side-to-side motion became larger. It rocked partway onto one door, then back the other way and partway onto the other, then back again—and full onto its left-hand door. There it balanced, precarious, for a few long seconds, as if getting its breath. And then it twitched hard, shuddered all the way over, and fell right-side down.

The scream that filled the air as the sports car came down on the fender-tangled right wheel was terrible to hear. Instantly it hunched up the fouled wheel, holding it away from the street, crouching on the three good wheels and shaking with its effort. Nita thought of an old sculpture she had seen once, a wounded lion favoring one forelimb—weary and in pain, but still dangerous.

Very slowly, as if approaching a hurt animal and not wanting to alarm it, Kit stepped away from the building and walked out into the street.

(Kit!)

(Ssssh,) he said silently. (Don't freak it.)

(Are you out of your—)

(Sssssshhh!)

The sports car watched Kit come, not moving. Now that it was right-side up, Nita could get a better idea of its shape. It was actually rather beautiful in its deadly looking way—sleekly swept-back and slung low to the ground. Its curves were battered in places; its once-shining hide was scored and dull. It stared at Kit from hunter's eyes, headlights wide with pain, and breathed shallowly, waiting.

(Lotus Esprit,) Kit said to Nita, not taking his eyes off the car, matching it stare for stare.

Nita shook her head anxiously. (Does that mean something? I don't know cars.)

(It's a racer. A mean one. What it is *here*— Look, Nita, there's your answer. Look at the front of it, under the head-lights.) He kept moving forward, his hands out in front of him. The Lotus held perfectly still, watching.

Nita looked at the low-sloping grille. (It's all full of oil or something.)

(It's a predator. These other cars, like that sedan—they must be what it hunts. This time its prey hurt the Lotus before it made its kill. Like a tiger getting gored by a bull or something. Ooops!)

Kit, eight or ten feet away from the Lotus's grille, took one step too many; it abruptly rolled back away from him a foot or so. Very quietly its engine stuttered to life and settled into a throaty growl.

(Kit, you're—)

(Shut up.) *"I won't hurt you,"* he said in the Speech, aloud. *"Let me see to that wheel."*

The engine growl got louder—the sound of the Speech seemed to upset the Lotus. It rolled back another couple of feet, getting close to the curb, and glared at Kit. But the glare seemed to have as much fear as threat in it now.

"I won't hurt you," Kit repeated, stepping closer, holding out his hands, one of them with the antenna in it. *"Come on, you know what this is. Let me do something about that wheel. You can't run on it. And if you can't run, or hunt—I bet there are other hunters here, aren't there? Or scavengers. I'm sure there are scavengers. Who'll be coming here to clean up this kill?*

And do you want them to find you here, helpless?"

The Lotus stared at him, shifting a little from side to side now, swaying uncertainly. The growl had not stopped, but it hadn't gotten any louder either. *"If I were going to hurt you, I would have by now,"* Kit said, getting closer. The car was four feet away, and its headlights were having to look up at Kit now. *"Just let me do something about that fender stuck in you, then you'll go your way and I'll go mine."*

The dark eyes stared at the antenna, then at Kit, and back at the antenna again. The Lotus stopped swaying, held very still. Kit was two feet away. He reached out with his free hand, very slowly, reached down to touch the scratched fiberglass hide.

The engine raced, a sudden startling roar that made Nita stifle a scream and made Kit flinch all over—but he didn't jump away, and neither did the Lotus. For a second or two he and the car stood there just looking at each other—small trembling boy, large trembling predator. Then Kit laid his hand carefully on the brown hide, a gingerly gesture. The car shook all over, stared at him. Its engine quieted to an uncertain rumbling.

"*It's okay,*" he said. "*Will you let me take care of it?*"

The Lotus muttered deep under its hood. It still stared at Kit with those fearsome eyes, but its expression was mostly perplexed now. So was Kit's. He rubbed the curve of the hurt wheel well in distress. (I can't understand why it's mute,) he said unhappily. (The Edsel wasn't. All it took was a couple of sentences in the Speech and it was talking.)

(It's bound,) Nita said, edging out of the shadow of the building she stood against. (Can't you feel it, Kit? There's some kind of huge binding spell laid over this whole place to keep it the way it is.)

She stopped short as the Lotus saw her and began to growl again. "*Relax,*" Kit said. "*She's with me, she won't hurt you either.*"

Slowly the growl dwindled, but the feral headlight-eyes stayed on Nita. She gulped and sat down on the curb, where she could see up and down the street. "Kit, do what you're going to do. If another of those cabs comes along—"

"Right. Fred, give me a hand? No, no, no," he said hastily, as Fred drifted down beside him and made a light pattern and a sound as if he was going to emit something. "Not *that* kind. Just make some light so I can see what to do down here."

Kit knelt beside the right wheel, studying the damage, and Fred floated in close to lend his light to the business, while the Lotus watched the process sidelong and suspiciously. "Mmmfff—nothing too bad, it's mostly wrapped around the tire. Lucky it didn't get fouled with the axle.

"*Come on, come on,*" Kit said in the Speech, patting the bottom of the tire, "*relax it, loosen up. You're forcing the scrap into yourself, holding the wheel up like that. Come on.*" The Lotus moaned softly and with fearful care relaxed the uplifted wheel a bit. "*That's better.*" Kit slipped the antenna up under the Lotus's wheel well, aiming for some piece of chrome that was out of sight. "Fred, can you get in there so I can see? Good. *Okay, this may sting a little.*" Molten light, half-seen, sparked under the Lotus's fender. It jumped, and an uneven half-circle-shaped piece of chrome fell clanging onto the pavement. "*Now hunch the wheel up again. A little higher—*" Kit reached in with both hands and, after a moment's tugging and twisting, freed the other half of the piece of metal. "*There,*" Kit said, satisfied. He tossed the second piece of scrap to the ground.

The engine roared again with terrible suddenness, deafening. This time Kit scrambled frantically backward as the Lotus leaped snarling away from him. With a screech of tires it swept so close past Nita that she fell over backward onto the sidewalk. Its engine screaming, the Lotus tore away down Fiftieth toward Madison, flung itself left around the corner in a cloud of blue exhaust, and was gone.

Very slowly Kit stood up, pushed the antenna into his pants pocket, and stood in the street dusting his hands off on his shirt as he gazed in disappointment after the Lotus. Nita sat back up again, shaking her head and brushing at herself. (I thought maybe it was going to stay long enough to thank you,) she said.

Kit shook his head, evidently in annoyance at himself for having thought the same thing. (Well, I don't know—I was thinking of what Picchu said. 'Don't be afraid to help.') He shrugged. (Doesn't really matter, I guess. It was hurting; fixing it was the right thing to do.)

(I hope so,) Nita said. (I'd hate to think the grateful creature might run off to—*you* know—and tell everybody about the people who helped it instead of hurting it. I have a feeling that doing good deeds sticks out more than usual around here.)

Kit nodded, looking uncomfortable. (Maybe I should've left well enough alone.)

(Don't be dumb. Let's get going, huh? The . . . whatever the place is where the dark Book's kept, it's pretty close. I feel nervous standing out here.)

They recrossed Madison and again started the weary progression from doorway to driveway to shadowed wall, heading north.

At Madison and Fifty-second, Nita turned right and paused. (It's on this block somewhere,) she said, trying to keep even the thought quiet. (The north side, I think. Fred, you feel anything?)

Fred held still for a moment, not even making a flicker. (The darkness feels thicker up ahead, at the middle of the block.)

Kit and Nita peered down the block. (It doesn't look any different,) Kit said. (But you're the expert on light, Fred. Lead the way.)

With even greater care than usual they picked their way down Fifty-second. This street was stores and office buildings again; all the store windows empty, all the windows dark. But here, though external appearances were no different, the feeling slowly began to grow that there was a reason for the grimy darkness of the windows. Something watched, something peered out those windows, using the darkness as a cloak, and no shadow was deep enough to hide in; the silent eyes would see. Nothing happened, nothing stirred anywhere. No traffic was in sight. But the street felt more and more like a trap, laid open for some unsuspecting creature to walk into. Nita tried to swallow as they ducked from one hiding place to another, but her mouth was too dry. Kit was sweating. Fred's light was out.

(This is it,) he said suddenly, his thought sounding unusually muted even for Fred. (This is the middle of the darkness.)

(This?) Kit and Nita thought at the same time, in shock, and then simultaneously hushed themselves. Nita edged out to the sidewalk to get a better look at the place. She had to crane her neck. They were in front of a skyscraper, faced completely in black plate glass, an ominous, windowless monolith.

(Must be about ninety stories,) Nita said. (I don't see any lights.)

(Why would you?) Fred said. (Whoever lives in this place doesn't seem fond of light at all. How shall we go in?)

Nita glanced back up the street. (We passed a driveway that might go down to a delivery entrance.)

(I'll talk to the lock,) Kit said. (Let's go!)

They went back the way they had come

and tiptoed down the driveway. It seemed meant for trucks to back into. A flight of steps at one side led up to a loading platform about four feet above the deepest part of the ramp. Climbing the stairs, Kit went to a door on the right and ran his hands over it as Nita and Fred came up behind. (No lock,) Kit said. (It's controlled from inside.)

(We can't get in? We're dead.)

(We're not dead yet. There's a machine in there that makes the garage doors go up. That's all I need.) Kit got out the antenna and held it against the door as he might have held a pencil he was about to write with. He closed his eyes. (If I can just feel up through the metal and the wires, find it . . .)

Nita and Fred kept still while Kit's eyes squeezed tighter and tighter shut in fierce concentration. Inside one garage door something rattled, fell silent, rattled again, began to grind. Little by little the door rose until there was an opening at the bottom of it, three feet high. Kit opened his eyes but kept the antenna pressed against the metal. (Go on in.)

Fred and Nita ducked through into darkness. Kit came swiftly after them. Behind him, the door began to move slowly downward again, shutting with a thunderous clang. Nita pulled out the rowan wand, so they could look around. There were wooden loading pallets stacked on the floor, but nothing else—bare concrete walls, bare ceiling. Set in the back wall of the huge room was one normal-sized double door.

(Let's see if this one has a lock,) Kit said as they went quietly up to it. He touched the right-hand knob carefully, whispered a word or two in the Speech, tried it. The right side of the double door opened.

(Huh. Wasn't even locked!) Through the open door, much to everyone's surprise, light spilled—plain old fluorescent office-building light, but cheery as a sunny day after the gloom outdoors. On the other side of the door was a perfectly normal-looking corridor with beige walls and charcoal-colored doors and carpeting. The normality came as something of a shock. (Fred, I thought you said it was *darker* here!)

(*Felt* darker. And colder. And it does,) Fred said, shivering, his faint light rippling as he did so. (We're very close to the source of the coldness. It's farther up, though.)

(Up?) Nita looked at Kit uneasily. (If we're going to get the dark Book and get out of here fast, we can't fool with stairs again. We'll have to use the elevators somehow.)

Kit glanced down at the antenna. (I think I can manage an elevator if it gets difficult. Let's find one.)

They slipped through the door and went down the hall to their right, heading for a lobby at its far end. There they peered out at a bank of elevators set in the same dark green marble as the rest of the lobby. No one was there.

Kit walked to the elevators, punched the call button, and hurriedly motioned Nita and Fred to join him. Nita stayed where she was for a moment. (Shouldn't we stay out of sight here?)

(Come on!)

She went out to him, Fred bobbing along beside. Kit watched the elevator lights to see which one was coming down and then slipped into a recess at the side. Nita took the hint and joined him. The elevator bell chimed; doors slid open.

The perytons piled out of the middle elevator in a hurry, five of them together, not looking left or right, and burst out the front door into the street. Once outside they began their awful chorus of howls and snarls, but Nita and Kit and Fred weren't sitting around to listen. They dove into the middle elevator, and Kit struck the control panel with the antenna, hard. *"Close up and take off!"*

The elevator doors closed, but then a rumbling, scraping, gear-grinding screech began—low at first, then louder, a combination of every weird, unsettling noise Nita had ever heard an elevator make. Cables twanged and ratchets ratcheted, and, had they been moving, she would have sworn they were about to go plunging down to crash in the cellar.

"Cut it out or I'll snap your cables myself when I'm through with you!" Kit yelled in the Speech. Almost immediately the elevator jerked slightly and then started upward.

Nita tried again to swallow and had no better luck than the last time. "Those perytons are going to pick up our scent right outside that door, Kit! And they'll track us inside, and it won't be five minutes before—"

"I know, I know. Fred, how well can you feel the middle of the darkness?"

(We're closer.)

"Good. You'll have to tell me when to stop."

The elevator went all the way up to the top, the eighty-ninth floor, before Fred said, (This is it!)

Kit rapped the control panel one last time with his antenna. *"You stay where you are,"* he said.

The elevator doors opened silently to reveal another normal-looking floor, this one more opulent than the floor downstairs. Here the carpets were ivory white and thick; the wall opposite the elevators was one huge bookcase of polished wood, filled with hundreds of books, like volumes of one huge set. Going left they came to another hallway, stretching off to their left like the long stroke of an *L;* this one too was lined with bookcases. At the far end stood a huge polished desk, with papers and Dictaphone equipment and an intercom and a multiline phone jumbled about on it. At the desk sat . . .

It was hard to know *what* to call it. Kit and Nita, peering around the corner, were silent with confusion and fear. The thing sitting in a secretary's swivel chair and typing on an expensive electric typewriter was dark green and warty, and sat about four feet high in the chair. It had limbs with tentacles and claws, all knotted together under a big eggplant-shaped head, and goggly, wicked eyes. All the limbs didn't seem to help the creature's typing much, for every few seconds it made a mistake and went grumbling and fumbling over the top of its messy desk for a bottle of correcting fluid. The creature's grumbling was of more interest than its typing. It used the Speech, but haltingly, as if it didn't care much for the language—and indeed the smooth, stately rhythms of the wizardly tongue suffered somewhat, coming out of that misshapen mouth.

Kit leaned back against the wall. (We've

gotta do something. Fred, are you *sure* it's up here?)

(Absolutely. And past that door, behind that—) Fred indicated the warty typist. From down the hall came another brief burst of typing, then more grumbling and scrabbling on the desk.

(We've got to get it away from there.) Nita glanced at Fred.

(I shall create a diversion,) Fred said, with relish. (I've been good at it so far.)

(Great. Something big. Something alive again, if you can manage it— Then again, forget that.) Nita breathed out unhappily. (I wouldn't leave anything alive here.)

(Not even Joanne?) Kit asked with a small but evil grin.

(Not even her. This place has her outclassed. Fred, just—)

A voice spoke, sounding so loud that Kit and Nita stopped breathing, practically stopped thinking. "Akthanath," it called, a male voice, sounding weary and hassled and bored, "come in here a moment."

Nita glanced at Kit. They carefully peeked down the hall once more and saw the tentacled thing hunch itself up, drop to the floor behind the desk, and wobble its way into the inner office.

(Now?) Fred said.

(No, save it! But come on, this is our best chance!) Nita followed Kit down the hall to the door, crouched by it, and looked in. Past it was another room. They slipped into it and found themselves facing a partly open door that led to the office the typist had gone into. Through the slit they could just see the tentacled creature's back and could hear the voice of the man talking to it. "Hold all my calls for the next hour or so, until they get this thing cleared up. I don't want everybody's half-baked ideas of what's going on. Let Garm and his people handle it. And here, get Mike on the phone for me. I want to see if I can get something useful out of him."

Nita looked around, trying not even to think loudly. The room they were in was lined with shelves and shelves of heavy, dark, leather-bound books with gold-stamped spines. Kit tiptoed to one book-shelf, pulled out a volume at random, and opened it. His face registered shock; he held out the book for Nita to look at. The print was the same as that in Carl's large Advisory manual, line after line of the clear graceful symbols of the Speech—but whatever was being discussed on the page Nita looked at was so complicated she could only understand one word out of every ten or twenty. She glanced at Kit as he turned back to the front of the book and showed her the title page. UNIVERSES, PARAUNIVERSES, AND PLANES—ASSEMBLY AND MAINTENANCE, it said. A CREATOR'S MANUAL. And underneath, in smaller letters, *Volume 108—Natural and Supernatural Laws.*

Nita gulped. Beside her, Fred was dancing about in the air in great agitation. (What is it?) she asked him.

(It's in *here.*)

(Where?) Kit said.

(One of *those.* I can't tell which, it's so dark down that end of the room.) Fred indicated a bookcase on the farthest wall. (It's worst over *there.*) Nita stopped dead when she saw the room's second door, which was wide open and led to the inner office.

Nita got ready to scoot past the door. The man who sat at the desk in the elegant office had his back to the door and was staring out the window into the dimness. His warty secretary handed him the phone, and he swiveled around in the high-backed chair to take it, showing himself in profile. Nita stared at him, confused, as he picked up the phone. A businessman, young, maybe thirty, and very handsome—red-gold hair and a clean-lined face above a trim, dark three-piece suit. *This* was the Witherer, the Kindler of Wildfires, the one who decreed darkness, the Starsnuffer?

"Hi, Michael," he said. He had a pleasant voice, warm and deep. "Oh, nothing much—"

(Never mind *him*,) Kit said. (We've got to get that Book.)

(We can't go past the door till he turns around.)

"—the answer to that is pretty obvious, Mike. I can't do a bloody thing with this place unless I can get some more power for it. I can't afford streetlights, I can barely afford a little electricity, much less a star. The entropy rating—"

The young man swiveled in his chair

again, leaning back and looking out the window. Nita realized with a chill that he had a superb view of the downtown skyline, including the top of the Pan Am Building, where even now wisps of smoke curled black against the lowering gray. She tapped Kit on the elbow, and together they slipped past the doorway to the bookshelf.

(Fred, do you have even a *little* idea—)

(Maybe one of those up there.) He indicated a shelf just within reach. Kit and Nita started taking down one book after another, looking at them. Nita was shaking—she had no clear idea what they were looking for.

(What if it's one of those up there, out of reach?)

(You'll stand on my shoulders. Kit, hurry!)

"—Michael, don't you think you could talk to the rest of Them and get me just a *little* more energy? —Well, They've *never* given me what I asked for, have They? All I wanted was my own Universe where everything *works*— Which brings me to the reason for this call. Who's this new operative you turned loose in here? This Universe is at a very delicate stage, interference will—"

They were down to the second-to-last shelf, and none of the books had been what they were looking for. Nita was sweating worse. (Fred, are you *sure*—)

(It's dark there, it's *all* dark. What do you *want* from me?)

Kit, kneeling by the bottom shelf, suddenly jumped as if shocked. (Huh?) Nita said.

(It stung me. *Nita!*) Kit grabbed at the volume his hand had brushed, yanked it out of the case, and knelt there, juggling it like a hot potato. He managed to get it open and held it out, showing Nita not the usual clean page, close-printed with the fine small symbols of the Speech, but a block of transparency like many pages of thinnest glass laid together. Beneath the smooth surface, characters and symbols seethed as if boiling up from a great depth and sinking down again.

Nita found herself squinting. (It hurts to look at.)

(It hurts to *hold!*) Kit shut the book

hurriedly and held it out to Fred for him to check, for externally it looked no different from any other book there. (Is this what we're looking for?)

Fred's faint glimmer went out like a blown candle flame with the nearness of the book. (The darkness—it blinds—)

Kit bundled the book into his backpack and rubbed his hands on his jacket. (Now if we can just get out of here . . .)

"Oh, come on, Mike," the voice was saying in the other office. "Don't get cute with me. I had an incident on top of one of my buildings. One of my favorite constructs got shot up and the site stinks of wizardry. *Your* brand, moonlight and noon-forged metal." The voice of the handsome young man in the three-piece suit was still pleasant enough, but Nita, peering around the edge of the door, saw his face going hard and sharp as the edge of a knife. He swiveled around in his chair again to look out the window at that thin plume of ascending smoke, and Nita waved Kit past the door, then scuttled after him herself. "That's a dumb question to be asking *me*, Michael. If I knew, would I tell you where the bright *Book* was? And how likely is it that I know at all? You people keep such close tabs on it, at least that's what I hear. Anyway, if it's not read from every so often, don't *I* go ffft! like everything else?— You're absolutely right, that's not a responsive answer. Why should *I* be responsive, *you're* not being very helpful—"

Kit and Nita peeked back into the hall. Fred floated up to hang between them. (I get a feeling—) Kit started to say, but the sudden coldness in the voice of the man on the phone silenced him.

"Look, Mike, I've had about enough of this silliness. The Bright Powers got miffed because I wanted to work on projects of my own instead of playing follow the leader like you do, working from their blueprints instead of drawing up your own. You can do what you please, but I thought when I settled down in this little pittance of a Universe that They would let me be and let me do things my way. They said They didn't need me when They threw me out—well, I've done pretty well without Them, too. Maybe They don't like that, because now all of a sudden I'm getting interference. You say this operative isn't one of your sweetness-and-light types? Fine. Then you won't mind if when I catch him, her, or it, I make his stay interesting and permanent. Whoever's disrupting my status quo will wish he'd never been born, spawned, or engendered. And when you see the rest of Them, you tell Them from me that— Hello? Hello?"

The phone slammed down. There was no sound for a few seconds. "Akthanath," the young man's voice finally said into that silence, "someone's soul is going to writhe for this."

The slow cold of the words got into Nita's spine. She and Kit slipped around the door and ran for it, down the hall and into the elevator. "He's playing it close to the chest," that angry voice floated down the hall to them. "I don't know what's going on. The Eldest still has it safe? —Good, then see that guards are mounted at the usual accesses. And have Garm send a pack of his people backtime to the most recent gate opening. I want to know which universe these agents are coming from."

In the elevator, Kit whipped out the

antenna and rapped the control panel with it. *"Down!"*

Doors closed, and down it went. Nita leaned back against one wall of the elevator, panting. Now she knew why that first crowd of perytons had come howling after them on top of the Pan Am Building, but the solution of that small mystery made her feel no better at all. "Kit, they'll be waiting downstairs, for sure."

He bit his lip. "Yeah. Well, we won't be where they think we'll be, that's all. If we get off a couple of floors too high and take the stairs—"

"Right."

"Stop at four," Kit said to the elevator.

The elevator stopped, opened its doors. Kit headed out the door fast and tripped— the elevator had stopped several inches beneath the fourth floor. *"Watch your step,"* the elevator said, snickering.

Kit turned and smacked the open elevator door with his antenna as Nita and Fred got out. *"Very funny. You stay here until I give the word.* C'mon, let's get out of here!"

They ran down the hall together, found the stairs, and plunged down them. Kit was panting as hard as Nita now. Fred shot down past landing after landing with them, his light flickering as if it were an effort to keep up. "Kit," Nita said, "where are we going to go after we leave this building? We need time, and a place to do the spell to find the bright *Book*."

Kit sounded unhappy. "I dunno. How about Central Park? If we hid in there—"

"But you saw what it looks like from the top of Pan Am. It's all dark in there, there were things moving—"

"There's a lot of room to hide. Look, Nita, if I can handle the machines here, it's a good bet you can handle the plants. You're good with plants and live stuff, you said."

She nodded reluctantly. "I guess we'll find out how good."

They came to the last landing, the ground floor. Nita pushed the door open a crack and found that they were almost directly across from the green lobby and the elevators.

(What's the situation?) Kit said silently.

(They're waiting.) Six perytons—black-coated, brown-coated, one a steely gray—were sitting or standing around the middle elevator with their tongues hanging out and looks of anticipation and hunger in their too-human eyes.

(Now?) Fred said, sounding eager.

(Not yet. We may not need a diversion, Fred.) *"Go!"* he whispered then in the Speech. The antenna in his hand sparked and sputtered with molten light, and Kit pressed close behind Nita. (Watch them!)

There was no bell, but even if there had been one, the sound of it and of the elevator doors opening would have been drowned out in snarls as the perytons leaped in a body into the elevator. The moment the perytons were out of sight, Nita pushed the door open and headed for the one to the garage. It stuck and stung her as the dark Book had; she jerked her hand away from it. Kit came up behind her and blasted it with the antenna, then grabbed it himself. This time it came open. They dashed through and Kit sealed the door behind them.

No one was in the garage, but a feeling was growing in the air as if the storm of rage they'd heard beginning upstairs was about to break over their heads. Kit raised the antenna again, firing a line of hot light that zapped the ceiling-mounted controls of the delivery door. With excruciating slowness the door began to rumble upward. (Now?) Fred said anxiously as they ran toward it.

(No, not yet, just—)

They bent over double, ducked underneath the opening door, and ran up the driveway. It was then that the perytons leaped at them from both sides, howling, and Nita grabbed for her wand and managed one slash with it, yelling, "Now, Fred! *Now!*"

All she saw clearly was the peryton that jumped at her, a huge, blue-eyed, brindled she-wolf, as the rowan wand spat silver moonfire and the peryton fell away screaming. Then came the explosion, and it hurled both her and Kit staggering off to their right. The street shook as if lightning struck, and part of the front of the dark building was demolished in a shower of shattered plate glass as tons and tons and tons of red bricks came crashing down from somewhere to fill the street from side to side, burying sidewalks and perytons and doors and the delivery bay twenty feet deep.

Nita picked herself up. A few feet away Kit was doing the same, and Fred bobbed over to them as an ominous stillness settled over everything. (How was I?) Fred asked, seeming dazed but pleased.

"Are you all right?" Kit asked.

(I'm alive, but my gnaester will never be the same,) Fred said. (You two?)

"We're fine," Kit said.

"And I think we're in trouble," Nita added, looking at the blocked street. "Let's get going!"

They ran toward Fifth Avenue, and the shadows took them.

Contractual
Magic:

AN INTRODUCTION

A FOUR-FOOT-HIGH wall ran down the west side of Fifth Avenue, next to a sidewalk of gray hexagonal paving stones. Nita and Kit crouched behind it, just inside Central Park, under the shadows of barren-branched trees, and tried to catch their breath. Fred hung above them, watching both Fifth Avenue and Sixty-fourth Street for signs of pursuit.

Nita leaned against the dirty wall, careless of grime or roughness or the pigeon droppings that streaked it. She was scared. All through her life, the one thing she knew she could always depend on was her energy—it never gave out. Even after being beaten up, she always sprang right back. But here and now, when she could less afford exhaustion than she had ever been able to in her life, she felt it creeping up on her. She was even afraid to rest, for fear it would catch up with her quicker. But her lungs were burning, and it felt so good to sit still, not have death or something worse chasing her. And there was another spell to be cast....

If I'd known I was going to get into a situation like this, she thought, *would I ever have picked that book up at all? Would I have taken the Oath?* Then she shook her head and tried to think about something else, for she got an inkling of the answer, and it shocked her. She had always been told that she wasn't brave. At least that's what Joanne and her friends had always said: *Can't take a dare, can't take a joke, crybaby, crybaby. We were only teasing....*

She sniffed and rubbed her eyes, which stung. "Did you find the spell?"

Kit had been paging through his wizards' manual. Now he was running a finger down one page, occasionally whispering a word, then stopping himself to keep from using the Speech aloud. "Yeah. It's pretty simple." But he was frowning.

"What's the matter?"

Kit slumped back against the wall, looked over at her. "I keep thinking about what—you know who—was talking about on the phone."

"Sounded like he was hiding something."

"Uh-huh. They know where the bright *Book* is, all right. And somebody's watching it. Whoever the 'Eldest' is. And now there're going to be more guards around it."

"'The usual accesses,' he said. Kit, there might be an *un*usual access, then."

"Sure. If we had any idea where the thing was hidden."

"Won't the spell give us a vision, a location, like the last one?"

"No. It's a directional." Kit dropped his hands wearily on the book in his lap, sighed, looked over at Nita. "I don't know . . . I just don't get it."

"What?" She rolled the rowan wand between her hands, watching the way its light shone between her fingers and through the skin.

"He didn't look evil. Or sound that way, at least not till right at the end there."

(The Snuffer was always glorious to look at before it scorned the light,) Fred said. (And it kept the beauty afterward— that's what the stars always used to say. That's one reason it's dangerous to deal with that one. The beauty ... seduces.) Fred made a small feeling of awe and fear. (What a blaze of darkness, what a flood of emissions. I was having a hard time keeping my composure in there.)

"Are you all right now?"

(Oh yes. I was a little amazed that you didn't perceive the power burning around the shell he was wearing. Just as well—you might have spoken to him, and everything would have been lost. That one's most terrible power, they say, is his absolute conviction that he's right in what he does.)

"He's not right, then?" Kit asked.

(I don't know.)

"But," Nita said, confused, "if he's fighting with ... with Them ... with the ones who made the bright *Book,* isn't he in the wrong?"

(I don't know,) Fred said again. (How am I supposed to judge? But you're wizards, you should know how terrible a power belief is, especially in the wrong hands—and how do you tell which hands are wrong? *Believe* something and the Universe is on its way to being changed. Because *you've* changed, by believing. Once you've changed, other things start to follow. Isn't that the way it works?)

Nita nodded as Fred looked across the dark expanse of Central Park. The branches of trees were knotted together in tangled patterns of strife. Ivy strangled what it climbed. Paths were full of pitfalls; copses clutched themselves full of threat and darkness. Shadows moved secretively through shadows, making unnerving noises. (This is what—he—believes in,) Fred said sadly, (however he justifies the belief.)

Nita could find nothing to say. The wordless misery of the trees had been wearing at her ever since she set foot inside the wall. All the growing things there longed for light, though none of them knew what it was; she could feel their starved rage moving sluggishly in them, slow as sap in the cold. Only in one place was their anger muted—several blocks south, at Fifth and Central Park South, where in her own New York the equestrian statue of General Sherman and the Winged Victory had stood. Here the triumphant rider cast in black bronze was that handsome young man they had seen in the black glass building, his face set in a cold proud conqueror's smile. The creature he rode was a skull-faced eight-legged steed, which the wizards' manual said brought death with the sound of its hooves. And Victory with her palm branch was changed to a grinning Fury who held a dripping sword. Around the statue group the trees were silent, not daring to express even inarticulate feelings. They knew their master too well.

Nita shook her head and glanced at Kit, who was looking in the same direction. "I thought it'd be fun to know the Mason's Word and run around bringing statues to life," he said unhappily, "but somehow I don't think there's any statue here I'd want to use the Word on... You ready? We should start this."

"Yeah."

The spell was brief and straightforward, and Nita turned to the right page in her manual and drew the necessary circle and diagram. Kit got the dark Book out of his backpack and dropped it in the middle of the circle. Nita held up her wand for light. They began to recite the spell.

It was only three sentences long, but by the end of the first sentence Nita could feel the trees bending in close to watch—not with friendly, secretive interest, as in her first spell with Kit, but in hungry desperation. Even the abstract symbols and words of the Speech must have tasted of another Universe where light was not only permitted, but free. The rowan wand was blazing by the end of the second sentence, maybe in reaction to being so close to something of the dark powers, and Nita wondered whether she should cover it up to keep them from being noticed. But the spell held her immobile as usual. For another thing, the trees all around were leaning in with such piteous feelings of hunger that she would as soon have eaten in front of starving children and not offered them some of what she had. Branches began to toss and twist, reaching down for a taste of the light. Nita and Kit finished the spell.

Kit reached right down to pick up the dark Book, which was as well, for immediately after the last word of the spell was spoken it actually hitched itself a little way along the ground, southward. Kit could only hold it for a moment before stuffing it back into his backpack. It no longer looked innocent. It burned, both to touch and to look at. Even when Kit had it hidden away and the backpack slung on, neither of them felt any easier. It was as if they were all now visible to something that was looking eagerly for them.

"Let's get out of here," Kit said, so subdued that Nita could hardly hear him. Nita stood and laid a hand against the trunk of the nearest tree, a consoling gesture. She was sorry she couldn't have left them more light. (I wish there was something I could do,) she said silently. But no answer came back. These trees were bound silent, like the car Kit had tended.

She rejoined Kit, who was looking over the wall. "Nothing," he said. Together they swung over the dropping-streaked stone and hurried down Fifth Avenue, crossing the street to get a safe distance between them and the strange cries and half-seen movements of the park. "Straight south?" Nita said.

"Pretty nearly. It's pushing straight that way on my back. The bright *Book* looked like it was way downtown, didn't it, in that spell?"

"Uh-huh. The financial district, I think." She gulped. It *was* a long way to walk—miles—even without having to worry about someone chasing you.

"Well, we'd better hurry," Kit said. He paused while they both stopped at the corner of Fifth and Sixty-first. When they were across, he added, "What gets me is that he's so sure that we're interference from the bright side. We haven't done anything yet."

"Huh," Nita said, gently scornful. "Sure we haven't. And anyway, whaddaya mean we aren't 'interference from the bright side'? *You* were the one who said we'd been had."

Kit mulled this over as they approached Sixtieth. "Well . . . maybe. If they know about us, do you think they'll send help?"

"I don't know. I get the feeling that maybe we *are* the help."

"Well, we're not dead yet," Kit said, and peered around the corner of Sixtieth and Fifth—and then jumped back, pale with shock. "We're dead," he said, turned around, and began running back the way they had come, though he limped doing it. Nita looked around that corner just long enough to see what he had seen—a whole pack of big yellow cabs, thundering down Sixtieth. The one in front had a twisted fender that stuck out slightly on one side, a jagged piece of metal. She turned and ran after Kit, frantic. "Where can we hide?"

"The buildings are locked here, too," Kit said from up ahead. He had been trying doors. "Fred, can you do something?"

(After that last emission? So soon?) Fred's thought was shaken. (It's all I can do to radiate light. I need time to recover.)

"Crud! Kit, the park, maybe the trees'll slow them down."

They both ran for the curb, but there was no time. Cabs came roaring around the corner from Sixtieth, and another pack of them leaped around the corner of Sixty-first and hurtled down Fifth toward them; they would never make it across the street.

Kit grabbed for his antenna, and Nita yanked out the wand, but without much hope—it hadn't worked that well on the helicopter. The cabs slowed, closed in from both sides, forming a half-circle with Kit and Nita and Fred at the center, backing them against the wall of a dingy building. The cordon tightened until there were no gaps, and one cab at each side was up on the sidewalk, blocking it. No matter where Nita looked, all she saw were chromed grilles like gritted teeth, hungry headlights staring. One of the cabs shouldered forward, its engine snarling softly. The jagged place at one end of its front fender wore a brown discoloration. Not rust—Kit's blood, which it had tasted. Kit lifted the antenna, the hand that gripped it shaking.

The high-pitched yowl of rage and defiance from outside the circle jerked Kit's head up. Nita stared. Fenders scraped and rattled against one another as the tight-wedged cabs jostled, trying to see what was happening. Even the bloodstained cab, the pack leader, looked away from Kit. But none of them could move any way but backward, and one cab paid immediately for that limitation as a fanged grille bit deep into its hindquarters and dragged it screaming out of the circle. Metal screeched and tore, glass shattered as the Lotus Esprit's jaws crushed through the cab's trunk, ripped away its rear axle, and with a quick sideways shake of its front end flung the bitten-off axle crashing down Fifth Avenue. Then the Lotus slashed sideways, its fangs opening up the side of another cab like a can opener. The circle broke amid enraged roaring; cabs circled and feinted while the first victim dragged itself away by its front wheels to collapse in the street.

Everything started happening at once. Nita slashed at the front of the cab closest to her. The whip of moonfire cracking across its face seemed to confuse and frighten it, but did no damage. *I hope it doesn't notice that right away,* she thought desperately, for there was no use yelling for help. Kit had his hands full. He had the antenna laid over his forearm again and was snapping off shot after shot of blinding-hot light, cracking headlights, burning holes in hoods, and exploding tires, a hit here, a hit there—nothing fatal, Nita noticed with dismay. But Kit was managing to hold the cabs at their distance as they harried him.

Out in the street one cab lunged at the Lotus, a leap, its front wheels clear of the ground and meant to come crashing down on the racer's hood—until suddenly the Lotus's nose dipped under the cab and heaved upward, sending the cab rolling helplessly onto its back. A second later the Lotus came down on top of the cab, took a great shark bite out of its underbelly, and then whirled around, whipping gas and transmission fluid all over, to slash at another cab about to leap on it from behind. This was the king cab, the pack leader, and as the Lotus and the Checker circled one another warily in the street, the other cabs drew away from Kit and Nita to watch the outcome of the combat.

There were two more cabs dead in the street that Nita hadn't seen fall—one with everything from right rear door to right front fender torn away, another horribly mangled in its front end and smashed sideways into a tree on the other side of Fifth, as if it had been thrown there. Amid the wreckage of these and the other two cabs, the cab and the Lotus rolled, turning and backing, maneuvering for an opening that would end in a kill. The Lotus was scored along one side but otherwise un-hurt, and the whining roar of its engine sounded hungry and pleased. Infuriated, the Checker made a couple of quick rushes at it, stopping short with a screech of tires and backing away again each time in a way that indicated it didn't want to close in. The Lotus snarled derisively, and without warning the Checker swerved around and threw itself full speed at Kit and Nita, still braced against the wall.

This is it, Nita thought with curious calm. She flung up the rowan wand in one last useless slash and then was thrown back against the wall with terrible force as a thunderstorm of screaming metal flew from right to left in front of her and crashed not five feet away. She slid down the wall limp as a rag doll, stunned, aware that death had gone right past her face. When her eyes and ears started working again, the Lotus was standing off to her left, its back scornfully turned to the demolished pack leader, which it had slammed into the wall. The Checker looked like the remains of a front-end collision test—it was crumpled up into itself like an accordion, and bleeding oil and gas in pools. The Lotus roared triumphant disdain at the remaining two cabs, then threatened them with a small mean rush. They turned tail and ran a short distance, then slowed down and slunk away around the corner of Sixty-first. Satisfied, the Lotus bent over the broken body of one dead cab, reached down, and with casual fierceness plucked away some of the front fender, as a falcon plucks its kill before eating.

Nita turned her head to look for Kit. He was several feet farther down the wall, looking as shattered as she felt. He got up slowly and walked out into the street. The Lotus glanced up, left its kill, and went to meet him. For a moment they simply looked at each other from a few feet apart. Kit held one hand out, and the Lotus slowly inched forward under the hand, permitting the caress. They stood that way for the space of four or five gasps, and then the Lotus rolled closer still and pushed its face roughly against Kit's leg, like a cat.

"How about that," Kit said, his voice cracking. "How about that."

Nita put her face down in her hands, wanting very much to cry, but all she could manage were a couple of crooked, whooping sobs. She had a feeling that much worse was coming, and she couldn't break down all the way. Nita hid her eyes until she thought her voice was working again, then let her hands fall and looked up. "Kit, we've got to—"

The Lotus had rolled up and was staring at her—a huge, dangerous, curious, brown-hided beast. She lost what she was saying, hypnotized by the fierce, interested stare. Then the Lotus smiled at Nita, a slow, chrome smile, silver and sanguine. "Uhh," she said, disconcerted, and glanced up at Kit, who had come to stand alongside the racer. "We've gotta get out of here, Kit. It has to be the spell that brought these things down on us. And when those two cabs let you-know-who know that we didn't get caught, or killed—"

Kit nodded, looked down at the Lotus; it glanced sideways up at him, from headlights bright with amusement and triumph. *"How about it?"* Kit said in the Speech. *"Could you give us a lift?"*

In answer the Lotus shrugged, flicking its doors open like a bird spreading its wings.

Nita stood up, staggering slightly. "Fred?"

He appeared beside her, making a feeling of great shame. "Fred, what's the matter?" Kit said, catching it too.

(I couldn't do anything.)

"Of course not," Nita said, reaching up to cup his faint spark in one hand. "Because you just *did* something huge, dummy. We're all right. Come on for a ride." She perched Fred on the upstanding collar of her down vest; he settled there with a sigh of light.

Together she and Kit lowered themselves into the dark seats of the Lotus, into the dim, warm cockpit, alive with dials and gauges, smelling of leather and metal and oil. They had barely strapped themselves in before the Lotus gave a great glad shake that slammed its doors shut, and burned rubber down Fifth Avenue—out of the carnage and south toward the joining of two rivers, and the oldest part of Manhattan.

Nita sat at ease, taking a breather and watching the streets of Manhattan rush by. Kit, behind the steering wheel, was holding the dark Book in his lap, feeling it carefully for any change in the directional spell. He was reluctant to touch it. The farther south they went, the more the Book burned the eyes that looked at it. The wizards' manual had predicted this effect—that, as the two Books drew closer to one another, each would assert its own nature more and more forcefully. Nita watched the Book warping and skewing the very air around it, blurring its own outlines, and found it easy to believe the manual's statement that even a mind of terrible enough purpose and power to wrench this Book to its use might in the reading be devoured by what was read. She hoped for Kit's sake that it wouldn't devour someone who just touched it.

"We're close," Kit said at last, in a quiet, strained voice.

"You okay?"

"I've got a headache, but that's all. Where are we?"

"Uh—that was just Pearl Street. Close to City Hall." She tapped the inside of her door, a friendly gesture. "Your baby *moves.*"

"Yeah," Kit said affectionately. The Lotus rumbled under its hood, sped on.

"Fred? You feeling better?"

Fred looked up at her from her collar. (Somewhat. I'd feel better still if I knew what we were going to be facing next. If I'm to make bricks again, I'm going to need some notice.)

"Your gnaester, huh?" Kit said.

(I'm not sure I *have* a gnaester anymore, after that last emission. And I'm afraid to find out.)

"Kit, scrunch down," Nita said suddenly, doing the same herself. The Lotus roared past the corner of Broadway and Chambers, pointedly ignoring a pair of sullen-looking cabs that stared and snarled as it passed. They were parked on either side of an iron-railed stairway leading down to a subway station. About a block farther along Broadway, two more cabs were parked at another subway entrance.

From his slumped-down position, Kit glanced over at Nita. "Those are the first we've seen."

" 'The usual accesses,' " Nita said. "They've got it down in the subway somewhere."

"Oh no," Kit muttered, and (Wonderful,) Fred said. Nita swallowed, not too happy about the idea herself. Subway stations, unless they were well lighted and filled with people, gave her the creeps. Worse, even in her New York, subways had their own special ecologies—not just the mice and rats and cats that everybody knew about, but other less normal creatures, on which the wizards' manual had had a twenty-page chapter. "They're all over the place," she said aloud, dealing with the worst problem first. "How are we going to—"

"Ooof!" Kit said, as the dark Book, sitting on his lap, sank down hard as if pushed. The Lotus kept driving on down Broadway, past City Hall, and Kit struggled upward to look out the back window, noting the spot. "That was where the other *Book* was—straight down from that place we just passed."

The Lotus turned right onto a side street and slowed as if looking for something. Finally it pulled over to the left-hand curb and stopped. "What—" Kit started to say, but the racer flicked open first Kit's door, then Nita's, as if it wanted them to get out.

They did, cautiously. The Lotus very quietly closed its doors. Then it rolled forward a little way, bumping up onto the sidewalk in front of a dingy-looking warehouse. It reached down, bared its fangs, and with great delicacy sank them into a six-foot-long grille in the sidewalk. The

Lotus heaved, and with a soft scraping groan, the grillwork came up to reveal an electric-smelling darkness and stairs leading down into it.

"It's one of the emergency exits from the subway, for when the trains break down," Kit whispered, jamming the dark Book back into his backpack and dropping to his knees to rub the Lotus enthusiastically behind one headlight. "It's perfect!"

The Lotus's engine purred as it stared at Kit with fierce affection. It backed a little and parked itself, its motions indicating it would wait for them. Kit got up, pulling out his antenna, and Nita got out her wand. "Well," she said under her breath, "let's get it over with..."

The steps were cracked concrete, growing damp and discolored as she walked downward. Nita held out the wand to be sure of her footing and kept one hand on the left wall to be sure of her balance—there was no banister or railing on the right, only darkness and echoing air. (Kit—) she said silently, wanting to be sure he was near, but not wanting to be heard by anything that might be listening down there.

(Right behind you. Fred?)

His spark came sailing down behind Kit, looking brighter as they passed from gloom to utter dark. (Believe me, I'm not far.)

(Here's the bottom,) Nita said. She turned for one last glance up toward street level and saw a huge sleek silhouette carefully and quietly replacing the grille above them. She gulped, feeling as if she were being shut into a dungeon, and turned to look deeper into the darkness. The stairs ended in a ledge three feet wide and perhaps four feet deep, recessed into the concrete wall of the subway. Nita held up the wand for more light. The ledge stretched away straight ahead, with the subway track at the bottom of a wide pit to the right of it. (Which way, Kit?)

(Straight, for the time being.)

The light reflected dully from the tracks beside them as they pressed farther into the dark. Up on the streets, though there had been darkness, there had also been sound. Here there was a silence like black water, a silence none of them dared to break. They slipped into it holding their breaths. Even the usual dim rumor of a subway tunnel, the sound of trains rumbling far away, the ticking of the rails, was missing. The hair stood up all over Nita as she walked and tried not to make a sound. The air was damp, chilly, full of the smells of life—too full, and the wrong kinds of life, at least to Nita's way of thinking: mold and mildew; water dripping too softly to make a sound, but still filling the air with a smell of leached lime, a stale, puddly odor; wet trash, piled in trickling gutters or at the bases of rusting iron pillars, rotting quietly; and always the sharp ozone-and-scorched-soot smell of the third rail. Shortly there was light that did not come from Nita's wand. Pale splotches of green-white radiance were splashed irregularly on walls and ceiling—firefungus, which the wizards' manual said was the main food source of the subway's smallest denizens, dun mice and hidebehinds and skinwings. Nita shuddered at the thought and walked faster. Where there were hidebehinds, there would certainly be rats to eat them. And where there were rats, there would also be fireworms and thrastles....

(Nita.)

She stopped and glanced back at Kit. He was holding his backpack in one arm now and the antenna in the other, and looking troubled in the wand's silver light. (That way,) he said, pointing across the tracks at the far wall with its niche-shaped recesses.

(Through the *wall*? We don't even know how thick it is!) Then she stopped and thought a moment. (I wonder— You suppose the Mason's Word would work on concrete? What's in concrete, anyhow?)

(Sand—quartz, mostly. Some chemicals—but I think they all come out of the ground.)

(Then it'll work. C'mon.) Nita hunkered down and very carefully let herself drop into the wide pit where the tracks ran. The crunch of rusty track cinders told her Kit was right behind. Fred floated down beside her, going low to light the way. With great care Nita stepped over the third rail and balanced on the narrow ledge of the wall on the other side. She stowed the wand and laid both hands flat on the concrete to begin implementation of the lesser usage of the Word, the one that merely manipulates stone rather than giving it the semblance of life. Nita leaned her head against the stone too, making sure of her memory of the Word, the sixteen syllables that would loose what was bound. Very fast, so as not to mess it up, she said the Word and pushed.

Door, she thought as the concrete melted under her hands, and a door there was; she was holding the sides of it. (Go ahead,) she said to Kit and Fred. They ducked through under her arm. She took a step forward, let go, and the wall re-formed behind her.

(Now what the—) Kit was staring around him in complete confusion. It took Nita a moment to recover from the use of the Word, but when her vision cleared, she understood the confusion. They were standing in the middle of another track, which ran right into the wall they had just come through and stopped there. The walls there were practically one huge mass of firefungus. It hung down in odd green-glowing lumps from the ceiling and layered thick in niches and on the poles that held the ceiling up. Only the track and ties and the rusty cinders between were bare, a dark road leading downward between eerily shining walls for perhaps an eighth of a mile before curving around to the right and out of view.

(I don't get it,) Kit said. (This track just starts. Or just stops. It would run right into that one we just came off! There aren't any subway lines in the city that do that! Are there?)

Nita shook her head, listening. The silence of the other tunnel did not persist here. Far down along the track, the sickly green light of the firefungus was troubled by small shadowy rustlings, movements, the scrabbling of claws. (What about the *Book?*) she asked.

Kit nodded toward the end of the track. (Down there, and a little to the right.)

They walked together down the long aisle of cold light, looking cautiously into the places where firefungus growth was sparse enough to allow for shadow. Here and there small sparks of brightness peered out at them, paired sparks—the eyes of dun mice, kindled to unnatural brightness by the fungus they fed on. Everywhere was the smell of dampness, old things rotting or rusting. The burning-ozone smell grew so chokingly strong that Nita realized it couldn't be just the third rail producing it—even if the third rail were alive in a tunnel this old. The smell grew stronger as they approached the curve at the tunnel's end. Kit, still carrying the backpack, was gasping. She stopped just before the curve, looked at him. (Are you okay?)

He gulped. (It's close, it's really close. I can hardly see, this thing is blurring my eyes so bad.)

(You want to give it to me?)

(No, you go ahead. This place seems to be full of live things. Your department—)

(Yeah, right,) Nita agreed unhappily, and made sure of her grip on the rowan wand. (Well, here goes. Fred, you ready for another diversion?)

(I think I could manage something small if I had to.)

(Great. All together now . . .)

They walked around the curve, side by side. Then they stopped.

It was a subway station. Or it had been

at one time, for from where they stood at one end of the platform, they could see the tons of rubble that had choked and sealed the tunnel at the far end of the platform. The rubble and the high ceiling were overgrown with firefungus enough to illuminate the old mosaics on the wall, the age-cracked tiles that said CITY HALL over and over again, down the length of the platform wall. But the platform and tracks weren't visible from where they stood. Heaped up from wall to wall was a collection of garbage and treasure, things that glittered, things that moldered. Nita saw gems, set and unset, like the plunder of a hundred jewelry stores, tumbled together with moldy kitchen garbage; costly fabric in bolts or in shreds, half buried by beer cans and broken bottles; paintings in ornate frames, elaborately carved furniture, lying broken or protruding crookedly from beneath timbers and dirt fallen from the old ceiling; vases, sculpture, crystal, silver services, a thousand kinds of rich and precious things, lying all together, whole and broken, among shattered dirty crockery and base metal. And lying atop the hoard, its claws clutched full of cheap costume jewelry, whispering to itself in the Speech, was the dragon.

Once more Nita tried to swallow and couldn't manage it. This looked nothing like the fireworm her book had mentioned—a foot-long mouse-eating lizard with cigarette-lighter breath. But if a fireworm had had a long, long time to grow— she remembered the voice of the young man in the three-piece suit, saying with relief, "The Eldest has it." There was no telling how many years this creature had been lairing here in the darkness, growing huger and huger, devouring the smaller creatures of the underground night and dominating those it did not devour, sending them out to steal for its hoard—or to bring it food. Nita began to tremble, looking at the fireworm-dragon's thirty feet of lean, scaled, tight-muscled body, looking at the size of its dark-stained jaws, and considering what kind of food it must eat. She glanced down at one taloned hind foot and saw something that lay crushed and forgotten beneath it—a subway repairman's reflective orange vest, torn and scorched; a wrench, half melted; the bones, burned black. . . .

The dragon had its head down and was raking over its hoard with huge claws that broke what they touched half the time. Its tail twitched like a cat's as it whispered to itself in a voice like hissing steam. Its scales rustled as it moved, glowing faintly with the same light as the firefungus, but colder, greener, darker. The dragon's eyes were slitted as if even the pale fungus light was too much for it. It dug in the hoard, nosed into the hole, dug again, nosed about, as if going more by touch than sight. *"Four thousand and ssix,"* it whispered, annoyed, hurried, angry. *"It was here sssomewhere, I know it was. Three thousand—no. Four thousand and—and—"*

It kept digging, its claws sending coins and bottle caps rolling. The dragon reached into the hole and with its teeth lifted out a canvas bag. Bright things spilled out, which Nita first thought were more coins but that turned out to be subway tokens. With a snarl of aggravation the fireworm-dragon flung the bag away, and tokens flew and bounced down the hoard-hill, a storm of brassy glitter. One rolled right to Nita's feet. Not taking her eyes off the dragon, she bent to pick it up. It was bigger than the subway token the New York transit system used these days, and the letters stamped on it were in an old-time style. She nudged Kit and passed it to him, looking around at the mosaics on the walls. They were *old.* The City Hall motif repeated in squares high on the train side wall of the platform looked little like the City Hall of today. This station had to be one of those that were walled up and forgotten when the area was being rebuilt long ago. The question was ...

(The problem is—) Kit started to say in his quietest whisper of thought. But it wasn't quiet enough. With an expression of rage and terror, the dragon looked up from its digging, looked straight at them. Its squinted eyes kindled in the light from Nita's wand, throwing back a frightful violet reflection. *"Who's there? Who's there!"* it screamed in the Speech, in a voice like an explosion of steam. Without waiting for an answer it struck forward with its neck as a snake strikes and spat fire at them. Nita was ready, though; the sound of the scream and the sight of many tiny shadows running for cover had given her enough warning to put up the shield spell for both herself and Kit. The firebolt, dark red shot with billowing black like the output of a flamethrower, blunted against the shield and spilled sideways and down like water splashing on a window. When the bolt died away, the dragon was creeping and coiling down the hoard toward them; but it stopped, confused, when it saw that Kit and Nita and Fred still stood unhurt. It reared back its head for another bolt.

"You can't hurt us, Eldest," Nita said hurriedly, hoping it wouldn't try; the smell of burned firefungus was already enough to turn her stomach. The dragon crouched low against the hoard, its tail lashing, staring at them.

"You came to ssteal," it said, its voice quieter than before but angrier, as it realized it *couldn't* hurt them. *"No one ever comes here but to ssteal. Or to try,"* it added, glancing savagely over at another torn and fire-withered orange vest. *"What*

do you want? You can't have it. Mine, all thiss is mine. No one takes what'ss mine. He promissed, he ssaid he would leave me alone when I came here. Now he breakss the promiss, is that it?"

The Eldest squinted wrathfully at them. For the second time that day, Nita found herself fascinated by an expression. Rage was in the fireworm-dragon's face, but also a kind of pain; and its voice was desperate in its anger. It turned its back, then, crawling back up onto the hoard. *"I will not let him break the promiss. Go back to him and tell him that I will burn it, burn it all, ssooner than let him have one ring, one jewel. Mine, all thiss is mine, no hoard has been greater than thiss in all times, he will not diminishhh it—"* The Eldest wound itself around the top of the hoard-mound like a crown of spines and scales, digging its claws protectively into the gems and the trash. A small avalanche of objects started from the place where it had been laying the hoard open before. Gold bars, some the small collectors' bars, some large ones such as the banks used, clattered or crashed down the side of the mound. Nita remembered how some $10 million worth of Federal Reserve gold had vanished from a bank in New York some years before—just vanished, untraceable—and she began to suspect where it had gone.

"*Mine,*" hissed the Eldest. "*I have eight thousand six hundred forty-two cut diamonds. I have six hundred—no. I have four hundred eight emeralds. I have eighty-nine black opals—no, fifteen black opals. I have eighty-nine—eighty-nine—*" The anxiety in its voice was growing, washing out the anger. Abruptly the Eldest turned away from them and began digging again, still talking, its voice becoming again as it had been when they first came in: hurried, worried. "*Eighty-nine pounds of silver plate. I have two hundred fourteen pounds of gold—no, platinum. I have six hundred seventy pounds of gold—*"

"Nita," Kit said, very softly, in English, hoping the Eldest wouldn't understand it. "You get the feeling it's losing its memory?"

She nodded. "Lord, how awful." For a creature with the intense possessiveness of a fireworm to be unable to remember what it had in its hoard must be sheer torture. It would never be able to be sure whether everything was there; if something was missing, it might not be able to tell. And to a fireworm, whose pride is in its defense of its hoard from even the cleverest thieves, there was no greater shame than to be stolen from and not notice and avenge the theft immediately. The Eldest must live constantly with the fear of that shame. Even now it had forgotten Kit and Nita and Fred as it dug and muttered frantically, trying to find something, though uncertain of what it was looking for.

Nita was astonished to find that she was feeling sorry for a creature that had tried to kill her a few minutes before. "Kit," she said, "what about the bright *Book?* Is it in there?"

He glanced down at the dark Book, which was straining in his backpack toward the piled-up hoard. "Uh-huh. But how are we going to find it? And are you sure that defense shield is going to hold up at close range, when it comes after us? You know it's not going to just let us *take* something."

(Why not trade it something?) Fred asked suddenly.

Nita and Kit both looked at him, struck by the idea. "Like what?" Kit asked.

(Like another Book?)

"Oh no," they said in simultaneous shock.

"Fred," Kit said then, "we can't do that. The—you-know-who—he'll just come right here and get it."

(So where did *you* get it from, anyway? Doubtless he could have read from it anytime he wanted. If you can get the bright *Book* back to the Senior wizards in your world, can't they use it to counteract whatever he does?)

Nita and Kit both thought about it. "He might have a point," Nita said after a second. "Besides, Kit—if we *do* leave the dark Book here, can you imagine you-know-who getting it back without some trouble?" She glanced up at the mound, where the Eldest was whispering threats of death and destruction against whoever might come to steal. "He wouldn't have put the bright *Book* here unless the Eldest was an effective guardian."

Even through the discomfort of holding the dark *Book*, Kit managed to crack a small smile. "Gonna try it?"

Nita took a step forward. Instantly the dragon paused in its digging to stare at her, its scaly lips wrinkled away from black fangs in a snarl, but its eyes frightened. *"Eldest,"* she said in the Speech, *"we don't come to steal. We're here to make a bargain."*

The Eldest stared at Nita a moment more, then narrowed its eyes further. *"Hss, you're a clever thiefff,"* it said. *"Why ssshould I bargain with you?"*

Nita gulped. *Wizardry is words,* the book had said. *Believe, and create the truth; but be careful what you believe.* "Because only your hoard, out of all the other hoards from this world to the next, has what we're interested in," she said carefully. "Only you ever had the taste to acquire and preserve this thing."

"Oh?" said the Eldest. Its voice was still suspicious, but its eyes looked less threatened. Nita began to feel a glimmer of hope. *"What might thiss thing be?"*

"*A book,*" Nita said, "*an old book something like this one.*" Kit took a step forward and held up the dark Book for the Eldest to see. This close to its bright counterpart, the dark volume was warping the air and light around it so terribly that its outlines writhed like a fistful of snakes.

The Eldest peered at the dark Book with interest. "*Now there is ssomething I don't have,*" it said. "*Sssee how it changes. That would be an interessting addition.... What did you ssay you wanted to trade it for?*"

"*Another Book, Eldest. You came by it some time ago, we hear. It's close in value to this one. Maybe a little less,*" Nita added, making it sound offhand.

The dragon's eyes brightened like those of a collector about to get the best of a bargain. "*Lesss, you say. Hsss ... Sssome-one gave me a book rather like that one, ssome time ago, I forget just who. Let me ssseee ...*" It turned away from them and began digging again. Nita and Kit stood and watched and tried to be patient while the Eldest pawed through the trash and the treasure, making sounds of possessive affection over everything it touched, mumbling counts and estimating values.

"I wish it would hurry up," Kit whispered. "I can't believe that after we've been chased this far, they're not going to be down here pretty quick. We didn't have too much trouble getting in—"

"*You* didn't open the wall," Nita muttered back. "Look, I'm still worried about leaving this here."

"Whaddaya want?" Kit snapped. "Do I have to carry it all the way home?" He breathed out, a hiss of annoyance that sounded unnervingly like the Eldest, and then rubbed his forearm across his eyes. "This thing burns. I'm sorry."

"It's okay," Nita said, slightly embarrassed. "I just wish there were some way to be *sure* that you-know-who wouldn't get his hands on it anytime soon."

Kit looked thoughtful and opened his mouth to say something. It was at that moment that the Eldest put its face down into the hole it had been digging and came up again with something bright.

The *Book of Night with Moon* fell with

a thump onto a pile of gold and gems and made them look tawdry, outshone them in a way that seemed to have nothing to do with light. Its cover was the same black leather as that of the dark Book—but as one looked at it, the blackness seemed to gain depth; light seemed hidden in it like a secret in a smiling heart. Even the dim green glow of the firefungus looked healthier now that the *Book* lay out in it. Where page edges showed, they glittered as if brushed with diamond dust rather than gilding. The Eldest bent over the bright *Book*, squinting as if into a great light but refusing to look away. *"Aaaaaahhhh,"* it said, a slow, caressing, proprietary sigh. *"Thisss is what you wisshed to trade your book ffor?"*

"Yes, Eldest," Nita said, starting to worry.

The dragon laid its front paws on either side of the Book. *"Ffair, it is ssso ffair. I had fforgotten how ssweet it was to look on. No. No, I will not trade. I will not. Mine, mine..."* It nosed the bright *Book* lovingly.

Nita bit her lip and wondered what in

the world to try next. *"Eldest,"* Kit said from beside her, *"we have something more to trade."*

"Oh?" The dragon looked away from the *Book* with difficulty and squinted at Kit. *"What might that be?"*

(Yeah, what?) Nita said silently.

(Sssh.) *"If you will take our book in trade for that one, we'll work such a wizardry about this place that no thief will ever enter. You'll be safe here for as long as you please. Or forever."*

(What are you talking about!) Nita said, amazed. (We don't have the supplies for a major wizardry like that. The only one you could possibly manage would be one of—)

(The blank-check spells, I know. Nita, *shaddup!*)

The Eldest was staring at Kit. *"No one would ever come in again to ssteal from me?"* it said.

"That's right."

Nita watched the dragon's face as it looked away from Kit, thinking. It was old and tired, and terrified of losing what it had amassed; but now a frightened hope was awakening in its eyes. It looked back at Kit after a few seconds. *"You will not come back either? No one will trouble me again?"*

"*Guaranteed,*" Kit said, meaning it.

"Then I will trade. Give me your book, and work your spell, and go. Leave me with what is mine." And it picked up the *Book of Night with Moon* in its jaws and dropped it off the hoard-hill, not far from Kit's feet. *"Give me, give me,"* the Eldest said. Warily, Nita dropped the shield spell. Kit took a couple of uneasy steps forward and held out the dark Book. The dragon shot its head down, sank teeth in the dark Book, and jerked it out of Kit's hands so fast that he stared at them for a moment, counting fingers.

"Mine, mine," it hissed as it turned away and started digging at another spot on the hoard, preparing to bury the dark Book. Kit stooped, picked up the *Book of Night with Moon*. It was as heavy as the dark Book had been, about the size of an encyclopedia volume, and strange to

hold—the depth of the blackness of its covers made it seem as if the holding hands should sink right through. Kit flipped it open as Nita and Fred came up behind to look over his shoulder. (But the pages are blank,) Fred said, puzzled.

(It needs moonlight,) Kit said.

(Well, this is moonlight.) Nita held up the rowan wand over the opened *Book*. Very vaguely they could make out something printed, the symbols of the Speech, too faint to read. (Then again, maybe secondhand moonlight isn't good enough. Kit, what're you going to do? You *have* to seal this place up now. You promised.)

(I'm gonna do what I said. One of the blank-check wizardries.)

(But when you do those you don't know what price is going to be asked later.)

(We have to get this *Book*, don't we? That's why we're here. And this is something that has to be done to get the *Book*. I don't think the price'll be too high. Anyway, *you* don't have to worry, I'll do it myself.)

Nita watched Kit getting out his wizards' manual and bit her lip. (Oh no, you're not,) she said. (If you're doing it, I'm doing it too. Whatever you're doing . . .)

(One of the Moebius spells,) Kit said, finding the page. Nita looked over his shoulder and read the spell. It would certainly keep thieves out of the hoard. When recited, a Moebius spell gave a specified volume of space a half-twist that left it permanently out of synch with the spaces surrounding it. The effect would be like stopping an elevator between floors, forever. (You read it all through?) Kit asked.

(Uh-huh.)

(Then let's get back in the tunnel and do it and get out of here. I'm getting this creepy feeling that things aren't going to be quiet on ground level when we get up there.)

They wanted to say good-bye to the Eldest, but it had forgotten them already "*Mine, mine, mine,*" it was whispering a garbage and gold flew in all directions from the place where it dug.

(Let's go,) Fred said.

Out in the tunnel, the firefungus

seemed brighter to Nita—or perhaps that was only the effect of looking at the *Book of Night with Moon.* They halted at the spot where the tunnel curved and began with great care to read the Moebius spell. The first part of it was something strange and unsettling—an invocation to the Powers that governed the arts of wizardry, asking help with this piece of work and promising that the power lent would be returned when They required. Nita shivered, wondering what she was getting herself into, for use of the Speech made the promise more of a prediction. Then came the definition of the space to be twisted, and finally the twisting itself. As they spoke the words Nita could see the Eldest, still digging away at his hoard, going pale and dim as if with distance, going away, though not moving. The words pushed the space farther and farther away, toward an edge that could be sensed more strongly though not seen—then, suddenly, over it. The spell broke, completed. Nita and Kit and Fred were standing at the edge of a great empty pit, as if someone had reached into the earth and scooped out the subway station, the hoard, and the Eldest, whole. Someone had.

"I think we better get out of here," Kit said, very quietly. As if in answer to his words came a long, soft groan of strained timber and metal—the pillars and walls of the tunnel where they stood and the tunnel on the other side of the pit, bending under new stresses that the pillars of the station had handled and that these were not meant to. Then a rumble, something falling.

Nita and Kit turned and ran down the tunnel, stumbling over timbers and picking themselves up and running again. Fred zipped along beside like a shooting star looking for the right place to fall. They slammed into the wall at the end of the track as the rumble turned to a thunder and the thunder started catching up behind. Nita found bare concrete, said the Mason's Word in a gasp, and flung the stone open. Kit jumped through with Fred behind him. The tunnel shook, roared, blew out a stinging, dust-laden wind, and went down in ruin as Nita leaped through the opening and fell to the tracks beside Kit.

He got to his knees slowly, rubbing

himself where he had hit. "Boy," he said, "if we weren't in trouble with you-know-who before, we are now..."

Hurriedly Kit and Nita got up and the three of them headed for the ledge and the way to the open air.

Major Wizardries:

TERMINATION
AND RECOVERY

WITH GREAT CAUTION AND a grunt of effort, Kit pushed up the grille at the top of the concrete steps and looked around. "Oh, brother," he whispered, "sometimes I wish I wasn't right."

He scrambled up out of the tunnel and onto the sidewalk, with Nita and Fred following right behind. The street was a shambles reminiscent of Fifth and Sixty-second. Corpses of cabs and limousines and even a small truck were scattered around, smashed into lampposts and the fronts of buildings, overturned on the sidewalk. The Lotus Esprit was crouched at

guard a few feet away from the grille opening, its engine running in long, tired-
sounding gasps. As Kit ran over to it, the
Lotus rumbled an urgent greeting and
shrugged its doors open.

"They know we're here," Nita said as
they hurriedly climbed in and buckled up.
"They have to know what we've done.
Everything feels different since the dark
Book fell out of this space."

(And they must know we'll head back
for the worldgate at Pan Am,) Fred said.
(Wherever that is.)

"We've gotta find it—oof!" Kit said, as
the Lotus reared back, slamming its doors
shut, and dove down the street they were
on, around the corner and north again.
"Nita, you up for one more spell?"

"Do we have a choice?" She got her
manual out of her pack, started thumbing
through it. "What I want to know is what
we're supposed to try on whatever they
have waiting for us at Grand Central. You-
know-who isn't just going to let us walk in
there and leave with the bright *Book*—"

"We'll burn that bridge when we come
to it." Kit had his backpack open in his lap

and was peeking at the *Book of Night with Moon.* Even in the sullen dimness that leaked in the Lotus's windows, the edges of the pages of the *Book* shone, the black depths of its covers glowed with the promise of light. Kit ran a finger along the upper edge of one cover, and as Nita watched his face settled into a solemn stillness, as if someone spoke and he listened intently. It was a long moment before the expression broke. Then Kit glanced over at her with a wondering look in his eyes. "It really doesn't look like that much," he said. "But it feels— Nita, I don't think they can hurt us while we have this. Or if they can, it won't matter much."

"Maybe not, if we read from it," Nita said, reading down through the spell that would locate the worldgate for them. "But you remember what Tom said—"

"Yeah." But there was no concern in Kit's voice, and he was looking soberly at the *Book* again.

Nita finished checking the spell and settled back in the seat to prepare for it, then started forward again as a spark of heat burned into her neck. "Ow!"

(Sorry.) Fred slid around from behind her to perch farther forward on her shoulder.

"Here we go," Nita said.

She had hardly begun reading the imaging spell before a wash of power such as she had never felt seized her and plunged her into the spell headfirst. And the amazing thing was that she couldn't even be frightened, for whatever had so suddenly pulled her under and into the magic was utterly benevolent, a huge calm influence that Nita sensed would do her nothing but good, though it might kill her doing it. The power took her, poured itself into her, made the spell *part* of her. There was no longer any need to work it; it *was*. Instantly she saw all Manhattan laid out before her again in shadow outlines, and there was the worldgate, almost drowned in the darkness created by the Starsnuffer, but not hidden to her. The power let her go then, and she sat back gasping. Kit was watching her strangely.

"I think I see what you mean," she said. "The *Book*—it made the spell happen by itself, almost."

"Not 'almost,' " Kit said. "No wonder you-know-who wants it kept out of the hands of the Senior wizards. It can make even a beginner's spell happen. It did the same thing with the Moebius spell. If someone wanted to take this place apart—or if someone wanted to make more places like it, and they had the *Book*—" He gulped. "Look, where's the gate?"

"Where it should be," Nita said, finding her breath. "Underground—under Grand Central. Not in the deli, though. It's down in one of the train tunnels."

Kit gulped again, harder. "Trains . . . And you *know* that place'll be guarded. Fred, are you up to another diversion?"

(Will it get us back to the Sun and the stars again? Try me.)

Nita closed her eyes to lean back and take a second's rest—the power that had run through her for that moment had left her amazingly drained—but nearly jumped out of her skin the next moment as the Lotus braked wildly, fishtailing around a brace of cabs that leaped at it out of a side street. With a scream of engine and a cloud of exhaust and burned rubber it found its traction again and tore out of the intersection and up Third Avenue, leaving the cabs behind.

"They know, they *know*," Nita moaned. "Kit, what're we going to do? Is the *Book* going to be enough to stand up to him?"

"We'll find out, I guess," Kit said, though he sounded none too certain. "We've been lucky so far. No, not lucky, we've been ready. Maybe that'll be enough. We both came prepared for trouble, we both did our reading—"

"You did, maybe." Nita looked sheepish. "I couldn't get past Chapter Forty. No matter how much I read, there was always more."

Kit smiled just as uncomfortably. "I only got to Thirty-three myself, then I skimmed a lot."

"Kit, there's about to be a surprise quiz. *Did we study the right chapters?*"

"Well, we're gonna find out," Kit said. The Lotus turned left at the corner of Third and Forty-second, speeding down toward Grand Central. Forty-second seemed empty; not even a cab was in sight. But a great looming darkness was gathered down the street, hiding the iron overpass. The Lotus slowed, unwilling to go near it.

"Right here is fine," Kit said, touching the dashboard reassuringly. The Lotus stopped in front of the doors to Grand Central, reluctantly shrugging first Nita's, then Kit's door open.

They got out and looked around them. Silence. Nita looked nervously at the doors and the darkness beyond, while the Lotus crowded close to Kit, who rubbed its right wheel well absently.

The sound came. A single clang, like an anvil being struck, not too far away. Then another clang, hollow and metallic, echoing from the blank-eyed buildings, dying into bell-like echoes. Several more clangs, close together. Then a series of them, a slow drumroll of metal beating on stone. The Lotus pulled out from under Kit's hand, turning to face down Forty-second the way they had come, growling deep under its hood.

The clangor grew louder; echoes bounced back and forth from building to building so that it was impossible to tell from what direction the sound was coming. Down at the corner of Lexington and Forty-second, a blackness jutted suddenly from behind one of the buildings on the uptown side. The shape of it and its unlikely height above the pavement, some fifteen feet, kept Nita from recognizing what it was until more of it came around the corner, until the blackness found its whole shape and swung it around into the middle of the street on iron hooves.

Eight hooves, ponderous and deadly, dented the asphalt of the street. They belonged to a horse—a huge, misproportioned beast, its head skinned down to a skull, leaden-eyed and grinning hollowly. All black iron, that steed was, as if it had stepped down from a pedestal at its rider's call; and the one who rode it wore his own darkness on purpose, as if to reflect the black mood within. The Starsnuffer had put aside his three-piece suit for chain mail like hammered onyx and a cloak like night with no stars. His face was still handsome, but dreadful now, harder than any stone. His eyes burned with the burning of the dark Book, alive with painful memory about to come real. About the feet of his mount the perytons milled, not quite daring to look in their master's face, but staring and slavering at the sight of Kit and Nita, waiting the command to course their prey.

Kit and Nita stood frozen, and Fred's light, hanging small and constant as a star behind them, dimmed down to its faintest.

The cold, proud, erect figure on the black mount raised what it held in its right hand, a steel rod burning dark and skewing the air about it as the dark Book had. *"You have stolen something of mine,"* said a voice as cold as space, using the Speech with icy perfection and hating it. *"No one steals from me."*

The bolt that burst from the rod was a red darker than the Eldest's fiery breath. Nita did not even try to use the rowan wand in defense—she might as well have tried to use a sheet of paper to stop a laser beam. But as she and Kit leaped aside, the air around them went afire with sudden clarity, as if for a moment the darkness inherent in it was burned away. The destroying bolt went awry, struck up sideways and

blasted soot-stained blocks out of the facade of Grand Central. And in that moment the Lotus screamed wild defiance and
leaped down Forty-second at the rider and
his steed.

"NO!" Kit screamed. Nita grabbed
him, pulled him toward the doors. He
wouldn't come, wouldn't turn away as the
baying perytons scattered, as the Lotus
hurtled into the forefront of the pack,
flinging bodies about. It leaped up at the
throat of the iron beast, which reared on
four hooves and raised the other four and
with them smashed the Lotus flat into the
street.

The bloom of fire that followed blotted
out that end of the street. Kit responded to
Nita's pulling then, and together they ran
through the doors, up the ramp that led
into Grand Central, out across the floor.

Nita was busy getting the rowan wand
out, had gotten ahead of Kit, who couldn't
move as fast because he was crying—but it
was his hand that shot out and caught her
by the collar at the bottom of the ramp,
almost choking her, and kept her from falling into the pit. There was no floor. From

one side of the main concourse to the other was a great smoking crevasse, the floor and lower levels and tunnels beneath all split as if with an ax. Ozone smell and cinder smell and the smell of tortured steel breathed up hot in their faces, while from behind, outside, the thunder of huge hooves on concrete and the howls of perytons began again.

Below them severed tunnels and stairways gaped dark. There was no seeing the bottom. It was veiled in fumes and soot, underlit by the blue arcs of shorted-out third rails and an ominous deep red, as if the earth itself had broken open and was bleeding lava. The hooves clanged closer.

Nita turned to Kit, desperate. Though his face still streamed with tears, there was an odd, painful calm about it. "I know what to do," he said, his voice saying that he found that strange. He drew the antenna out of his back pocket, and it was just as Nita noticed how strangely clear the air was burning about him that Kit threw the piece of steel out over the smoking abyss. She would have cried out and grabbed him, except that he was watching it so intently.

The hoofbeats stopped and were followed by a sound as of iron boots coming down on the sidewalk, immensely heavy, shattering the stone. Despite her own panic, Nita found she couldn't look away from the falling antenna either. She was gripped motionless in the depths of a spell again, while the power that burned the air clear now poured itself through Kit and into his wizardry. There was something wrong with the way the antenna was falling. It seemed to be getting bigger with distance instead of smaller. It stretched, it grew, glittering as it turned and changed. It wasn't even an antenna anymore. Sharp blue light and diffuse red gleamed from flat, polished faces, edges sharp as razors. It was a sword blade, not even falling now, but laid across the chasm like a bridge. The wizardry broke and turned Nita loose. Kit moved away from her and stepped out onto the flat of the blade, fear and pain showing in his face again.

"Kit!"

"It's solid," he said, still crying, taking another step out onto the span, holding his arms out for balance as it bent slightly under his weight. "Come on, Nita, it's noon-forged steel, he can't cross it. He'll have to change shape or seal this hole up."

(Nita, come on,) Fred said, and bobbled out across the crevasse, following Kit. Though almost blind with terror, her ears full of the sound of iron-shod feet coming after them, she followed Fred, who was holding a straight course out over the sword blade—followed him, arms out as she might have on a balance beam, most carefully not looking down. This was worse than the bridge of air had been, for that hadn't flexed so terribly under each step she or Kit took. His steps threw her off balance until she halted long enough to take a deep breath and step in time with him. Smoke and the smell of burning floated up around her; the shadows of the dome above the concourse stirred with wicked eyes, the open doors to the train platforms ahead of her muttered, their mouths full of hate. She watched the end of the blade, looked straight ahead. Five steps: Kit was off. Three. One—

She reached out to him, needing desperately to feel the touch of a human hand.

He grabbed her arm and pulled her off the bridge just as another blast of black-red fire blew in the doors on the other side of the abyss. Kit said one sharp word in the Speech, and the air went murky around his body again as the *Book* ceased to work through him. Nita let go, glanced over her shoulder in time to see the sword blade snap back to being an antenna, like a rubber band going back to its right size. It fell into the fuming darkness, a lone glitter, quickly gone.

They ran. Nita could still see in her mind the place where the worldgate was hidden; the *Book*'s power had burned it into her like a brand. She took the lead, racing down a flight of stairs, around a corner and down another flight, into echoing beige-tiled corridors where Fred and the rowan wand were their only light. Above them they could hear the thunderous rumor of iron footsteps, slow, leisurely, inexorable, following them down. The howls of perytons floated down to them like the voices of lost souls, hungry for the blood and pain they needed to feel alive again.

"Here!" Nita shouted, not caring what might hear, and dodged around a corner, and did what she had never done in all her life before—jumped a subway turnstile. Its metal fingers made a grab for her, but she was too fast for them, and Kit eluded them too, coming right behind. At full speed Nita pounded down the platform, looking for the steps at the end of it that would let them down onto the tracks. She took them three at a time, two leaps, and then was running on cinders again, leaping over ties. Behind her she could hear Kit hobbling as fast as he could on his sore leg, gasping, but keeping up. Fred shot along beside her, pacing her, lighting her way. Eyes flickered in his light—hidebehinds, dun mice, ducking under cover as the three of them went past. Nita slowed and stopped in the middle of the tracks. "Here!"

Kit had his manual out already. He found the page by Fred's light, thumped to a stop beside Nita. "*Here?* In the middle of the—"

"Read! Read!" she yelled. There was more thunder rolling in the tunnel than just the sound of their pursuer's footsteps. Far away, she could hear what had been missing from the other tunnel beneath City Hall: trains. Away in the darkness, wheels slammed into the tracks they rode—even now the rails around them were clacking faintly in sympathy, and a slight cool wind breathed against Nita's face. A train was coming. On *this* track. Kit began the worldgating spell, reading fast. Again the air around them seemed clearer, fresher, as the power of the *Book of Night with Moon* seized the spell and its speaker, used them both.

That was when the Starsnuffer's power came down on them. It seemed impossible that the dank close darkness in which they stood could become any darker, but it did, as an oppressive blanket of clutching, choking hatred fell over them, blanketing everything. The rowan rod's silver fire was smothered. Fred's light went out as if he had been stepped on. Kit stopped reading, struggled for breath. Nita tried to resist, tried to find air, couldn't, collapsed to her knees, choking. The breeze from the dark at the end of the tunnel got stronger: the onrushing train, pushing the air in front of it, right up the track, right at them.

(I—will—*not*,) Fred said, struggling, angry, (I will—*not*—go out!) His determination was good for a brief flare, like a match being struck. Kit found his voice, managed to get out a couple more words of the spell in Fred's wavering radiance, grew stronger, managed a few more. Nita found that she could breathe again. She clutched the rowan wand, thinking with all her might of the night Liused had given it to her, the clear moonlight shining down between the branches. The wand came alive again. Shadows that had edged forward from the walls of the tunnel fled again. Kit read, hurrying. *Two-thirds done,* Nita thought. *If he can just finish—*

Far away down the tunnel, there were eyes. They blazed. The headlights of a train, coming down at them in full career. The clack of the rails rose to a rattle, the breeze became a wind, and the roar of the train itself echoed not just in the other tunnels, but in this one. Nita got to her feet, facing those eyes down. She would not look away. Fred floated by her shoulder;

she gathered him close, perching him by her ear, feeling his terror of the over-whelming darkness as if it were her own but having nothing to comfort him with. *Kit,* she thought, not daring to say it aloud for fear she should interrupt his concentra-tion. The sound of his words was getting lost in the thunder from above, iron-shod feet, the thunder from below, iron wheels on iron rails.

Suddenly Kit's voice was missing from the mélange of thunders. Without warning the worldgate was there, glistening in the light of the rowan wand and Fred and the train howling down toward them—a great jagged soap bubble, trembling with the pressure of sound and air. Kit wasted no time, but leaped through. Fred zipped into the shimmering surface and was gone. Nita made sure of her grip on the rowan wand, took a deep breath, and jumped through the worldgate. A hundred feet away, fifty feet away, the blazing eyes of the train glared at her as she jumped; its horn screamed in delight, anticipating the feel of blood beneath its wheels; sudden thunder rocked the platform behind her, black-red fire more sensed than seen. But the rainbow shimmer of the gate broke across her face first. The train roared through the place where she had been, and she heard the beginnings of a cry of frustrated rage as she cheated death, and anger, and fell and fell and fell....

... And came down *slam* on nothing. Or it seemed that way, until opening her eyes a little wider she saw the soot and smog trapped in the hardened air she lay on, the only remnant of her walkway. Kit was already getting up from his knees beside her, looking out from their little island of air across to the Pan Am Building. Everything was dark, and Nita started to groan, certain that something had gone wrong and that the worldgate had simply dumped them back in the Starsnuffer's world—but no, her walkway *was* there. Greatly daring, she looked down and saw far below the bright yellow glow of sodium-vapor streetlights, long straight streams of traffic, the white of headlights and red of taillights. City noise, roaring, ca-cophonous and alive, floated up to them. *We're back. It worked!*

Kit was reading from his wizards' man-ual, as fast as he had read down in the train tunnel. He stopped and then looked at Nita in panic as she got up. "I can't close the gate!"

She gulped. "Then he can follow us . . . through . . ." In an agony of haste she fumbled her own book out of her pack, checked the words for the air-hardening spell one more time, and began reading herself. Maybe panic helped, for this time the walkway spread itself out from their feet to the roof of the building very fast indeed. "Come on," she said, heading out across it as quickly as she dared. *But where will we run to?* she thought. *He'll come be-hind, hunting. We can't go home, he might follow. And what'll he do to the city?*

She reached up to the heliport railing and swung herself over it. Kit followed, with Fred pacing him. "What're we gonna do?" he said as they headed across the gravel together. "There's no time to call the Senior wizards, wherever they are—or even Tom and Carl. *He'll* be here shortly."

"Then we'll have to get away from here and find a place to hole up for a little. Maybe the bright *Book* can help." She paused as Kit spoke to the lock on the roof door, and they ran down the stairs. "Or the manuals might have something, now that we need it."

"Yeah, right," Kit said as he opened the second door at the bottom of the stairs, and they ran down the corridor where the elevators were. But he didn't sound convinced. "The park?"

"Sounds good."

Nita punched the call button for the elevator, and she and Kit stood there panting. There was a feeling in the air that all hell was about to break loose, and the sweat was breaking out all over Nita because *they* were going to have to stop it somehow. "Fred," she said, "did you ever hear anything, out where you were, any stories of someone getting the better of you-know-who?"

Fred's light flickered uncomfortably as he watched Kit frantically consulting his manual. (Oh yes,) he said. (I'd imagine that's why he wanted a Universe apart to himself—to keep others from getting in and thwarting him. It used to happen fairly frequently when he went up against life.)

Fred's voice was too subdued for Nita's liking. "What's the catch?"

(Well ... it's possible to win against him. But usually someone dies of it.)

Nita gulped again. Somehow she had been expecting something like that. "Kit?"

The elevator chimed. Once inside, Kit went back to looking through his manual. "I don't see anything," he said, sounding very worried. "There's a general information chapter on him here, but there's not much we don't know already. The only thing he's never been able to dominate was the *Book of Night with Moon.* He tried— that's what the dark Book was for; he thought by linking them together he could influence the bright *Book* with it, diminish its power. But that didn't work. Finally he was reduced to simply stealing the bright *Book* and hiding it where no one could get at it. That way no one could become a channel for its power, no one could possibly defeat him ..."

Nita squeezed her eyes shut, not sure whether the sinking feeling in her stomach was due to her own terror or the elevator going down. *Read from it? No, no. I hope I never have to,* Tom's voice said in her mind. . . . *Reading it, being the vessel for all that power—I wouldn't want to. Even good can be terribly dangerous.*

And that was an Advisory, Nita thought, miserable. There was no doubt about it. One of them might have to do what a mature wizard feared doing: read from the *Book* itself.

"Let me do it," she said, not looking at Kit.

He glanced up from the manual, stared at her. "Bull," he said, and then looked down at the manual again. "If you're gonna do it, *I'm* gonna do it."

Outside the doors another bell chimed as the elevator slowed to a stop. Kit led the way out across the black stone floor, around the corner to the entrance. The glass door let them out onto a street just like the one they had walked onto in the Snuffer's otherworld—but here windows had lights in them, and the reek of gas and fumes was mixed with a cool smell of evening and a rising wind, and the cabs that passed looked blunt and friendly. Nita could have cried for relief, except that there was no reason to feel relieved. Things would be getting much worse shortly.

Fred, though, felt no such compunctions. (The stars, the stars are back,) he almost sang, flashing with delight as they hurried along.

"Where?" Kit said skeptically. As usual, the glow of a million streetlights was so fierce that even the brightest stars were blotted out by it. But Fred was too cheerful to be suppressed.

(They're there, they're *there!*) he said, dancing ahead of them. (And the Sun is there, too. I don't care that it's on the other side of this silly place, I can feel—feel—)

His thought cut off so abruptly that Nita and Kit both stopped and glanced over their shoulders. A coldness grabbed Nita's heart and wrung it. The sky, even though clear, did have a faint golden glow to it, city light scattered from smog—and against that glow, high up atop the Pan Am Building, a form, half unstarred night and half black iron, glowered down at them like a statue from a dauntingly high pedestal. Nita and Kit froze like moths pinned to a card as the remote clear howl of perytons wound through the air.

"He'll just jump down," Nita whispered, knowing somehow that he could do it. But the rider did not leap, not yet. Slowly he raised his arms in summons. One hand still held the steel rod about which the air twisted and writhed as if in pain; as the arm lifted, that writhing grew more violent, more tortured.

And darkness answered the gesture. It flowed forward around the feet of the dark rider's terrible mount, obscuring the perytons peering down over the roof's edge, and poured down the surface of the building like a black fog. What it touched, changed. Where the darkness passed, metal tarnished, glass filmed over or shattered, lighted windows were quenched, went blind. Down all the sides of the building it flowed, black lava burning the brightness out of everything it touched.

Kit and Nita looked at each other in despair, knowing what would happen when that darkness spilled out onto the ground. The streets would go desolate and dark, the cabs would stop being friendly; and when all the island from river to river was turned into his domain, the dark rider would catch them at his leisure and do what he pleased with them. And with the bright *Book*—and with everything else under the sky, perhaps. This was no other-world, frightening but remote. This was their home. If this world turned into *that* one...

"We're dead," Kit said, and turned to run. Nita followed him. Perhaps out of hope that another Lotus might be waiting innocently at some curbside, the way Kit ran retraced their earlier path. But there was no Lotus—only bright streets, full of people going about their business with no idea of what was about to happen to them, cars honking at one another in cheerful ignorance. Fat men running newsstands and bemused bag ladies watched Nita and Kit run by as if death and doom were after them, and no one really noticed the determined spark of light keeping pace. They ran like the wind down West Fiftieth, but no Lotus lay there, and around the corner onto Fifth and up to Sixty-first, but the carnage left in the otherworld was not reflected here—the traffic on Fifth ran unperturbed. Gasping, they waited for a break in it, then ran across, hopped the wall into the park, and crouched down beside it as they had in the world they'd left.

The wind was rising, not just a night breeze off the East River, but a chill wind with a hint of that other place's coldness to it. Kit unslung his pack as Fred drew in close, and by his light Kit brought out the *Book of Night with Moon*. The darkness of its covers shone, steadying Kit's hands, making Fred seem to burn brighter. Kit and Nita sat gasping for breath, staring at each other.

"I'm out of ideas," Kit said. "I think we're going to have to read from this to keep the city the way it should be. We can't just let him change things until he catches us. Buildings are one thing, but what happens to *people* after that black hits them?"

"And it might not stop here either," Nita said between gasps, thinking of her mother and father and Dairine, of the quiet street where they lived, the garden, the rowan, all warped and darkened—if they would survive at all.

Her eyes went up to the Moon shining white and full between the shifting branches. All around them she could feel the trees stirring in that new, strange, cold wind, whispering uneasily to one another. It was so good to be in a place where she could hear the growing things again.

The idea came. "Kit," she said hurriedly, "that dark was moving pretty fast. If we're going to read from the *Book* we may need something to buy us time, to hold off the things that'll come with it, the perytons and the cabs."

"We're out of Lotuses," Kit said, his voice bleak.

"I know. But look where we are! Kit, this is *Central Park!* You know how many trees there are in here of the kinds that went to the Battle in the old days? They don't forget."

He stared at her. "What can they—"

"The *Book* makes everything work better, doesn't it? There's a spell that—I'll do it, you'll see. But you've got to do one, too, it's in your specialty group. The Mason's Word, the long version—"

"To bring stone or metal to life." He scrubbed the last tears out of his eyes and managed ever so slight and slow a smile. "There are more statues within screaming distance of this place—"

"Kit," Nita said, "how loud can you scream?"

"Let's find out."

They both started going through their manuals in panicky haste. Far away on the East Side, lessened by all the buildings and distance that lay between, but still much too clear, there was a single, huge, deep-pitched *clang,* an immense weight of metal hitting the ground with stone-shattering force. Fred bobbled a little in the air, nervously. (How long do you think—)

"He'll be a while, Fred," Kit said, sounding as if he hoped it would be a long while. "He doesn't like to run; it's beneath his dignity. But I think—" He broke off for a moment, reading down a page and forming the syllables of the Mason's Word without saying them aloud. "I think we're going to have a few friends who'll do a little running for us."

He stood up, and Fred followed him, staying close to light the page. "Nita, hand me the *Book.*" She passed it up to him, breaking off her own frantic reading for a moment to watch. "It'll have to be a scream," he said as if to himself. "The more of them hear me, the more help we get."

Kit took three long breaths and then shouted the Word at the top of his lungs, all twenty-seven syllables of it without missing a one. The sound became impossibly more than the yell of a twelve-year-old boy as the *Book* seized the sound and the spell together and flung them out into the city night. Nita had to hold her ears. Even when it seemed safe to uncover them again, the echoes bounced back from buildings on all sides and would not stop. Kit stood there amazed as his voice rang and ricocheted from walls blocks away. "Well," he said, "they'll feel the darkness. They'll know what's happening. I think."

"My turn," Nita said, and stood up beside Kit, making sure of her place. Her spell was not a long one. She fumbled for the rowan wand, put it in the hand that also held her wizards' manual, and took the bright *Book* from Kit. "I hope—" she started to say, but the words were shocked out of her as the feeling that the *Book* brought with it shot up her arm. Power, such sheer joyous power that no spell could fail, no matter how new the wizard was to the Art. Here, under moonlight and freed at last from its long restraint, the *Book* was more potent than even the dark rider who trailed them would suspect, and that potency raged to be free. Nita bent her head to her manual and read the spell.

Or tried to. She saw the words, the syllables, and spoke the Speech, but the moonfire falling on the *Book* ran through her veins, slid down her throat, and turned the words to song more subtle than she had ever dreamed of, burned behind her eyes and showed her another time, when another will had voiced these words for the first time and called the trees to battle.

All around her, both now and then, the trees lifted their arms into the wind, breathed the fumes of the new-old Earth and breathed out air that humans could use; they broke the stone to make ground for their children to till and fed the mold with themselves, leaf and bough, for generation upon generation. They knew to what end their sacrifice would come, but they did it anyway, and they would do it again in the Witherer's spite. They were doing it now. Oak and ash and willow, birch and alder, elm and maple, they felt the darkness in the wind that tossed their branches and would not stand still for it. The ground shook all around Nita, roots heaved and came free—first the trees close by, the counterparts of the trees under which she and Kit and Fred had sheltered in the dark otherworld. White oak, larch, twisted crabapple, their leaves glittering around the edges with the flowering radiance of the rowan wand, they lurched and staggered as they came rootloose, and then crowded in around Kit and Nita and Fred, whispering with wind, making a protecting circle through which nothing would pass but moonlight. The effect spread out and away from Nita, though the spell itself was finished, and that relentless power let her sag against one friendly oak, gasping.

For yards, for blocks, as far as she could see through the trunks of the trees that crowded close, branches waved green and wild as bushes and vines and hundred-year monarchs of the park pulled themselves out of the ground and moved heavily to the defense. Away to the east, the clangor of metal hooves and the barks and howls of the dark rider's pack were coming closer. The trees waded angrily toward the noise, some hobbling along on top of the ground, some wading through it, and just as easily through sidewalks and stone walls. In a few minutes there was a nearly solid palisade of living wood between Kit and Nita and Fred and Fifth Avenue. Even the glare of the streetlights barely made it through the branches.

Kit and Nita looked at each other. "Well," Kit said reluctantly, "I guess we can't put it off any longer."

Nita shook her head. She moved to put her manual away and was momentarily shocked when the rowan wand, spent, crumbled to silver ash in her hand. "So much for that," she said, feeling unnerv-ingly naked now that her protection was gone. Another howl sounded, very close by, and was abruptly cut off in a rushing of branches as if a tree had fallen on some-thing on purpose. Nita fumbled in her pocket and pulled out a nickel. "Call it," she said.

"Heads."

She tossed the coin, caught it, slapped it down on her forearm. Heads. "Crud," she said, and handed the bright *Book* to Kit.

He took it uneasily, but with a glitter of excitement in his eye. "Don't worry," he said. "You'll get your chance."

"Yeah, well, don't hog it." She looked over at him and was amazed to see him re-garding her with some of the same worry she was feeling. From outside the fence of trees came a screech of brakes, the sound of a long skid, and then a great splintering crashing of metal and smashing of glass as an attacking cab lost an argument with some tree standing guard. Evidently rein-forcements from that other, darker world were arriving.

"I won't," Kit said. "You'll take it away from me and keep reading if—"

He stopped, not knowing what might happen. Nita nodded. "Fred," she said, "we may need a diversion. But save yourself till the last minute."

(I will. Kit—) The spark of light hung close to him for a moment. (Be careful.)

Suddenly, without warning, every tree around them shuddered as if violently struck. Nita could hear them crying out in silent anguish, and cried out in terror herself as she felt what they felt—a great numbing cold that smote at the heart like an ax. Kit, beside her, sat frozen with it, aghast. Fred went dim with shock. (Not again!) he said, his voice faint and horrified. (Not *here*, where there's so much life!)

"The Sun," Nita whispered. "He put out the Sun!" *Starsnuffer*, she thought. *That tactic's worked for him before. And if the Sun is out, pretty soon there won't be moonlight to read by, and he can—*

Kit stared up at the Moon as if at someone about to die. "Nita, how long do we have?"

"Eight minutes, maybe a little more, for

light to get here from the Sun. Eight minutes before it runs out..."

Kit sat down hurriedly, laid the bright *Book* in his lap, and opened it. The light of the full Moon fell on the glittering pages. This time the print was not vague as under the light of Nita's wand. It was clear and sharp and dark, as easily read as normal print in daylight. The *Book*'s covers were fading, going clear, burning with that eye-searing transparency that Nita had seen about Kit and herself before. The whole *Book* was hardly to be seen except for its printing, which burned in its own fashion, supremely black and clear, but glistening as if the ink with which the characters were printed had moonlight trapped in them too. *"Here's an index,"* Kit whispered, using the Speech now. *"I think—the part about New York—"*

Yes, Nita thought desperately, as another cab crashed into the trees and finished itself. *And what then? What do we do about...* She would not finish the thought, for the sound of those leisurely, deadly hoofbeats was getting closer, and mixing with it were sirens and the panicked sound of car horns. She thought of that awful dark form crossing Madison, kicking cars aside, crushing what tried to stop it, and all the time that wave of blackness washing alongside, changing everything, stripping the streets bare of life and light. *And what about the Sun? The Earth will freeze over before long, and he'll have the whole planet the way he wants it—* Nita shuddered. Cold and darkness and nothing left alive—a storm-broken, ice-locked world, full of twisted machines stalking desolate streets forever. . . .

Kit was turning pages, quickly but gently, as if what he touched was a live thing. Perhaps it was. Nita saw him pause between one page and the next, holding one bright-burning page draped delicately over his fingers, then letting it slide carefully down to lie with the others he'd turned. *"Here,"* he whispered, awed, delighted. He did not look up to see what Nita saw, the wave of darkness creeping around them, unable to pass the tree wall, passing onward, surrounding them so that they were suddenly on an island of grass in a sea of wrestling naked tree limbs and bare-seared dirt and rock. *"Here—"*

He began to read, and for all her fear Nita was lulled to stillness by wonder. Kit's voice was that of someone discovering words for the first time after a long silence, and the words he found were a song, as her spell to free the trees had seemed. She sank deep in the music of the Speech, hearing the story told in what Kit read.

Kit was invoking New York, calling it up as one might call up a spirit; and obedient to the summons, it came. The skyline came, unsmirched by any blackness—a crown of glittering towers in a smoky sunrise, all stabbing points and jeweled windows, precipices of steel and stone. City Hall came, brooding over its colonnades, gazing down in weary interest at the people who came and went and governed the island through it. The streets came, hot, dirty, crowded, but flowing with voices and traffic and people, bright lifeblood surging through concrete arteries. The parks came, settling into place one by one as they were described, free of the darkness under the night—from tiny paved vest-pocket niches to the lake-set expanses of Central Park, they all came, thrusting the black fog back. Birds sang, dogs ran and barked and rolled in the grass, trees were bright with wary squirrels' eyes. The Battery came, the crumbling old first-defense fort standing peaceful now at the southernmost tip of Manhattan—the rose-gold of some remembered sunset glowed warm on its bricks as it mused in weedy silence over old battles won and nonetheless kept an eye on the waters of the harbor, just in case some British cutter should try for a landing when the colonists weren't looking. Westward over the water, the Palisades were there, shadowy cliffs with the Sun behind them, mist blue and mythical-looking though New Jersey was only a mile away. Eastward and westward the bridges were there, the lights of their spanning suspension cables coming out blue as stars in the twilight. Seabirds wheeled pale and graceful about the towers of the George Washington Bridge and the Verrazano Narrows and the iron crowns of the 59th Street Bridge, as the soft air of evening settled over Manhattan, muting the city roar to a quiet breathing rumble. Under the starlight and the risen Moon, an L-1011 arrowed out of LaGuardia Airport and soared over the city, screaming its high song of delight in the cold upper airs, dragging the thunder along behind. . . .

Nita had to make an effort to pull herself out of the waking dream. Kit read on, while all around the trees bent in close to hear, and the air flamed clear and still as a frozen moment of memory. He read on, naming names in the Speech, describing people and places in terrifying depth and detail, making them real and keeping them that way by the *Book*'s power and the sound of the words. But no sign of any terror at the immensity of what he was doing showed in Kit's face—and that frightened Nita more than the darkness that still surged and whispered around them and their circle of trees. Nita could see Kit starting to burn with that same unbearable clarity, becoming more real, so much so that he was not needing to be visible anymore. Slowly, subtly, the *Book*'s vivid transparency was taking him too. Fred, hanging beside Kit and blazing in defiance of the dark, looked pale in comparison. Even Kit's shadow glowed, and it occurred to Nita that shortly, if this kept up, he wouldn't have one. *What do I do?* she thought. *He's not having trouble, he seems to be getting* stronger, *not weaker, but if this has to go on much longer...*

Kit kept reading. Nita looked around her and began to see an answer. The darkness had not retreated from around them. Out on the Fifth Avenue side of the tree-wall, the crashes of cabs were getting more frequent, the howls of perytons were closer, the awful clanging hoofbeats seemed almost on top of them. There was nowhere to run, and Nita knew with horrible certainty that not all the trees in the park would be enough to stop the Starsnuffer when he came there. Keeping New York real was one answer to this problem, but not *the* answer. The darkness and the unreality were symptoms, not the cause. Something had to be done about *him.*

The iron hooves paused. For an awful moment there was no sound; howls and screeching tires fell silent. Then metal began to smash on stone in a thunderous canter, right across the street, and with a horrible screeching neigh the rider's iron steed smashed into the tree wall, splintering wood, bowing the palisade inward. Nita wanted to shut her mind against the screams of the trees broken and flung aside in that first attack, but she could not. All around her the remaining trees sank their roots deep in determination, but even they knew it would be hopeless. There were enough cracks in the wall that Nita could see the black steed rearing back for another smash with its front four hooves, the rider smiling, a cold cruel smile that made Nita shudder. One more stroke and the wall would be down. Then there would be wildfire in the park. Kit, oblivious, kept reading. The iron mount rose to its full height. "Fred," Nita whispered, "I think you'd better—" The sound of heavy hoofbeats, coming from behind them, from the park side, choked her silent. *He has a twin brother*, Nita thought. *We are dead.*

But the hoofbeats divided around the battered circle of trees and poured past in a storm of metal and stone, the riders and steeds marble pale or bronze dark, every equestrian statue in or near Central Park

gathered together into an impossible cav-
alry that charged past Nita and Kit and
Fred and into the street to give battle.
Perytons and cabs screamed as General
Sherman from Grand Army Plaza crashed
in among them with sword raised, closely
followed by Joan of Arc in her armor, and
Simón Bolívar and General San Martin
right behind. King Wladislaw was there in
medieval scale mail, galloping on a knight's
armored charger; Don Quixote was there,
urging poor broken-down Rosinante to
something faster than a stumble and shouting threats against the whole breed of sor-
cerers; Teddy Roosevelt was there, cracking
off shot after shot at the cabs as his huge
horse stamped them into the pavement; El
Cid Campeador rode there, his bannered
lance striking down one peryton after another. Behind all these came a wild assortment of creatures, pouring past the tree
circle and into the street—eagles, bears,
huge dogs, a hunting cat, a crowd of
doughboys from the first World War with
bayoneted rifles—all the most warlike of
the nearby statuary—even some not so
warlike, such as several deer and the Ugly

Duckling. From down Fifth Avenue came striding golden Prometheus from his pedestal in Rockefeller Center, bearing the fire he brought for mortals and using it in bolt after bolt to melt down cabs where they stood; and from behind him, with a stony roar like the sky falling, the great white lions from the steps of the Public Library leaped together and threw themselves upon the iron steed and its dark rider. For all its extra legs, the mount staggered back and sideways, screaming in a horrible parody of a horse's neigh and striking feebly at the marble claws that tore its flanks.

Under cover of that tumult of howls and crashes and the clash of arms, Nita grabbed Kit to pull him away from the tree wall, behind another row of trees. She half expected her hands to go right through him, he was becoming so transparent. Unresisting, he got up and followed her, still holding the *Book* open, still reading as if he couldn't stop, or didn't want to, still burning more and more fiercely with the inner light of the bright *Book*'s power. "Fred," she said as she pushed Kit down onto the ground again behind a looming old maple,

"I've got to do this now. I may not be able to do anything else. If a diversion's needed—"

(I'll do what's necessary,) Fred said, his voice sounding as awed and frightened as Nita felt at the sight of what Kit was becoming. (You be careful, too.)

She reached out a hand to Fred. He bobbed close and settled at the tip of one finger for a moment, perching there delicately as a firefly, energy touching matter for a moment as if to reconfirm the old truth that they were just different forms of the same thing. Then he lifted away, turning his attention out to the street, to the sound of stone and metal wounding and being wounded; and in one quick gesture Nita grabbed the *Book of Night with Moon* away from Kit and bent her head to read.

An undertow of blinding power and irresistible light poured into her, over her, drowned her deep. She couldn't fight it. She didn't want to. Nita understood now the clear-burning transfiguration of Kit's small plain human face and body, for it was not the wizard who read the *Book;* it was the other way around. The silent Power that had written the *Book* reached through it now and read what life had written in her body and soul—joys, hopes, fears, and failings all together—then took her intent and read that too, turning it into fact. She was turning the bright pages without even thinking about it, finding the place in the *Book* that spoke of creation and rebellion and war among the stars—the words that had once before broken the terrible destroying storm of death and darkness that the angry Starsnuffer had raised to break the new-made worlds and freeze the seas where life was growing, an eternity ago. *"I am the wind that troubles the water,"* Nita said, whispering in the Speech. The whisper smote against the windowed cliffs until they echoed again, and the clash and tumult of battle began to grow still as the wind rose at her naming. *"I am the water, and the waves; I am the shore where the waves break in rainbows; I am the sunlight that shines in the spray—"*

The power rose with the rhythms of the old, old words, rose with the wind as all about her the earth and air and waters of the park began to remember what they were—

matter and energy, created, indestructible, no matter what darkness lay over them. *"I am the trees that drink the light; I am the air of the green things' breathing; I am the stone that the trees break asunder; I am the molten heart of the world—"*

"NO!" came his scream from beyond the wall of trees, hating, raging, desperate. But Nita felt no fear. It was as it had been in the Beginning; all his *no*'s had never been able to stand against life's *I Am*. All around her trees and stones and flesh and metal burned with the power that burned her, self-awareness, which death can seem to stop but can never keep from happening, no matter how hard it tries. *"Where will you go? To what place will you wander?"* she asked sorrowfully, or life asked through her, hoping that the lost one might at last be convinced to come back to his allegiance. Of all creatures alive and otherwise, he had been and still was one of the mightiest. If only his stubborn anger would break, his power could be as great for light as for darkness—but it could not happen. If after all these weary eons he still had not realized the hopelessness of his position,

that everywhere he went, life was there before him.... Still she tried, the ancient
words speaking her solemnly. "... *in vale
or on hilltop, still I am there...*"

Silence, silence, except for the rising
wind. All things seemed to hold their
breath to hear the words; even the dark
rider, erect again on his iron steed and bitter of face, ignoring the tumult around him.
His eyes were only for Nita, for only her
reading held him bound. She tried not to
think of him, or of the little time remaining
before the Moon went out, and gave herself
over wholly to the reading. The words
shook the air and the earth, blinding,
burning.

> "*Will you sound the sea's depth, or
> climb the mountain?
> In air or in water, still I am there;
> Will the earth cover you? Will the
> night hide you?
> In deep or in darkness, still I am
> there;
> Will you kindle the nova, or kill the
> starlight?
> In fire or in deathcold, still I am there—*"

The Moon went out.

Fred cried out soundlessly, and Nita felt the loss of light like a stab in the heart. The power fell away from her, quenched, leaving her small and cold and human and alone, holding in her hands a *Book* gone dark from lack of moonlight. She and Kit turned desperately toward each other in a darkness rapidly becoming complete as the flowing blackness put out the last light of the city. Then came the sound of low, satisfied laughter and a single *clang* of a heavy hoof, stepping forward.

Another *clang*.

Another.

(Now,) Fred said suddenly, (*now* I understand what all that emitting was practice for. No beta, no gamma, no microwave or upper-wavelength ultraviolet or X rays, is that all?)

"Fred?" Kit said, but Fred didn't wait. He shot upward, blazing, a point of light like a star falling the wrong way, up and up until his brightness was as faint as one more unremarkable star. "Fred, where are you *going?*"

(To create a diversion,) his thought came

back, getting fainter and fainter. (Nita, Kit—)

They could catch no more clear thoughts, only a great wash of sorrow and loss, a touch of fear—and then brightness intolerable erupted in the sky as Fred threw his claudication open, emitting all his mass at once as energy, blowing his quanta. He could hardly have been more than halfway to the Moon, for a second or two later it was alight again, a blazing, searing full Moon such as no one had ever seen. There was no looking at either Fred's blast of light or at the Moon that lit trees and statues and the astounded face of the Starsnuffer with a light like a silver sun.

The rider spent no more than a moment being astounded. Immediately he lifted his steel rod, pointing it at Fred this time, shouting in the Speech cold words that were a curse on all light everywhere, from time's beginning to its end. But Fred burned on, more fiercely, if possible. Evidently not even the Starsnuffer could quickly put out a white hole that was liberating all the bound-up energy of five or six blue-white giant stars at once.

"Nita, Nita, *read!*" Kit shouted at her. Through her tears she looked down at the *Book* again and picked up where she had left off. The dark rider was cursing them all in earnest now, knowing that another three lines in the *Book* would bring Nita to his name. She had only to pronounce it to cast him out into the unformed void beyond the Universes, where he had been cast the first time those words were spoken.

Cabs and perytons screamed and threw themselves at the barrier in a last wild attempt to break through, the statues leaped into the fray again, stone and flesh and metal clashed. Nita fell down into the bright power once more, crying, but reading in urgent haste so as not to waste the light Fred was giving himself to become.

As the power began again to read her, she could hear it reading Kit, too, his voice matching hers as it had in their first wizardry, small and thin and brave, and choked with grief like hers. She couldn't stop crying, and the power burned in her tears, too, an odd hot feeling, as she cried bitterly for Fred, for Kit's Lotus, for everything horrible that had happened all that day—all the fair things skewed, all the beauty twisted by the dark Lone Power watching on his steed. If only there were some way he could be otherwise if he wanted to. For here was his name, a long splendid flow of syllables in the Speech, wild and courageous in its own way—and it said that he had not always been so hostile; that he got tired sometimes of being wicked, but his pride and his fear of being ridiculed would never let him stop. *Never, forever,* said the symbol at the very end of his name, the closed circle that binds spells into an unbreakable cycle and indicates lives bound the same way. Kit was still reading. Nita turned her head in that nova moonlight and looked over her shoulder at the one who watched. His face was set, and bitter still, but weary. He knew he was about to be cast out again, frustrated again, and he knew that because of what he had bound himself into being, he would never know fulfillment of any kind. Nita looked back down to the reading, feeling sorry even for him, opened her mouth and along with Kit began to say his name.

Don't be afraid to make corrections!

Whether the voice came from her memory or was a last whisper from the blinding new star far above, Nita never knew. But she knew what to do. While Kit was still on the first part of the name she pulled out her pen, her best pen that Fred had saved and changed. She clicked it open. The metal still tingled against her skin, the ink at the point still glittered oddly—the same glitter as the ink with which the bright *Book* was written. Nita bent quickly over the *Book* and, with the pen, in lines of light, drew from that final circle an arrow pointing upward, the way out, the symbol that said change could happen—if, only if—and together they finished the Starsnuffer's name in the Speech, said the new last syllable, made it real.

The wind was gone. Fearfully Nita and Kit turned around, looked at Fifth Avenue—and found it empty. The creeping blackness was gone with the breaking of its master's magic and the sealing of the worldgate he had held open. Silent and somber, the statues stood among the bodies of the slain—crushed cabs and perytons, shattered trees—then one by one each paced off into the park or down Fifth Avenue, back to its pedestal and its long quiet regard of the city. The howl of sirens, lost for a while in the wind that had risen, now grew loud again. Kit and Nita stood unmoving as the trees ringing them moved away to their old places, sinking roots back into torn-up earth and raising branches to the burning Moon. Some ninety-three million miles away, the Sun had come quietly back to life. But its light would not reach Earth for another eight minutes yet, and as Nita and Kit watched, slowly the new star in the heavens faded, and the Moon faded with it—from daylight brilliance to silver fire, to steel gray glow, to earthlight shimmer, to nothing. The star went yellow, and red, and died. Nothing was left but a stunning, sky-wide aurora, great curtains and rays of rainbow light shivering and crackling all across the golden-glowing city night.

"He forgot the high-energy radiation again," Kit said, tears constricting his voice to a whisper.

Nita closed the *Book* she held in her hands, now dark and ordinary looking except for the black depths of its covers, the faint shimmer of starlight on page edges. "He always does," she said, scrubbing at her eyes, and then offered Kit the *Book*. He shook his head, and Nita dropped it into her backpack and slung it over her back again. "You think *he'll* take the chance?" she said.

"Huh? Oh." Kit shook his head unhappily. "I dunno. Old habits die hard. If he wants to..."

Above them the Moon flicked on again, full and silver bright through the blue-and-red shimmer of the auroral curtain. They stood gazing at it, a serene, remote brilliance, seeming no different than it had been an hour before, a night before, when everything had been as it should be. And now...

"Let's get out of here," Nita said.

They walked out of the park unhindered by the cops and firemen who were already arriving in squad cars and fire trucks and paramedic ambulances. Evidently no one felt that two grade-school kids could possibly have anything to do with a street full of wrecked cabs and violently uprooted trees. As they crossed Fifth

Avenue and the big mesh-sided Bomb Squad truck passed them, Nita bent to pick up a lone broken-off twig of oak, and stared at it sorrowfully. "There wasn't even anything left of him," she said as they walked east on Sixty-fourth, heading back to the Pan Am Building and the timeslide.

"Only the light," Kit said, looking up at the aurora. Even that was fading now.

Silently they made their way to Grand Central and entered the Pan Am Building at the mezzanine level. The one guard was sitting with his back to them and his feet on the desk, reading the *Post*. Kit went wearily over to one elevator, laid a hand on it, and spoke a word or three to it in the Speech. Its doors slid silently open, and they got in and headed upstairs.

The restaurant level was dark, for the place served only lunch, and there was no one to see them go back up to the roof. Kit opened the door at the top of the stairs, and together they walked out into peace and darkness and a wind off the ocean. A helicopter was moored in the middle of the pad with steel pegs and cables, crouching on its skids and staring at them with clear, sleepy, benevolent eyes. The blue high-intensity marker lights blazed about it like the circle of a protection spell. Nita looked away, not really wanting to think about spells or anything else to do with wizardry. *The book said it would be hard. That I didn't mind. But I hurt! And where's the good part? There was supposed to be happiness too...*

The bright *Book* was heavy on her back as she looked out across the night. All around, for miles and miles, was glittering light, brilliant motion, shining under the Moon; lights of a thousand colors gleaming from windows, glowing on streets, blazing from the headlights of cars. The city, breathing, burning, living the life they had preserved. Ten million lives and more. *If something should happen to all that life— how terrible!* Nita gulped for control as she remembered Fred's words of just this morning, an eternity ago. And this was what being a wizard was about. Keeping terrible things from happening, even when it hurt. Not just power, or control of what ordinary people couldn't control, or delight in being able to make strange things happen.

Those were side effects—not the reason, not the purpose.

She could give it up, she realized suddenly. In the recovery of the bright *Book*, she and Kit had more than repaid the energy invested in their training. If they chose to lay the Art aside, if *she* did, no one would say a word. She would be left in peace. Magic does not live in the unwilling soul.

Yet never to hear a tree talk again, or a stone, or a star...

On impulse Nita held out her hands and closed her eyes. Even without the rowan rod she could feel the moonfire on her skin as a tree might feel it. She could taste the restored sunlight that produced it, feel the soundless roar of the ancient atomic furnace that had burned just this way while her world was still a cloud of gas, nebulous and unformed. And ever so faintly she could taste a rainbow spatter of high-energy radiation, such as a white hole might leave after blowing its quanta.

She opened her eyes, found her hands full of moonlight that trembled like bright water, its surface sheened with fading aurora glow. "All right," she said after a moment. "All right." She opened her hands to let the light run out. "*Kit?*" she said, saying his name in the Speech.

He had gone to stand beside the helicopter and was standing with one hand laid against its side. It stared at him mutely. "*Yeah,*" he said, and patted the cool metal, and left the chopper to rejoin Nita. "*I guess we pass the test.*"

They took their packs off and got out the materials necessary for the timeslide. When the lithium-cadmium battery and the calculator chip and the broken teacup handle were in place, Kit and Nita started the spell—and without warning were again caught up by the augmenting power of the bright *Book* and plunged more quickly than they expected into the wizardry. It *was* like being on a slide, though they were the ones who held still, and the events of the day as seen from the top of the Pan Am Building rushed backward past them, a high-speed 3-D movie in reverse. Blinding white fire and the nova Moon grew slowly in the sky, flared, and were gone. The Moon, briefly out, came on again. Darkness flowed backward through the suddenly open worldgate, following its master on his huge dark mount, who also stepped backward and vanished through the gate. Kit and Nita saw *themselves* burst out of the roof door, blurred with speed; saw themselves run backward over the railing, a bright line of light pacing them as they plunged out into the dark air, dove backward through the gate, and vanished with it. The Sun came up in the west and fled back across the sky. Men in coveralls burst out of the roof door and unpegged the helicopter; two of them got into it and it took off backward. Clouds streamed and boiled past, jets fell backward into La Guardia. The Sun stood high. . . .

The slide let them go, and Kit and Nita sat back gasping. "What time have you got?" Kit said when he had enough breath.

Nita glanced at her watch. "Nine fortyfive."

"*Nine* forty-five! But we were supposed to—"

"It's this *Book*, it makes everything

work too well. At nine forty-five we were—"

They heard voices in the stairwell, behind the closed door. Kit and Nita stared at each other. Then they began frantically picking up the items left from their spelling. Nita paused with the lithium-cadmium battery in her hand as she recognized one of those voices coming up the stairs. She reared back, took aim, and threw the heavy battery at the closed door, hard. CRACK!

Kit looked at her, his eyes wide, and understood. "Quick, behind there," he said. Nita ran to scoop up the battery, then ducked around after Kit and crouched down with him behind the back of the stairwell. There was a long, long pause before the door opened and footsteps could be heard on the gravel. Kit and Nita edged around the side of the stairwell again to peer around the corner. Two small, nervous-looking figures were heading for the south-facing rail in the bright sunlight. A dark-haired girl, maybe thirteen, wearing jeans and a shirt and a down vest; a dark-haired boy, small and a touch stocky, also in jeans and parka, twelve years old or so.

The boy held a broken-off piece of antenna, and the girl held a peeled white stick, and they were being paced by a brilliant white spark like a will-o'-the-wisp plugged into too much current and about to blow out.

" 'There are no accidents,' " Kit whispered sadly.

The tears stung Nita's eyes again. "G'bye, Fred," she said softly in English, for fear the Speech should attract his attention, or hers.

Silently and unseen, Kit and Nita slipped through the door and went downstairs for the shuttle and the train home.

Timeheart

THE WALK HOME FROM the bus stop was weary and quiet. Three blocks from Nita's house, they reached the corner where their ways usually parted. Kit paused there, waiting for the light to change, though no traffic was in sight. "Call me tomorrow?" he said.

What for? Nita felt like saying, for there were no more spells in the offing, and she was deadly tired. Still ... "It's your turn," she said.

"Huh? Right." The light changed, and Kit headed across the street to Nita's left. In the middle of the street he turned, walking backward. "We should call Tom and Carl," he shouted, sounding entirely exhausted.

"Yeah." The light changed again, in Nita's favor; Kit jumped up onto the sidewalk on the other side and headed south toward his place. Nita crossed east, watching Kit as she went. Though the look on his face was tired and sad, all the rest of his body wore the posture of someone who'd been through so much fear that fear no longer frightened him. *Why's he so afraid of getting beat up?* Nita thought. *Nobody in their right mind would mess with him.*

In midstep she stopped, watching him walk away. *How about that. How about that. He got what he asked for.*

After a second she started walking home again. The weight at her back suddenly reminded her of something. (Kit!) she called silently, knowing he could hear even though he was now out of sight. (What about the *Book?*)

(Hang on to it,) he answered. (We'll give it to the Advisories. Or they'll know what to do with it.)

(Right. See ya later.)

(See ya.)

Nita was so tired that it took three or four minutes before the identity of the blond person walking up East Clinton toward her registered at all. By then Joanne was within yelling distance, but she didn't yell at Nita at all, much to Nita's surprise. This was such an odd development that Nita looked at Joanne carefully as they got closer, something she had never done before. There was something familiar about Joanne today, a look that Nita couldn't quite pin down—and then she recognized the expression and let out a tired, unhappy breath. The look was less marked, less violent, and terrible than that of the pride-frozen misery of the dark rider, but there all the same. The angry fear was there too—the terror of what had been until now no threat but was now out of control; the look of the rider about to be cast out by a power he had thought himself safe from, the look of a bully whose victim suddenly wasn't a victim anymore.

Nita slowed down and stopped where she was, in the middle of the sidewalk, watching Joanne. *Even he can be different now,* she thought, her heart beating fast—

her own old fear wasn't entirely gone. *But that was partly because we gave him the chance.*

She stood there, watching Joanne slow down warily as she got closer to Nita. Nita sweated. Doing something that would be laughed about behind her back was almost as bad as being beaten up. But she stood still until Joanne came to a stop four or five feet away from her. "Well?" Joanne said, her voice full of anger and uncertainty.

I don't know what to say to her, we have absolutely nothing in common, Nita thought frantically. *But it has to start somewhere.* She swallowed and did her best to look Joanne in the eye, calmly and not in threat. "Come on over to my place after supper sometime and look through my telescope," she said. "I'll show you Jupiter's moons. Or Mars—"

Joanne made that old familiar haughty face and brushed past Nita and away. "Why would I ever want to go to *your* house? You don't even have a wide-screen TV."

Nita stood still, listening to Joanne's footsteps hurrying away, a little faster

every second—and slowly began to realize
that she'd gotten what she asked for too—
the ability to break the cycle of anger and
loneliness, not necessarily for others, but at
least for herself. It wouldn't even take the
Speech; plain words would do it, and the
magic of reaching out. It would take a long
time, much longer than something simple
like breaking the walls between the worlds,
and it would cost more effort than even the
reading of the *Book of Night with Moon*.
But it would be worth it—and eventually
it would work. A spell always works.

Nita went home.

That night after supper she slipped outside to sit in Liused's shadow and watch
the sky. The tree caught her mood and, after greeting her, was quiet—until about ten
o'clock, when it and every other growing
thing in sight suddenly trembled violently
as if stricken at the root. They had felt the
Sun go out.

(It's all right,) she said silently, though
for someone whose tears were starting
again, it was an odd thing to say. She
waited the eight minutes with them, saw

the Moon blink out, and leaned back against the rowan trunk, sheltering from the wind that rose in the darkness. Branches tossed as if in a hurricane, leaves hissed in anguish—and then the sudden new star in the heavens etched every leaf's shadow sharp against the ground and set the Moon on fire. Nita squinted up at the pinpoint of brilliance, unwilling to look away though her eyes leaked tears of pain. She'd thought, that afternoon, that living through the loss a second time would be easier. She was wrong. The tears kept falling long after the star went out, and the Moon found its light again, and the wind died to a whisper. She stopped crying long enough to go back inside and go to bed, and she was sure she would start again immediately. But she was wrong about that too. Exhaustion beat down grief so fast that she was asleep almost as soon as her head touched the pillow under which she had hidden the *Book of Night with Moon*. . . .

The place where they stood was impossible, for there's no place in Manhattan where the water level in the East River comes right up to the railed path that runs alongside it. There they stood, though, leaning with their backs against the railing, gazing up at the bright city that reared against the silver sky, while behind them the river whispered and chuckled and slapped its banks. The sound of laughter came down the morning wind from the apartments and the brownstones and the towers of steel and crystal; the seabirds wheeled and cried over the white piers and jetties of the Manhattan shoreline, and from somewhere down the riverside came the faint sound of music—quiet rock, a deep steady backbeat woven about with guitars and voices in close harmony. A jogger went by on the running path, puffing, followed by a large black-and-white dog galloping to catch up with its master.

Are we early, or are they late? Kit asked, leaning back farther still to watch an overflying Learjet do barrel-roll after barrel-roll for sheer joy of being alive.

Who cares? Nita said, leaning back too and enjoying the way the music and the city sounds and the Learjet's delighted scream all blended. *Anyway, this is Timeheart. There's nothing here but Now...*

They turned their backs on the towers and the traffic and the laughter, and looked out across the shining water toward Brooklyn and Long Island. Neither was there just then—probably someone else in Timeheart was using them, and Kit and Nita didn't need them at the moment. The silver expanse of the Atlantic shifted and glittered from their feet to the radiant horizon, endless. Far off to their right, south and west of the Battery, the Statue of Liberty held up her torch and her tablet and looked calmly out toward the sunrise as they did, waiting. Nita was the first to see the dark bulge out on the water. She nudged Kit and pointed. *Look, a shark!*

He glanced at her, amused. *Even here I don't think sharks have wheels...*

The Lotus came fast, hydroplaning. Water spat up from its wheels as it skidded up to the railing and fishtailed sideways, grinning, spraying them both. On its wildly waving antenna rode a spark of light. Nita smiled at her friend, who danced off the antenna to rest momentarily on one of her fingers like a hundred-watt firefly. *Well,* Nita said, *is it confusing being dead?*

Fred chuckled a rainbow, up the spectrum and down again. *Not very.* Beside him, the Lotus stood up on its hind wheels, putting its front ones on the railing so that Kit could scratch it behind the headlights.

We brought it, Kit said.

Good, said the Lotus, as Nita got the bright *Book* out of her backpack and handed it to Kit. *The Powers want to put it away safe. Though the precaution may not really be necessary, after what you did.*

It worked? He's changed? Nita said.

Fred made a spatter of light, a gesture that felt like the shake of a head. *Not changed. Just made otherwise, as if he'd been that way from the beginning. He has back the option he'd decided was lost—to put aside his anger, to build instead of damn . . .*

Then if he uses that option—you mean every place could be like this some day? Kit looked over his shoulder at the city and all the existence behind it, preserved in its fullest beauty while still growing and becoming greater.

Possibly. What he did remains. Entropy's still here, and death. They look like waste and horror to us now. But if he chooses to have them be a blessing on the worlds, instead of anger's curse—who knows where those gates will lead then? . . . The Lotus sounded pleased by the prospect.

Kit held out the *Book of Night with Moon.* Most delicately the Lotus opened fanged jaws to take it, then rubbed its face against Kit and dropped to all four wheels on the water. It smiled at them both, a chrome smile, silver and sanguine—then backed a little, turned, and was off, spraying Kit and Nita again.

Fred started to follow, but Nita caught him in cupped hands, holding him back for a moment. *Fred! Did we do right?*

Even here she couldn't keep the pain out of her question, the fear that she could somehow have prevented his death. But Fred radiated a serene and wondering joy that took her breath and reassured her and filled her with wonder to match his, all at once. *Go find out,* he said.

She opened her hands and he flew out of them like a spark blown on the wind—a brightness zipping after the Lotus, losing itself against the dazzling silver of the sea, gone. Nita turned around to lean on the railing again, and after a moment Kit turned with her. They breathed out, relaxing, and settled back to gaze at the city transfigured, the city preserved at the heart of Time, as all things loved are preserved in the hearts that care for them—gazed up into the radiance, the life, the light unending, the light. . . .

The light was right in her eyes, mostly because Dairine had yanked the curtain open. Her sister was talking loudly, and Nita turned her head and quite suddenly felt what was not under her pillow. "You gonna sleep all morning? Get up, it's ten thirty! The Sun went out last night, you should see it, it was on the news. And somebody blew up Central Park; and Kit Rodriguez called, he wants you to call him back. How come you keep calling each other, anyhow?" Halfway out the bedroom door, realization dawned in her sister's eyes. "Maaaaa!" she yelled out the door, strangling on her own laughter. "Nita's got a *boyfriend!*"

"Oh, jeez, Dair*iiiiiiiine!*"

The wizard threw her pillow at her sister, got up, and went to breakfast.

Turn the page for an exciting peek at

Deep
Wizardry

The second book in the Young Wizards series

Summer
Night's Song

NITA SLIPPED OUT THE back door of the
beach house, careful not to let the rickety
screen door slam, and for a second stood silently on the back porch in the darkness. It
was no use. "Nita"—her mother's voice came
floating out from the living room—"where're
you going?"

"Out," Nita said, hoping to get away with
it just this once.

She might as well have tried to rob a bank.
"Out where?"

"Down to the beach, Mom."

There was a sigh's worth of pause from the
living room, broken by the sound of a crowd
on TV shouting about a base that had just

been stolen somewhere in the country. "I don't like you walking down there alone at night, Neets ..."

"Nhhnnnnn," Nita said, a loud noncommittal noise she had learned to make while her mother was deciding whether to let her do something. "I'll take Ponch with me," she said in a burst of inspiration.

"Mmmmmm ...," her mother said, considering it. Ponch was a large black-and-white dog, part Border collie, part German shepherd, part mutt—an intrepid hunter of water rats and gulls, and ferociously loyal to his master and to Nita because she was his master's best friend. "Where's Kit?"

"I dunno." It was at least partly the truth. "He went for a walk awhile ago."

"Well ... OK. You take Ponch and look for Kit, and bring him back with you. Don't want his folks thinking we're not taking care of him."

"Right, Ma," Nita said, and went pounding down the creaky steps from the house to the yard before her mother could change her mind, or her father, immersed in the ball game, could come back to consciousness.

"Ponch! Hey, Pancho!" Nita shouted, pounding through the sandy front yard, through the gate in the ancient picket fence, and out across the narrow paved road to the dune on the other side of the road. Joyous barking began on the far side of the dune as Nita ran up it. *He's hunting again*, Nita thought, and would have laughed for delight if running had left her any breath. *This is the best vacation we ever had...*

At the top of the dune she paused, looking down toward the long, dark expanse of the beach. "It's been a good year," her father had said a couple of months before, over dinner. "We can't go far for vacation—but let's go somewhere nice. One of the beaches in the Hamptons, maybe. We'll rent a house and live beyond our means. For a couple weeks, anyway..."

It hadn't taken Nita much begging to get her folks to let her friend Kit Rodriguez go along with them, or to get Kit's folks to say yes. Both families were delighted that their children had each finally found a close friend. Nita and Kit laughed about that sometimes. Their families knew only the surface of what was going on— which was probably for the best.

A black shape came scrabbling up the dune toward Nita, flinging sand in all directions in his hurry. "Whoa!" she shouted at Ponch, but it was no use; it never was. He hit her about stomach level with both paws and knocked her down, panting with excitement; then, when she managed to sit up, he started enthusiastically washing her face. His breath smelled like dead fish.

"Euuuuw, enough!" Nita said, making a face and pushing the dog more or less off her. "Ponch, where's Kit?"

"Yayayayayayayayaya!" Ponch barked, jumping up and bouncing around Nita in an attempt to get her to play. He grabbed up a long string of dead seaweed in his jaws and began shaking it like a rope and growling.

"Cut it out, Ponch. Get serious." Nita got up and headed down the far side of the dune, brushing herself off as she went. "Where's the boss?"

"He played with me," Ponch said in another string of barks as he loped down the dune alongside her. "He threw the stick. I chased it."

"Great. Where is he *now*?"

They came to the bottom of the dune together. The sand was harder there, but still dry; the tide was low and just beginning to turn. "Don't know," Ponch said, a bark with a grumble on the end of it.

"Hey, you're a good boy; I'm not mad at

you," Nita said. She stopped to scratch the dog behind the ears, in the good place. He stood still with his tongue hanging out and looked up at her, his eyes shining oddly in the light of the nearly full moon that was climbing the sky "I just don't feel like playing right now. I want to swim. Would you find Kit?"

The big brown eyes gazed soulfully up at her, and Ponch made a small beseeching whine. "A dog biscuit?"

Nita grinned. "Blackmailer. OK, you find the boss, I'll give you a biscuit. Two biscuits. Go get 'im!"

Ponch bounded off westward down the beach, kicking up wet sand. Nita headed for the waterline, where she shrugged off the windbreaker that had been covering her bathing suit and dropped it on the sand. Two months ago, talking to a dog and getting an answer back would have been something that happened only in Disney movies. But then one day in the library, Nita had stumbled on to a book called *So You Want to Be a Wizard*. She'd followed the instructions in the book, as Kit had in the copy he'd found in a used bookstore—and afterward, dogs talked back. Or, more accurately, she knew what language they spoke and how to hear it. There was nothing that *didn't* talk back, she'd found—only things she didn't yet know how to hear or how to talk to properly.

Like parents, Nita thought with mild amusement. If her mother knew Nita was going swimming, she'd probably pitch a fit: she'd had a terrible thing about night swimming after seeing *Jaws. But it's OK*, Nita thought. *There aren't any sharks here ... and if there were, I think I could talk them out of eating me.*

She made sure her clothes were above the high-water line, then waded down into the breakers. The water was surprisingly warm around her knees. The waxing moon, slightly golden from smog, made a silvery pathway on the water, everywhere else shedding a dull radiance that made both land and sea look alive.

What a great night, Nita thought. She went out another twenty paces or so, then crouched over and dived into an incoming wave. Waterborne sand scoured her, the water thundered in her ears; then she broke surface and lay in the roil and dazzle of the moonlit water, floating. There were no streetlights there, and the stars she loved were bright. After a while she stood up in the shoulder-high water, watching the sky. Back up on the beach, Ponch was barking, excited and noisy. *He can't have found Kit that fast,* Nita thought. *Probably something distracted him. A crab, maybe. A dead fish. A shark . . .*

Something pushed her in the back, *hard.* Nita gasped and whipped around in the water, thinking, *This is it, there are too sharks here and I'm* dead! The sight of the slick-skinned shape in the water stopped her breath—until she realized what she was looking at. A slender body, ten feet long; a blowhole and an amused eye that looked at her sidelong; and a long, beaked face that wore a permanent smile. She reached out a hesitant hand, and under her touch the dolphin turned lazily, rolling sideways, brushing her with skin like warm, moon lit satin.

She was immensely relieved. *"Dai'stiho,"* she said, greeting the swimmer in the Tongue that wizards use, the language that she'd learned from her manual and that all creatures understand. She expected no more answer than a fizz or squeak as the dolphin returned the greeting and went about its business.

But the dolphin rolled back toward her and looked at her in what seemed to be shock. *"A wizard!"* it said in an urgent whistle. Nita had no time to answer; the dolphin dived and its tail slapped the surface, spraying her. By the time Nita rubbed the salt sting out of her eyes, there was nothing near her but the usual roaring breakers. Ponch was bouncing frantically on the beach, barking something about sea monsters to the small form walking beside him.

"Neets?"

Nita waded out of the breakers. At the waterline Kit met her and handed Nita her windbreaker. He was smaller than she was, a year younger, dark-haired and brown-eyed and sharp of face and mind; *definitely sharper*, Nita thought with approval, *than the usual twelve-year-old*.

"He was hollering about whales," Kit said, nodding at Ponch.

"Dolphins," Nita said. "At least, *a* dolphin. I said hi to it and it said, 'A wizard!' and ran away."

"Great." Kit looked southward, across the ocean. "Something's going on out there, Neets. I was up on the jetty. The rocks are upset."

Nita shook her head. Her specialty as a wizard was living things; animals and plants talked to her and did the things she asked, at least if she asked properly. It still startled her sometimes when Kit got the same kind of result from "unalive" things like cars and doors and telephone poles, but that was where his talent lay. "What can a rock get upset about?" she said.

"I'm not sure. They wouldn't say. The stones piled up there remembered something. And they didn't want to think about it anymore. They were shook." Kit looked up sharply at Nita. "That was *it*. The earth shook once ... "

"Oh, come off it. This isn't California. Long Island doesn't have earthquakes."

"Once it did. The rocks remember ... I wonder what that dolphin wanted?"

Nita was wondering, too. She zipped up her windbreaker. "C'mon, we have to get back before Mom busts a gut."

"But the dolphin—"

Nita started down the beach, then turned and kept walking backward when she noticed that Kit wasn't following her. "The ball game was almost over," she said, raising her voice as she got farther from Kit and Ponch. "They'll go to bed early. They always do. And when they're asleep—"

Kit nodded and muttered something, Nita couldn't quite hear what. He vanished in a small clap of inrushing air and then reappeared next to Nita, walking with her; Ponch barked in annoyance and ran to catch up.

"He really hates that 'beam-me-up-Scotty' spell," Nita said.

"Yeah, when it bends space, it makes him itch. Look, I was practicing that other one—"

"With the water?" She grinned at him. "In the dark, I hope."

"Yeah. I'll show you later. And then—"

"Dolphins."

"Uh-*huh*. C'mon, I'll race you."

They ran up the dune, followed by a black shape barking loudly about dog biscuits.

Wizards' Song

THE MOON GOT HIGH. Nita sat by the window of her ground-floor room, listening through the stillness for the sound of voices upstairs. There hadn't been any for a while.

She sighed and looked down at the book she held in her lap. It looked like a library book—bound in one of those slick-shiny buckram library bindings, with a Dewey decimal number written at the bottom of the spine in that indelible white ink librarians use, and at the top of the spine, the words SO YOU WANT TO BE A WIZARD. But on opening the book, what one saw were the words *Instruction and Implementation Manual, General and Limited Special-Purpose Wizardries, Sorceries, and Spells: 933rd*

Edition. Or that was what you saw if you were a wizard, for the printing was done in the graceful, Arabic-looking written form of the Speech.

Nita turned a few pages of the manual, glancing at them in idle interest. The instructions she'd found in the book had coached her through her first few spells—both the kinds for which only words were needed and those that required raw materials of some sort. The spells had in turn led her into the company of other wizards—beginners like Kit and more experienced ones, typical of the wizards, young and old, working quietly all over the world. And then the spells had taken her right out of the world she'd known, into one of the ones "next door," and into a conflict that had been going on since time's beginning, in all the worlds there were.

In that other world, in a place like New York City but also terribly different, she had passed through the initial ordeal that every candidate for wizardry undergoes. Kit had been with her. Together they had pulled each other and themselves through the danger and the terror, to the successful completion of a quest into which they had stumbled. They saved their own world without attracting much notice;

they lost a couple of dear friends they'd met along the way; and they came into their full power as wizards. It was a privilege that had its price. Nita still wasn't sure why she'd been chosen as one of those who fight for the Worlds against the Great Death of entropy. She was just glad she'd been picked.

She flipped pages to the regional directory, where wizards were listed by name and address. Nita never got tired of seeing her own name listed there, for other wizards to call if they needed her. She overshot her own page in the Nassau County section, wanting to check the names of two friends, Senior Wizards for the area—Tom Swale and Carl Romeo. They had recently been promoted to Senior from the Advisory Wizard level, and as she'd suspected, their listing now read "On sabbatical: emergencies only." Nita grinned at the memory of the party they'd thrown to celebrate their promotion. The guests had been a select group. More of them had appeared out of nowhere than arrived through the front door. Several had spent the afternoon floating in midair; another had spent it in the fishpond, submerged. Human beings had been only slightly in the majority at the party, and Nita became very careful at the snack table after her

first encounter with the dip made from Penn-
sylvania crude oil and fresh-ground iron fil-
ings.

She paged back through the listing and
looked at her own name.

CALLAHAN, Juanita T. 243 E. Clinton Avenue
                      Hempstead, NY 11575
                      (555) 379-6786
     On active status   Assignment location:
                      38 Tiana Beach Road
                      Southampton, NY
                      11829
                      (555) 667-9084

Nita sighed, for this morning the status note
had said, like Carl's and Tom's, "Vacationing:
emergencies only." The book updated itself all
over that way—pages changing sometimes second to second, reporting the status of worldgates in the area, what spells were working
where, the cost of powdered newt at your local
Advisory. *Whatever's come up,* Nita thought,
we're expected to be able to handle it.

*Of course, last time out they expected us to
save the world, too...*

"Neets!"

She jumped, then tossed her book out the

window to Kit and began climbing out. "Sssh!"

"Shhh yourself, mouth. They're asleep. C'mon."

Once over the dune, the hiss and rumble of the midnight sea made talking safer. "You on active status, too?" Kit said.

"Yup. Let's find the dolphin and see what's up."

They ran for the breakers. Kit was in a bathing suit and windbreaker as Nita was, with sneakers slung over his shoulder by the laces. "Okay," he said, "watch this." He said something in the Speech, a long, liquid-sounding sentence with a curious even-uneven rhyme in it, all of which told the night and the wind and the water what Kit wanted of them. And without pause Kit ran right up to the water, which was retreating at that particular moment—and then onto it. Under his weight it bucked and sloshed the way a waterbed will when you stand on it; but Kit didn't sink. He ran four or five paces out onto the silver-slicked surface— then lost his balance and fell over sideways.

Nita started laughing, then hurriedly shut herself up for fear the whole beach should hear. Kit was lying on the water, his head propped up on one hand; the water bobbed him up and down while he looked at her with a sour expression. "It's not funny. I did it all last night and it never happened *once.*"

"Must be that you did the spell for two this time," Nita said, tempted to start laughing again, except that Kit would probably have punched her out. She kept her face as straight as she could and stepped out to the water, putting a foot carefully on an incoming, flattened-out wave. It took her weight, flattening more as she stepped up with the other foot and was carried backward. "It's like the slidewalk at the airport," she said, putting her arms out for balance and wobbling.

"Kind of." Kit got up on hands and knees, swaying. "Come on. Keep your knees bent a little. And pick up your feet."

It was a useful warning. Nita tripped over several breakers and sprawled each time, a sensation like doing a belly whopper onto a waterbed, until she got her sea legs. Once past the breakers she had no more trouble, and Kit led her at a bouncy trot out into the open Atlantic.

They both came to understand shortly why not many people, wizards or otherwise, walk on water much. The constant slip and slide of the water under their feet forced them to use leg muscles they rarely bothered with on land. They had to rest frequently, sitting, while they looked around them for signs of the dolphin.

At their first two rest stops there was nothing to be seen but the lights of Ponquogue and Hampton Bays and West Tiana on the mainland, three miles north. Closer, red and white flashing lights marked the entrance to Shinnecock Inlet, the break in the long strip of beach where they were staying. The Shinnecock horn hooted mournfully at them four times a minute, a lonely sounding call. Nita's hair stood up all over her as they sat down the third time and she rubbed her aching legs. Kit's spell kept them from getting wet, but she was chilly; and being so far out there in the dark and quiet was very much like being in the middle of a desert—a wet, hissing barrenness unbroken for miles except by the quick-flashing white light of a buoy or two.

"You okay?" Kit said.

"Yeah. It's just that the sea seems . . . safer near the shore, somehow. How deep is it here?"

Kit slipped his manual out of his windbreaker and pulled out a large nautical map. "About eighty feet, it looks like."

Nita sat up straight in shock. Something had broken the surface of the water and was arrowing toward them at a great rate. It was a triangular fin. Nita scrambled to her feet. "Uh, Kit!"

He was on his feet beside her in a second, staring, too. "A shark has to stay in the water," he said, sounding more confident than he looked. "We don't. We can jump—"

"Oh, yeah? How high? And for how long?"

The fin was thirty yards or so away. A silvery body rose up under it, and Nita breathed out in relief at the frantic, high-pitched chattering of a dolphin's voice. The swimmer leaped right out of the water in its speed, came down, and splashed them both. "I'm late, and you're late," it gasped in a string of whistles and pops, "and S'reee's about to be! Hurry!"

"Right," Kit said, and slapped his manual shut. He said nothing aloud, but the sea's surface instantly stopped behaving like a waterbed and started acting like water. "*Whoolp!*" Nita said as she sank like a stone. She didn't get wet—that part of Kit's spell was still working—but she floundered wildly for a moment before managing to get hold of the dolphin in the cold and dark of the water.

Nita groped up its side and found a fin. In-

stantly the dolphin took off, and Nita hoisted
herself up to a better position, hanging from
the dorsal fin so that her body was half out of
the water and her legs were safely out of the
way of the fiercely lashing tail. On the other
side, Kit had done the same. "You might have
warned me!" she said to him across the dolphin's back.

He rolled his eyes at her. "If you weren't
asleep on your feet, you wouldn't need warning."

"Kit—" She dropped it for the time being
and said to the dolphin, "What's S'reee? And
why's it going to be late? What's the matter?"

"She," the dolphin said. "S'reee's a wizard.
The Hunters are after her and she can't do
anything, she's hurt too badly. My pod and another one are with her, but they can't hold
them off for long. She's beached, and the tide's
coming in—"

Kit and Nita shot each other shocked looks.
Another wizard in the area—and out in the
ocean in the middle of the night? "What hunters?" Kit said; "Your pod?" Nita said at the
same moment.

The dolphin was coming about and heading
along the shoreline, westward toward Quogue.
"*The* Hunters," it said in a series of annoyed

squeaks and whistles. "The ones with teeth, who else? What kind of wizards are they turning out these days, anyway?"

Nita said nothing to this. She was too busy staring ahead of them at a long, dark bumpy whale shape lying on a sandbar, a shape slicked with moonlight along its upper contours and silhouetted against the dull silver of the sea. It was the look of the water that particularly troubled Nita. Shapes leaped and twisted in it, shapes with two different kinds of fins. "Kit!"

"Neets," Kit said, not sounding happy, "there really aren't sharks here, the guy from the Coast Guard said so last week—"

"Tell *them!*" the dolphin said angrily. It hurtled through the water toward the sandbar around which the fighting continued, silent for all its viciousness. The only sound came from the dark shape that lay partly on the bar, partly off it—a piteous, wailing whistle almost too high to hear.

"Are you ready?" the dolphin said. They were about fifty yards from the trouble.

"Ready to *what?*" Kit asked, and started fumbling for his manual.

Nita started to do the same—and then had an idea, and blessed her mother for having watched *Jaws* on TV so many times. "Kit, forget it! Remember a couple months ago and those guys who tried to beat you up? The freeze spell?"

"Yeah . . ."

"Do it, do it big. I'll feed you power!" She pounded the dolphin on the side. "Go beach! Tell your buddies to beach, too!"

"But—"

"Go do it!" She let go of the dolphin's fin and dropped into the water, swallowing hard as she saw another fin, of the wrong shape entirely, begin to circle in on her and Kit. "Kit, get the water working again!"

It took a precious second; and the next one—one of the longer seconds of Nita's life—for her and Kit to clamber up out of the "liquid" water onto the "solid." They made it and grabbed one another for both physical and moral support, as that fin kept coming. "The other spell set?" Nita gasped.

"Yeah—*now!*"

The usual immobility of a working spell came down on them both, with something added—a sense of being not one person alone, but part of a *one* that was somehow bigger than even Nita and Kit together could be. Inside that sudden oneness, she felt the freeze spell waiting like a phone number with all but one digit dialed. Kit said the one word in the Speech that set the spell free, the "last digit," then gripped Nita's hand hard.

Nita did her part, quickly saying the three most dangerous words in all wizardry—the words that give all of a wizard's power over into another's hands. She felt it going from her, felt Kit shaking as he wound her power, her trust, into the spell. And then she took all her fright, and her anger at the sharks, and her pity for the poor wailing bulk on the sand, and let Kit have those, too.

The spell blasted away from the two of them with a shock like a huge jolt of static....